Tall Tales & Short Fiction

A Multi-Genre Collection

by David Bowmore

Published by Clarendon House Publications
76 Coal Pit Lane Sheffield, England
Published in Sheffield 2020
First edition

Cover image © 2020 Wim Van't Einde
ISBN #: 9798678596987

for Mary Barton
Elegance and Education

with love
from David

TABLE OF CONTENTS

Who Killed Panama Harlan?

(First appeared in Grievous Bodily Harm by Zombie Pirate Publishing.)

The boys in blue took great pleasure in kicking the office door in. Before I could get off the sofa, which doubled as a bed these days, two of them had dragged me to my feet and another delivered a truncheon to the gut.

Of course, a blow like that on a tired and hung-over body is going to make the poor bloke receiving it bring up his last meal. Not that it looked much like battered fish as it landed on the copper's boots.

By the time they'd dragged me into the station, my lips were swollen and my back black and blue.

I made myself as comfortable as I could in the cell, which stank of its last resident. Flies buzzed around the bucket.

The little viewing portal shot open with a crack that echoed around the small space, an eye peered in and the viewing portal promptly closed again. Then the door swung inwards.

The crisp suit in front of me smiled and then held his arms wide.

'Ricky McCorkingdale, you old bastard. What you in here for?'

'I wish I knew, Spence,' I said, refusing the embrace. 'Nobody has said anything. Your boys did a good job of doing me over.'

'Oh come off it, Corky. We're not allowed to do that sort of thing.'

'Yeah — I know. Do you have any idea why I'm here?'

'I've just come on duty. There's a hell of a fuss going on, but I always takes a look at the charge sheet, check out who's in the cells. You taught me that, remember?'

'I remember.'

'I'll see what I can find out. Hang tight.'

Spence, or to use his correct moniker Ian Spencer, had been my partner when we were both in uniform. Now wearing a flash suit, he was desperate to make a name for himself in CID. Rumour was, he would be in the Met in under a year.

That's where I should have been, but five years ago it had all been flushed away. The reason? What else could it have been but a woman? The kind of woman you only see in films. I never saw her wearing anything but some sort of slinky number, except when I saw her wearing nothing at all. Diana Dors had nothing on her.

He was bound to find out — pity he found out the way he did. I resigned before I was formally dismissed. Well, it would have been difficult to stay, wouldn't it? I made a powerful enemy that day.

The Chief Constable was one of those men who made promotion on the fairways of golf courses with a secret handshake. His talent for keeping those hands clean was legendary; he hadn't felt a collar in years. Everyone has secrets and I knew he had some too. Now I know much more about him.

'Ya don't buy a dog and bark yerself, do ya lad?' he said to me once. I had always found the little man, with his big bravado and a small mind, difficult to like. How he'd managed to bag a prize like Krista, was one of the things I never found out. I think it was the security his wealth and position could provide her, and once he had her — he wasn't going to let go.

Krista had come to England as a refugee war child and by the time she was twenty-one had grown into a dangerous woman, a siren, what the movies called a femme fatale. I'd seen her perform jazz songs in classy night spots on a few occasions. She had a cracking pair of lungs, despite the twenty a day she got through and the atmosphere of the clubs where she sang. It was a beautiful, deep and powerful, smoke-filled voice that mesmerised the soul and stirred parts of the body that ought not to have been stirred.

After my disgraceful exit from the force, I set up as a Private Inquiry Agent; I ask questions that others find difficult and I investigate the ordinary. You know the sort of thing — divorce cases, following unfaithful spouses, evidence gathering in the form of unseemly photographs. At one point, I employed a secretary, but had to let her go. Business was far from good.

A week ago, five years after that fateful night with Krista on her knees and her old man bursting a blood vessel, she walked back into my life. Little had changed. You still had to ask yourself if a woman like this was real. But I was a mess. I'd seen it before, had even helped it come about — men fall apart without a woman to organise them. I'd deteriorated and I knew it when I saw the look of pity on her face as she glanced at the sheet and pillow thrown over the battered sofa.

'What happened?' Her breathy voice could make a man weep.

'What do you want, Krista?' I ran a comb through my hair, and slid the bottle back into a drawer. I'd need a new one by the end of the day.

'I need your help.'

'You still with him?'

'Yar.' Her accent was always more prominent when she was upset. 'I'm frightened, Rick.'

'I don't want to know.'

I was a fool, but when she looked at me with those big watery pools and said, 'There is no one else I can trust,' a bit of me cracked. I wanted to hide in her warmth and dive into her eyes.

'Why?'

She sat on the chair opposite, her straight back accentuating every curve. It was difficult to look her in the face, so I rested my feet on the desk, leaned back in the chair and closed my eyes while I listened to her beautiful voice.

The viewer shot across again bringing me back to the present. I sat up as Spence sauntered in, a grim look in his eyes.

'You're in trouble, Corky.'

'Can't be. I haven't worked for weeks. I haven't broken any laws in the pursuit of errant husbands, let alone justice, unless I'm here for not paying my rent.'

'It's no joke. We're looking at murder, old son.'

'Who?'

'Bloke called Panama Harlan. You heard of him?'

I hung my head in my heads. If I didn't play my cards right, I'd swing for this.

'You did then. How was that?'

'How was he killed?'

'You don't get to ask questions anymore, Richard.'

'Richard now, is it? And I thought we were friends?'

'You're in deep shit.'

I found myself echoing Krista's words of only a week earlier.

'I can't trust anyone. You're going to find lots out, but you must believe me when I say I didn't do this.'

He paced the room for a few seconds.

'I'll listen, but old man Austin is on the warpath. You better make it good.'

'Get me out of here, and I'll tell you everything I know.'

'What? Are you out of your mind?'

'You see the state I'm in,' I said pointing at my swollen face. 'Come tomorrow morning be lying on a slab in the morgue, after having "fallen down some stairs". Come on Spence; do an old mate a favour. I promise on my little girl's life that I won't run.'

He left the cell without any promises. But then again, no refusals.

The meeting with Krista and her lover, Panama Harlan, went around and around in my confused brain while I waited for Spence to return.

Panama was on stage at The Gaslight, blasting out some powerful tune on a shining silver trumpet inlaid with a delicate pattern around the rim of the tube. The decor hadn't changed much since I had been in there five or six years earlier. Pink lampshades cast a sultry hue over everyone. A mirror-ball left over from the pre-war jazz scene hung high above the old dance floor now dotted with small round tables.

He called a halt to rehearsal and joined us in one of the red leather tall-backed booths that lined one wall. He shook my hand and smiled at Krista. Then he sat next to me, resting the trumpet on the table between us. Sitting next to her would have been frowned upon by the club owner, even when the venue was closed to the public.

'Good of you to come, sir.' He had a pleasant southern drawl I hadn't heard since the country was overflowing with Americans ten years earlier.

'Call me, Corky.'

'This is Panama, who I told you about, Rick. We want get out of the country.'

'I told you already, I don't see how I can help?' I tapped the cigarette three times before raising it to my lips.

'You see, sir—' I stopped him by pointing at him with the two fingers that held the ciggie.

'I don't want to hear any of that cap-doffing "sir" shit, Panama. You're a talented boy and have probably had to eat a lot of humble pie in your time. But I have no power over you, so do me a favour and stop the grovelling minstrel act.'

He took a moment to light his own cigarette, taking a deep long drag.

'She tell you about me and her?' I asked.

'Yeah, she told me.' He let the smoke circle his head.

'And if you're any kind of man, you'll be torn up inside that she asked me to help, an old flame, who fucked up his life over a tight skirt and earthly pleasures. You'll have all kinds of images going on inside your head and you won't completely trust me. So forget about the past. It was a thing. It's over.'

'You can trust him, Pete,' she said reaching a hand across the table to Panama. He drew away from her.

'See, Corky. We can't relax here,' she said, while her eyes pleaded for understanding.

'I don't see how I can help,' I said again, I was beginning to hate the sound of my voice. 'Like I said, I have no power and there are no strings I can pull.'

'Austin won't let me go. He refuses to divorce me; he thinks he owns me. He has my passport. If I do anything to embarrass him, he even says he has proof that I am a Nazi sympathiser. I think he means letters from an old aunt.'

'These letters in German?'

'Yar.' She pulled a cigarette holder from her small bag and slotted an unfiltered in place.

'That might be enough with the right jury.'

'He is such a brute, Corky. I barely get a minute to myself. After...' she shot a sideways look at Panama, '...after us, he locked me up for a week. He did things, terrible things to me. It was only because the band needed me, and venues were booked that I'm still alive. His hold on me has slackened recently. But he would kill me if he found out about us, Panama too probably.'

'Then why carry on like this?'

'Everybody needs a bit of tenderness, Corky.'

'Does he know about you two?'

'No. I said he would kill us if he knew.'

'Don't count on it. The chances are that he knows.'

They shared a worried glance.

'I don't see what I can do,' I said again. God, how many times had I said that?

'We only need my passport,' she said, her eyes opening up and promising so much.

'You'll have to elaborate.'

'She's asking you to steal her passport from his study safe,' said Panama, his eyes ready to kill.

*

'Where were you last night, Corky?' Spencer asked after he had shut the cell door.

'Come on, Spencer. Am I really a suspect?'

'You need to answer the question to have any chance of my help.'

'I met Panama once, a week ago. I refused to do a job for him. That was it.'

'The chief wants your chopper on the block. And he's sharpening the cleaver.'

'He hasn't anything on me. I didn't do it.'

'Then tell me where you were last night.' He was an insistent bugger.

'I was with Krista.'

'What? You mean some other Krista, and not the Krista the guy with the cleaver is married to.' His look of concern gave me a little hope for the future.

'I mean Krista Austin, wife of your dear leader.'

'And she will corroborate this?'

'I don't think so. He has her pretty scared.'

'Jesus, Corky, you're a fuckin' madman.'

'Will you help me?'

He paced the small room, removed his hat, pushed his hair back and replaced the hat. Then he turned to look at me.

'I'll see what I can do. I'll tell the DI that I have a chance of getting you to open up to me. I'll insist you stay at my gaff. They don't have a weapon and found nothing in your office, so your solicitor will insist on bail. At least if you're released into my custody, there's a chance I can get information out of you. That sort of thing.'

'Thanks, Spencer.'

And then as he stood by the cell door, he asked, 'Did you do it?'

'Do you really have to ask?'

'You better be telling the truth, old son.'

After the meeting with Panama I went on a bender, visiting every respectable drinking dive in the vicinity and few others that were verboten to ex-coppers. But I was served their watered-down scotch and politely pushed on my way by the criminals that ran them. I woke up two days later with Krista throwing a glass of water on my face.

'If you are going to help me, you need to be better than this,' she said, stubbing her cigarette out in the stained Bakelite ashtray on my desk.

'I told you already, I'm not helping.' My head throbbed and my tongue was thick. 'I don't want to get involved with you again. I don't want to help your spade run away with you. And I don't want to get on the wrong side of your husband.' The long speech had left me breathless and I coughed up enough phlegm to float a boat. 'Just leave me alone Krista. You're bad for a man. You're bad for me.'

'Panama's gone.'

I rubbed my eyes and went to the sink in the corner of the room, took a leak in it and then splashed cold water over my face. I found my cleanest dirty shirt in a drawer and slipped into it.

'You're disgusting.'

'We all have our demons, luv,' I said, sitting behind my desk.

I shook a crumpled cigarette from the packet and tapped it three times before placing it between my lips and lighting it. Then I held the flame while she lit her own.

'Where's he gone?'

'I wouldn't be here if I knew. He should have been at The Gaslight last night, but never showed. We played it more low-key, but without a trumpet player like Panama, something is lost.'

'So you want me to find your trumpet player.'

'Yar.'

'And the passport thing?'

'That doesn't matter now. I'm more worried about Panama.'

'He probably took off on his own. What makes you think something is wrong?'

'Panama wouldn't do that. He was a good man and he wanted to help me. He said if we both got to Paris then we'd be free.'

'What was his poison?'

'People like you.'

'Me?'

'White men. White English men and American men. In Paris, he said they were more tolerant of the black man, accepting his skills and talents ahead of his skin colour.'

'I've got nothing against blacks.'

'Of course you do. It's in your blood, you instantly judge everything not British and white to be inferior.'

'That's a fine thing for a German to say.'

'I am a Jew,' she sneered at me, then stood and walked out the door.

As interviews go, I've had better.

*

The Gaslight had been around for more years than most remembered. The management liked to spread the rumour that even the bombs of the Luftwaffe hadn't shut them down, but I knew better. My borrowed suit didn't fool the doorman who stopped me with his big hand. Fortunately, an old Police ID card did the trick.

Lit by a single spotlight, Krista looked glorious standing on stage in front of the band. Her dress split so far up her long legs, one imagined the glimpse of the top of a stocking. Eyes couldn't help watching and ears couldn't help crying.

She had found a replacement for Panama — what was that saying 'the show must go on'? But he wasn't as good. Perhaps the magic was in Panama's fancy trumpet; perhaps it was Panama's talent.

When the band took their break, she took a stool next to mine at the bar.

'Buy you a drink?' I asked.

'Scotch.'

While we waited for the drinks to be poured, I apologised.

'What for? You can't help it. Somehow we all are capable of hatred.'

'But, if it weren't for the English, you might have...'

'I am aware of what I have to thank the English for.'

We sipped the drinks silently.

'I'll see if I can find your trumpet player.'

'Thank you. I'll come to your office tomorrow before noon. Make sure you are sober.'

'Can't we talk here?'

'Austin will be here soon. He makes sure I'm home with no opportunity to be with anyone else.'

'So how did you and Panama manage to find time together?'

'Rehearsals. Now go, please, before he gets here.'

'You could just go you know. Those diamonds around your neck would buy a fake passport and a place to live in Paris.'

'I don't want to live as someone else. I want my papers and I want Panama.'

I left as she returned to the stage and I seriously questioned my sanity for getting involved with this woman again.

*

'How was he killed?' I asked Spence from my seat at his kitchen table. For all his flash suits and style, he lived in a hole of a flat. Damp ran down the wall behind the sink and cooker, pulling greasy wallpaper with it. But a policeman's salary can only buy you so much.

'Run through with a knife, a big one. He was found floating in the canal.'

'Any other injuries? Was he in a fight?' I picked at the chipped Formica at the edge of the table.

'Large bruise to the temple.' He stood by the cooker waiting for the kettle to whistle.

'How do you know he was killed last night?'

'That's what the doc says and what the doc says goes.' The kettle began its shrill cry and, holding it with dirty tea towel, he poured the water into two mugs. The one thing the Americans left behind that I was grateful for was instant coffee. He passed on the milk after sniffing the rim of the bottle and grimacing. I prefer it black anyway.

'The doc play golf with old man Austin?'

'I don't know. Why do you ask?' The coffee slopped as he placed in it front of me.

'Cheers. Panama went missing three days ago and I was looking for him. Last I heard he left his digs for The Gaslight. A thirty-minute walk.'

'How do you know he didn't catch a bus?'

'Not all the drivers let blacks on. So rather than suffer the humiliation of being refused, he would walk. And that should not have taken him past the canal. One option could be that he was attacked for his trumpet or money. But a mugger would not have tried to dispose of the body. Where is the trumpet?'

'No idea. Not in his room. Could have been racial – plenty of stupid yobs do that sort of thing for fun.'

'Nah,' I said after sipping the coffee. 'It's not that.'

'What do you know? Why do you want to know who the chief plays golf with?'

'Krista and Panama were planning on doing a flit.'

'Jesus Christ. She knows how to pick 'em. And you think Fred Austin bumped him off, do you?'

'It's a possibility.'

'Bollocks. The old man isn't capable.'

'I know things about him, Spence. He does things to her.'

'He's her husband, and she's a Kraut.'

'And that make it alright?'

Spence shrugged his shoulders.

'He looked like he might kill me that night he found me with her.'

'Course he did. You were giving his missus a length. What do you expect? Cup of tea, congratulations on a job well done and then compare notes?'

'Believe me, he's capable. He's as crooked as they come.'

'Are you joking? Old man Austin.' He stood and went to his jacket where his smokes resided.

'I know, Spence. I've had to do a lot of listening since I became self-employed. He's as corrupt as they come and I would bet my last drop of whisky that he's behind this. He found out about their affair and put an end to it. Have you spoken to her yet?'

'It's not really my case. I'm too far down the pecking order. He's taken direct control of the investigation. I had to work very hard to get you out of the cells.'

'And you don't think that's a bit fishy? Why would he be bothered about a murdered spade?'

'Course it's fishy, but I just can't see him killing anyone.'

'Come on. Let's visit Krista.' I picked up my cigarettes and lighter and reached for my jacket.

'Whoa. Easy tiger. Tell me what you were doing with her last night.' He stopped with an arm half inside the jacket.

'Nothing.'

'Are you sure?'

'Yeah. I wasn't even with her. I met her during the day to give a progress report. But last night, no, I didn't see her.' Now my jacket was on and shrugged into place, I lit a smoke, bouncing it three times on the packet first.

'For crying out loud, Corky. Why would you lie to me?'

'I was playing for time.'

'It's put you right back in the frame.'

'I have alibis for every night of the week – ask any of the regulars in The Shepherd, or The Dog's Head. Let me ask you a question. Do you know where Fred Austin was last night or several nights before that?'

'No. Okay, let's pay a visit to the sultress of swing.'

We went to the Gaslight where Krista sat at the bar with a drink. She didn't see us arrive and for a moment she looked like a lost child. She dabbed at her eyes when she saw me, but her face hardened when she looked at Spence. The deep pools that I longed to dive into had iced over.

'Hello, Krista. May we join you?' I asked.

She gave permission with a nod of her head.

'You've heard?' I asked.

'About Panama, yes. Who is this?'

'This is Detective Sergeant Spencer. I'm in his custody until they find out who killed Panama.'

'Hello, Krista. Mind if I ask a few questions?' Spence said.

Again, she nodded.

'How well did you know Panama?'

'I think you know the answer, detective,' she said, blowing a smoke ring towards him.

'And when did you last see him?' Spence continued.

'And you know the answer to that one, too.'

'Listen, Krista—'

'Hold on, Spence,' I said. It was clear she wouldn't talk to him. 'How did you find out, Krista?'

'Austin told me.'

'When?'

'What?'

'When did he tell you about Panama?'

'This morning. He phoned.'

'What else did he tell you?'

21

'That you were in the cells and that you would be hanged for it.'

'Why would he tell you?'

She shrugged her shoulders. Her red lips formed a sulky pout.

'Was he gloating, do you think?'

'Perhaps.'

Spencer said, 'Obviously he was rubbing salt in old wounds.'

'But why? Why is he so interested in the case? He never takes personal charge of an investigation. He couldn't care less about who did what to whom, unless it's one of the local squires or the rotary club. Why did he send the boys round to do me over this morning? What made him want to frame me for this?' I turned to Krista. 'Is it possible he may have known about you and Panama?'

'But we were very careful. More than anything we were friends with plans for the future.'

'Did you ever discuss the plans anywhere you could have been overheard? Did anyone else know?'

'There was only us and then you.'

'Listen, Corky,' said Spence, 'you can't still think old man Austin did this. He's lazy, out of shape and only interested in climbing the greasy pole.'

'He has an interest in this place. Did either of you know that?' They both shook their heads. 'I wouldn't be surprised if he has someone reporting back to him about your friendliness with Panama. He probably knows that I've met you here on several occasions, Krista, once with Panama.'

'How do you know this?' Spence asked.

'It's my job to know. I am sorry about Panama, Krista, but it's too dangerous to be seen together in public. From now on, I suggest we only meet at my office. Come there when you're ready.'

*

My office looked like a storm had hit it. The police officers weren't searching; they were destroying, intimidating and humiliating me. It's an old tactic. Spence helped right chairs and pick up paperwork.

'If he did kill Panama,' he asked, while scooping paper back into the waste-paper basket, 'and he wants to fit you up for the murder, then why hasn't he planted the knife yet?'

'That's a good point.'

'Well?'

'I don't know.'

I too, had pondered on that exact problem. So I told Spence everything I knew about Austin's corrupt life.

'He blackmails the owners and managers of establishments. It's how he operates and he's very smooth about it. Nothing big, you understand. If, for instance, he found out about Mr Smith doing the Saturday girl, he would offer his silence in return for five percent of the business. He has a twenty-five percent stake in The Gaslight. God knows what he has on the management to secure that sort of silence. Once he has a stake, he conveniently ignores illegal activity.

'Now, if he knew about Krista and Panama, which is likely because he is good at finding out secrets, then he should be your prime suspect.'

'How can I prove this?'

'Find the murder weapon.'

'You think he'd be stupid enough to keep it?'

'He sure hasn't planted it on me. And I think he's arrogant enough to think he wouldn't be suspected. We need to search his house.'

'I can't just search the Chief Constable's house. Not without a warrant.'

'In that case we need to be sure the evidence is there first.'

'You better not be suggesting the planting of evidence.'

'Of course not. But we could search the house looking for genuine evidence, when he's not there, on the sly.'

'Break in! Jesus, my career's on the line.'

'Justice is on the line, Spence. He will find a way to get me for this, we both know it. And Krista deserves to be free of him.'

I poured him a drink. He shook his head and I smiled as he took a sip anyway. I remained quiet while the idea settled.

'Tonight then,' he said, 'but I'm not doing anything dodgy. I've never been a bent copper.'

'Pull the other one. When you were in uniform, there was that tart—'

'That was different. I was young and she wasn't doing any harm.'

'Have it your way.'

*

Dressed in black and looking like something from one of the war films that were so popular, we sat outside the walls of Fred Austin's house in Spence's new car waiting for the old man to leave. According to Krista, we would have about half an hour. After Austin had reversed his car down the drive at ten fifteen, we got out of Spence's Morris Minor and I gave Spence a leg up to the top of the garden wall, then he reached down to haul me up. Spence turned his back while I picked the backdoor lock. We slipped inside, silent as cats. We had already agreed that Spence would search the kitchen and garage while I went upstairs to search Austin's study and bedroom. We had a general idea of the layout from Krista. I quickly searched the tallboy and wardrobe of his bedroom before heading for his study, which was the next room along.

Austin's study was typical of the sort. A wall-to-wall burgundy carpet, with small gold-coloured diamond shapes, covering the floor. Above the wood panelling, several framed prints were illuminated by individual electric bulbs. One wall had floor to ceiling shelves lined with leatherbound books, probably never even opened. A suit of armour loomed in one corner. His mahogany desk stood not quite dead centre of the room, giving it an asymmetrical feel, which was wrong and somehow off-balance. But I had no time to inspect his interior design nuances too closely. What I had to do, I had to do without Spence knowing. I lowered a framed print—The Hay Wain by John Constable—to the floor, revealing the slightly recessed door of the safe. It should have been easy to crack as it was an old-style triple combination rotary dial, which only needed a good ear and a steady hand to unlock. But this wasn't my normal line of work and my hands shook terribly. I knew Spence wouldn't leave me alone for long. The two minutes it took to open the safe stretched on for an eternity. I had no idea what I'd say if Spence walked in on me. As I turned the handle I heard him call out to me in a hushed whisper.

I rammed everything I needed into the deep inside pocket of my jacket. I could hear him along the landing trying one of the doors. Thank God, he couldn't remember the layout too well.

As he opened the study door, I was closing a drawer in Austin's mahogany desk.

'Anything?' he asked.

'Nothing. You?'

'No. Come on, let's get out of here.'

'Hang on, what about a safe?' I said, in a feigned attempt at innocence. 'He must have a safe.'

'Do you know how to crack a safe?'

'Not especially.'

'Well, forget it then. It's a washout. Let's go.'

And it was a washout or so I thought until I asked, 'Why is his desk to piss?'

'I don't know. Come on let's go.' I shone my torch into Spence's face. Sweat stood in shiny dots on top of his boot-polished forehead. Of course he was worried, his whole career would fall apart if we were discovered, or if anyone ever found out.

'One more minute.' Shining the torch at the carpet, I could see the heavy desk had left imprints in the carpet. I knelt down and yes, the desk had been moved and was covering a stain. A tacky stain that was slightly darker than the carpet, which seeped out from under the new position of the desk.

This was better than a bloody knife. It put Panama right there in Austin's study. We had the old bastard. Spence and I looked at each other, me with a smile splitting my face in two and him with a look of fear.

'Let's go,' he said, dragging me to my feet.

'No,' I said, going over to the suit of armour. My mind was a whirl, picturing the scene. 'What's the betting that's the murder weapon?' I asked pointing at the four foot long-sword positioned centrally, tip down, in the grip of the suit of armour. Removing my glove, I ran the pad of my thumb across the edge of the blade.

'It's razor sharp.' I only saw fear in Spence's eyes.

We hurried down the wide stairs as the light from car headlights swept up the drive, partially illuminating the hallway. It was close; they were opening the front door as we were slipping out the back.

Spence and I talked long into the night. The implications were ground-breaking, and my friend was fearful of the outcome. Going up against the Chief Constable would make or break his career. But he agreed, once we'd met with Krista and found her somewhere safe to stay, that he would put a case forward to his DI or even the DCI to apply for a warrant to search Austin's house for evidence. He would have to tell his superiors that Krista had been having an affair with Panama and she would have to come clean about it, even if she couldn't bear witness against her husband. The fact the affair existed was a large motive. Spence would moot the point that the Chief Constable should not be in charge as there was a conflict of interest, and should in fact be considered a suspect. He would question why Austin had not made it known that Krista and Panama knew each other from the band, it was bound to come out. He would say that he had stumbled over the fact by accident, that when he quizzed her she was quite blatant about it.

And all the while we were planning, I couldn't let Spence know how anxious I was for Krista's safety. What would happen if Austin realised her papers and letters were missing? Would he care more about the missing cash? These questions dominated my thoughts, hindering my attempts at sleep.

But the next morning, she walked into my office looking like dynamite. Spence, sitting on the sofa, stopped thinking like a copper and started thinking like a man. She and I stood looking at each other.

'We found blood on his study carpet, Krista,' I said.

She looked from me to Spence, who quickly raised his eyes to nod his head in agreement.

'Panama's?'

'Bit early to say. But there was a lot of it. I imagine Austin is planning to get the carpet disposed of fairly soon, so we need to move quickly. Spence here is going into the station to present his findings to his superior.'

'How can he do that?' she asked. 'He can't let them know he broke in last night.'

'I'm going to tell them about you and Panama,' said Spence. 'The chief should have made it known you played in a band together. This very basic information led to you telling me about your affair with the trumpet player.'

'I would never tell you such a thing. They will see that you are lying.'

'We have to start somewhere. When they agree to the facts, we can search the house and find the bloody carpet and what we think is the murder weapon.'

'And how will they agree to the facts?' she asked.

'When you confirm it to them,' he said.

'No, I won't.'

'Please, Krista. It is the only way,' I said.

'No. Find another.'

'Why?' I asked.

'Because he will hurt me. That is why.'

'Interviews with the band then, back room rumours,' Spence continued. 'I'll say you have a certain way of avoiding the question. You'll have to come in though. Damn it, Krista, this is murder.' Spence was angry and prepared to use every tactic he had at his disposal.

'Do not try to scare me, little man. I remember what the uniformed police are truly capable of. My parents went away for questioning and never returned.' She turned her back on him and I couldn't help smiling as he sat deflated, the wind truly taken from his sails.

'Spence will think of something. We'll wait here.'

'No you won't. You're in my custody, Corky. When I turn up at the station, you better be with me.'

'Jesus, do we have to?'

'Yes. Get your coat. Krista, wait here. I'll think of a way to search his study.'

That was when I came to realise that the only chance was to let her go. It was apparent to me that as soon as the affair was made public knowledge, old man Austin would do for her, probably managing to frame me for her murder. Or maybe not, but knowing him the way I did and hearing her talk about him, I realised he was tapped in the head, mentally deranged and insane with jealously — she had driven him to it. I reached inside my jacket and pulled out a large envelope.

'Your passport, letters and some of his money. Just go, right now in the clothes you're wearing. You have that sparkler around your neck, use it. You can be out of the country by the end of the day.'

Spencer's police brain started working, he wound his tongue in, sprang to his feet, and twirling me around by the shoulder said, 'Damn it, Corky, she's a suspect. I can't let her go.'

The time for talking had passed, so I landed a right on his chin, his head snapped and he crumpled to the floor like a paper chain folding on top of itself. I made sure he was comfortable. When he woke a few minutes later, he found himself sitting with his hands tied behind his back and gag in his mouth.

'A plane leaves every day for Paris from London Airport, at one o'clock,' I said to her. 'Be on it, it will land just before three thirty. And you'll be beyond his reach.'

'But I can't go on my own.'

'You're a survivor, Krista. You'll be fine.'

'Come with me. It will be like the old days.'

'No, it won't. I'm not the man I used to be, but I'll make sure your husband pays for what he's done.'

The taxi collected her ten minutes later, taking her away forever. I hope she still sings and is happy. I would never have been enough for her.

*

'Now, you want to know for sure who killed Panama Harlan, don't you? I can tell you for certain that I didn't bump him off, no matter what the jury say next week. It wasn't Spence although he certainly left me floating in the shitter. As soon as I untied his wrists, he arrested me and dropped all plans of pursuing Austin and I couldn't convince him otherwise — I think his fear got to him. It could have been Krista, but she gained nothing from Panama's death, quite the opposite actually.

'Trust me, Austin did it. I see him coming in on Panama while he's attempting to crack the safe. I suspect he lashed out and landed a lucky blow. Panama might have hit his head on the corner of that big desk and then, mad with rage, Austin killed him with the nearest weapon, which happened to be a medieval sword.'

'Do you have anything else to confess, my child?'

'No, Father. Will you pass a message along?'

'That is not my role.'

'Please — I'm going to hang for something that I didn't do.'

'What's your message?'

'Will you remind Spence about friendship and justice? Convince him to come forward; tell the truth, shame the Devil.'

Tall Tales

(First appeared in Oceans by Black Hare Press.)

I'm only a simple fisherman, making a modest living alone in a small boat hauling cold, wet nets by hand.

I've had some rare old catches in my time. Pulled a mermaid in once, I did. Truth. Don't look at me like that.

She weren't no looker, anyway.

'nother night, a dead body ends up in the nets. Headless it were, naked and bloated too. Nearly shit myself, I did.

I threw it back. Nothing I could do for the poor sod, was there?

The look on your fizzog tells me ya don't believe me.

No one ever believes fishermen.

A Surfeit of Death

(First appeared in Enigma by Clarendon House. It is notable as the first appearance of Mortimer Marsh, Morty to his friends.)

Dramatis Personae

Richard Allinson, Superintendent, Criminal Investigation Department

Jimmy Monroe, Detective Sergeant, Criminal Investigation Department

Dr Sean Harris, Police Doctor / Surgeon

Isabelle Balantine, glamorous socialite

Sir Michael Melrose, the War Office

Reginald Balantine, millionaire industrialist

Lady Sisely Balantine, his wife

Jennifer Balantine, their daughter

Mortimer Marsh, cousin to Isabelle

Patrice Lombard, dress designer

Madeline Plunkett, friend of Jennifer

Timothy Sinclair, friend of Mortimer

Mr Ambrose, Butler

Percival Wilkins, Assistant Commissioner, Metropolitan Police Force

Hamish, an Aberdeen Terrier

Evening Chronicle July 21ˢᵗ, 1936

Heiress Dies Under Mysterious Circumstances
The family of Isabelle Balantine are in shock
today, after the glamorous socialite died under
unexplained circumstances, at a private party for
her 23rd birthday at the family's Mayfair house.
We are reliably informed that Scotland Yard
have sent their finest detective. You can be sure
the culprit won't be able to avoid the long arm
of the law with Superintendent Richard Allinson
on the case.

Superintendent Allinson stepped from the car into a puddle. The rain poured incessantly. He raised his umbrella in a feeble attempt to keep dry, but as he seemed to be wading through a foot of water, wondered why he bothered. His sodden feet climbed the steps beyond the white pillars with the number '25' neatly presented on each.

He was greeted by a uniform, miraculously drier than himself, who stood guard outside the residence. The uniform opened the door for him with an informal salute. Once inside, Allinson stamped his feet and shook out the umbrella. A stand for such a utensil to his right allowed him to deposit the awkward thing.

He observed the layout of the house while waiting — without much hope — to be greeted by a member of staff. The hallway with large black and white chequered floor tiles, was dominated by a wide set of stairs carpeted in blood-red Axminster, which ascended to a minstrel gallery. Canvases adorned the burgundy walls, mostly country scenes, mainly themed around the hunt. Illumination was provided by a chandelier with what must have been a hundred electric light bulbs.

From the hallway, two doors either side of the aforementioned stairs led to what he imagined were various reception rooms. One door under these impressive risers would no doubt descend into a dark and grim basement kitchen and butler's rooms, various.

Hearing raised voices in a room to his left, and being a detective, he decided to investigate.

Allinson opened the door to see Detective Sergeant Monroe asking for calm. A butler was serving brandy. Men and women in various stages of evening or night attire were scattered about the room. Everyone stopped to watch the newcomer as he hesitantly observed the tableau.

'Er,' he said.

'Who are you?' said a woman of battleship proportions.

After finally getting up the nerve to fully step into the room, he replied, 'Superintendent Allins—'

'Good, then kindly tell this impudent youth to let us return to our rooms,' she continued in an unpleasant, supercilious manner.

'If you could bear with us for just a few more minutes,' Allinson said to the room at large. Looking to DS Monroe, he added, 'A minute of your time, Sergeant.'

'Yes, sir.'

When they were both in the hallway, he said, 'Better take me to the body, Monroe.'

'Upstairs, sir. Might not be a straightforward one this time, sir,' Monroe said as they trudged up the stairs.

'Seen a few dead bodies in my time, Monroe, I'm sure we'll cope. Police doctor here yet?'

'Any minute now, sir.'

They heard the door open behind them and turned to see a little man in a bowler hat and long trench coat that dragged on the floor. He carried the usual doctor's kit — stethoscope, hip flask, sedative for the ladies — in a leather Gladstone.

'Hello, Dickie,' he called up to the two policemen, his warm Irish lilt filling the cavernous space.

'I'm on duty, Dr Harris. Try to be a bit more formal.'

'Right you are, old son. Where's the cadaver?'

'We're on our way up to take a look now.'

'Jolly good,' said the doctor as he skipped up to join them.

The body of Isabelle Balantine lay on the right-hand side of the double bed, completely concealed by the quilted eiderdown, except for the head, which had a neat hole in the temple, and a right arm that dangled toward the floor. Held loosely in the hand was a small feminine pistol. As well as her eyes being open, dark scorch marks surrounded the hole, blood trickled from both the wound and the ear, and froth had dried around her mouth and run down her chin.

'Straightforward enough. Suicide, wouldn't you say, Harris?' said Allinson.

The doctor moved the head slightly to look into the eyes.

'Strange, I think her pupils are dilated,' said Harris.

'I thought that, sir. Perhaps—' interjected Monroe.

'Quiet, Monroe,' Allinson said sharply.

'But there's another thing, sir,' Monroe persisted.

'Monroe, I'm talking with the doctor.'

'The doctor will find out anyways, sir.'

'Go on. What is it?' he said, mentally raising his eyes to the heavens.

DS Monroe pulled the bed cover back.

'Oh my, oh my, oh my,' said the doctor, with a chuckle. 'This does complicate matters, although it doesn't explain her dilated eyes or why she has dried vomit on her chin.'

'But that's blood, Monroe.' Allinson rubbed the back of his neck, a familiar gesture that Monroe had become used to. The superintendent was perplexed.

'Yes, sir. She's been stabbed as well.'

'Yes, Monroe, I can see that, thank you. Well, Harris, what is it? Murder or suicide?' asked Allinson.

'My dear fellow, it's too early to say. I'll carry out the post-mortem. Run all the usual tests. Let you know tomorrow, er… later today. But it does beg the question, if she was stabbed first, why didn't she scream out or struggle?' He picked up the Gladstone bag and asked Monroe, 'How are the ladies bearing up? Any hysteria?'

'I don't think so, Dr Harris.'

'Hmm, pity.' The little man turned and plodded away.

Allinson led the way out of the room. 'Better fill me in on the details, Monroe.'

'Earlier tonight, a group was gathered to celebrate the deceased's twenty-third birthday. Present was her father, Reginald Balantine, a millionaire industrialist, something of a name in rivets; his wife, the deceased's step-mother, Sisely Balantine — she's a lady, youngest daughter of an earl, I think; Jennifer Balantine, step-sister of the deceased, and her friend Madeline Plunkett.'

'You don't have to keep saying deceased, Monroe. I am capable of keeping up.'

'Yes, sir. Also present was Mortimer Marsh, cousin, more or less brought up by the family; his friend Timothy Sinclair; Sir Michael Melrose of The War Office, not happy about being kept waiting, and Mr Patrice Lombard, a dress designer. They'd announced their engagement tonight, sir.'

'Sir Michael and Lombard are engaged?'

'No, sir. Lombard and the er, deceased were engaged, sir.'

'Okay, we have eight suspects. So, she either killed herself with a bullet and someone stabbed a dead body, or she was killed twice and someone tried to make it look like suicide not knowing she had already been stabbed. Tricky, Monroe, very tricky. I'd better go and have a brief word. Arrange for the body to be taken away, would you?'

'The ambulance is waiting outside, sir. I've arranged for the rooms to be searched for the knife.'

'Good.'

*

Allinson entered the drawing room for the second time to find everyone where he remembered them to be. A tall broad-shouldered man with grey wavy hair and a bristling moustache quickly advanced on him.

'Sorry for your loss, Mr Balantine. If I can keep you all here for a few more minutes while formalities are concluded?'

'I'm Sir Michael Melrose. Balantine's over there,' he said, indicating a shorter, plumper man standing next to the woman of supercilious nature. 'Look here, Superintendent, it's vital that I'm allowed to leave at once and that no one else knows of my presence here tonight. I shall a take a very dim view if the press find out.'

'I see. Perhaps there is a room where we can talk privately before you go,' said the superintendent with a questioning look toward Reginald Balantine.

'Use the library, directly opposite. Michael knows it well,' said Mr Balantine, with a wave of his hand.

They made their way across the hall and into the library. Once inside, Allinson quickly interrupted the minister's self-important protestations.

'Sir, may I assume that you're here on confidential, if not secret business?'

'What makes you say that?'

'It is usually the way with these things. A meeting held while a more innocent gathering is taking place.'

'Your supposition is correct. But I cannot talk about it with you. It is a matter of national security. I'm sure you understand.'

Allinson nodded his head in compliance and said, 'But I do have to ask, did you have any other dealings with the family? When did you first become acquainted with them, and did you know Isabelle Balantine before this evening?'

'Balantine and I are members of the Ballona club; we've known each other for four or five years. I've dined here on three previous occasions, and I have only encountered members of the family here on those occasions.' He twitched at the ends of his moustache.

'Do you know who was first on the scene, that is to say, who found the body?'

'It was me, Superintendent. Balantine and I were talking here, in the library. We both heard the shot and raced out of here and up the stairs. I reached the room slightly ahead of him. Balantine had to break the news to Sisely; she'd slept through it.'

'Where were the rest of the party?'

'Dancing. In fact, they arrived back just as it dawned on us all what had happened. We could hear them making a damn awful racket as they came in.'

'And you didn't see anyone unexpected?'

'No. Now, if you really don't mind, Superintendent?' said Sir Michael as he picked his briefcase up from beside the sofa.

'Just one more thing, Sir Michael. Would you give me a brief overview of the party guests?'

'Really, this is intolerable.'

'Your impartial view would a valuable insight.'

'Oh, very well. Reginald: important industrialist, self-made man, sound fellow if a little uncouth. Lady Sisely: self-obsessed, self-important, resents marrying below her station. Jennifer Balantine: spoilt in much the same mould as her mother, if a little mannish. Mortimer Marsh: cousin of the family, brought up by them, not the brightest button. Timothy Sinclair: a nobody, not my sort of man. A girl called Madeline, another nobody. Patrice Lombard: a popinjay, designs dresses or some such thing, took the dandy quite some time to find the right girl.'

'And what were your thoughts on Isabelle?'

'Nice girl, full of life, always a twinkle in her eye. Now, may I leave?'

'Of course, sir. Thank you.'

They left the library together as the body of Isabelle Balantine was being stretchered down the stairs, a white hospital sheet covering her. Sir Michael stopped and respectively lowered his head.

'Sad day,' he said and followed the stretcher out into the night after the butler handed him his hat and coat.

*

Sergeant Monroe joined Allinson in the drawing room, where the guests immediately started to harangue the superintendent. 'Prisoners in our own home,' ... 'Little man thinks he can keep us prisoner,' ... 'I shall be speaking with the Assistant Commissioner about this dreadful treatment,' ... 'Dashed silly way to treat people, if you ask me,' ... 'Nobody asked you anything, Morty.'

He had to raise his voice to be heard above the din.

'Ladies and gentlemen, please, calm yourselves. Please.'

The hubbub died down, allowing Allinson to return to a quieter tone of voice. 'Am I to take it that some of you are house guests for the weekend?'

Lady Sisely stepped forward, forcing Allinson to take a step back. 'Indeed they are, and as my guests, I find your treatment of them very poor. I shall be having words with my friend, Sir Percival...'

'That is your prerogative, ma'am. You are all free to return to your rooms, but I request that you don't leave the house for a day or two until our inquiries are concluded.' The party started to head for the door to the hallway and from there up to their individual rooms.

'Er, pardon me, Mr Balantine. A word before you retire,' said Allinson, to the short, plump industrialist.

'What?'

'A word, sir, before you go to bed.'

'Well, what is it?'

'Would you mind describing the scene when you arrived with Sir Michael?'

'Bloody stupid question. Pretty much what you saw, Superintendent. I arrived at the same time as Melrose, and Isabelle was lying there like she was sleeping. We were unsure at first, but the gun in her hand was still smoking.' He wiped at one eye with his thumb.

'The room had been searched, had it?'

'I don't know; yes, I think so. Why would she do that? She had everything to live for. It must have been an intruder, a tramp perhaps. You should arrest all the tramps, Superintendent, force them to work.'

'We might, sir. I'm not entirely convinced it was suicide.'

'But that would mean —'

'Yes, sir. I have a few questions. The sheets of the bed were covering her body, were they?'

'What? Yes, of course they were.'

'And your wife didn't hear the gunshot.'

'No, she'd taken a sedative. I had to rouse her pretty vigorously.'

'And, before the gunshot, Sir Michael and yourself were together the whole time?'

'Yes…no, not the whole time. He had to get papers from his room, but he was gone for no more than ten minutes.'

'And what time would that have been?'

'Oh, about eleven o'clock.'

'And some of your guests went dancing. What time was that?'

'About ten o'clock.'

'And why did Miss Balantine not go with them?'

'She had a headache, felt a bit nauseous. Cried off early and took herself off to bed.'

'Really,' said Allinson. 'And what time was that?'

'Not sure, between nine-fifteen and nine-thirty I think.'

'One more thing. Are you aware of Miss Balantine's testamentary disposition?'

'Her what?'

'A will, did she have a will?'

'She didn't have much of her own. She survived on an annual allowance from the trust set up by her mother's father. She comes into full possession of the capital on her twenty-fifth birthday or when she's married. The sticking point for modern girls was there was an additional clause stipulating that her husband would have full access to her accounts. He didn't believe women could control their own affairs. Something to do with the size of their brains apparently.'

'And if she didn't marry?'

'Isabelle would not have remained unmarried. She was a modern beauty. But I see your point, Superintendent. I suppose it has to be assumed she would die an old maid having frittered away all her money.'

'How much money would that be?'

'About a hundred thousand pounds.'

'And now what happens to the trust?'

'I suppose it all goes to Mortimer. His mother was Isabelle's aunt, I mean Isabelle's mother's sister. Their father made his money in coal and set up the trust for his two grandchildren.'

'Thank you, Mr Balantine, and may I say once again how sorry I am to meet in such circumstances?'

'Are there any other circumstances we are likely to meet under?'

'Er, no. Probably not.'

When the two policemen were left alone, Monroe said, 'A hundred thousand pounds is a very large motive, sir.'

'It certainly is, but Mortimer is due for the same amount when he turns twenty-five. It's no motive at all.'

'What next, sir?'

'No murder weapon yet, I suppose?'

'No, not yet, but these did turn up in the deceased's room. In her dresser, looked like they'd been hidden away.'

'Love letters. That's my reading material for the night then,' Allinson said, placing them in a pocket of his jacket. 'Are the staff still up?'

'All downstairs.'

'Fine. Ask them the usual questions. Don't mention the stabbing, not yet anyway. Then get some rest. Back here at seven. Did you put a man outside the girl's room?'

'Yes, sir.'

*

DS Monroe arrived on the dot of seven, springing with youth and vigour. By contrast, Allinson hadn't been home and looked as if he hadn't slept. His clothes had taken on that lived-in look, which only policemen unable to lay their head on a comforting pillow for the night tend to find themselves wearing.

'Morning, Monroe. What did the servants have to say for themselves?'

'Morning, sir. The cook and her assistant, and one footman who helped serve dinner, saw and heard nothing unusual or did anything they didn't normally do. The butler arrived on the scene after the two gentlemen, only after the bell to the butler's pantry had been rung from the deceased's bedroom. Apparently, he didn't hear the shot all the way down there. And I believe him. Upon his arrival at the scene, he was told to telephone for the police, so he returned to the library to put the call through. While he was making the call, Balantine was rousing his wife. It was about then that the dancing party arrived back.'

'She can't have committed suicide, the room had already been searched by the time Sir Michael and her father arrived. And a living person wouldn't let that happen, would they? Besides, no one would try to kill what is on first impressions a suicide. My thinking is the girl must have been dead from the stabbing when the room was searched. The real question is, did that person stab

Isabelle Balantine before they searched the room, or did they ignore the corpse?'

'Are the letters enough of a motive, sir?'

'Possibly. They're initialled "M.M."'

'Mortimer Marsh or Sir Michael Melrose.'

'The guests should be down for breakfast soon. I'll question Marsh, you tackle Timothy Sinclair and Madeline Plunkett.'

'But they was dancing, sir. Surely, they are alibied by each other. It's more likely to be Sir Michael. He was here at the time.'

'I know, Sergeant. I know. And, Monroe, we keep the stabbing to ourselves. Tell them we're not happy with her suicide. That's all.'

'Yes, sir.'

*

As it happened, Mortimer Marsh was the first down to breakfast. He found the superintendent hovering by the doors to the patio.

'What ho, Super,' he said, with a bounce in his step.

'Good morning, Mr Marsh. Sleep well?'

'Like the proverbial log,' he said, lifting the lids of terrines and helping himself to sausage, bacon and devilled kidneys.

'Good. Would you come along to the library for a quick chat?'

'Oh, fine, fine. Shall I bring this with me?' he asked, holding up his morning's nourishment.

In the library, Marsh sat at his uncle's desk and complimented Allinson for all the clever brain-work the police do. How they got the time to run around catching burglars and thieves and who-knows-what, as well as bend the bean as to how the crimes were actually done staggered him.

'Thank you. Now please, if you don't mind, what was your relationship with Isabelle like?'

'Oh, you know,' he said with a wobble of the head.

'No, sir, I don't.'

'Oh, yes, I see, ha-ha. Ah well, me and Izzy — that's what I called her, Izzy — got on fine. In fact, when we were ankle-biters we used to pretend we were going to get married to each other. You know, set up shop together, feed from the same trough and all that guff.'

'So you were on friendly terms.'

'Good lord, no!' ejaculated Mortimer. 'She could be a complete menace. Always wanting me to set her up with some poor unsuspecting fellow. Always getting me to walk her blasted hound. Always landing yours truly in the *potage*.'

'So you're not upset by her death then, Mr Marsh?'

'Ah, well, I am and all that. Stiff upper lip; you know, the British way in the face of adversity and all that rot.'

'I see. Now, to last night, you went dancing. Is that correct?'

'Yes, Café de Paris. Jennifer's idea; she goes absolutely head-over-heels for Cole Porter. I prefer Al Bowlly; there's only so much "Let's Do It" a chap can take, but that new one of his is much more my sort of thing. Have you heard it yet?' Mortimer broke into song, the words of 'Anything Goes' muffled by bacon.

'No, sir,' Allinson interrupted. 'And you were *all* there *all* the time: Miss Balantine, Timothy Sinclair, Madeline Plunkett and Patrice Lombard?'

'Well, I think so. There was quite a bit of foot shaking and talking to other chaps, don't-cha-know.'

'One more thing. Do you recognise these, Mr Marsh?' Allinson said, removing the letters from his inside pocket and laying them on the desk.

'Never seen 'em before, old fruit. Incriminating evidence, is it? But she shot herself, didn't she?'

'I'm not entirely satisfied that it was suicide, Mr Marsh.'

'You mean murder, eh? Well, I'd no reason to see young Izzy snuffed out, no matter how much of a pill she could be.'

'Thank you, Mr Marsh. You can return to the breakfast room. Please ask Miss Balantine to come along if she's there.'

'Righto,' he said, leaving the dirty plate for someone else to attend to.

As Mortimer left the library, the telephone sounded its abrupt clang. Allinson grabbed it before the second round of tinnitus-inducing clanging began.

'Allinson here…Good morning, Doctor…Really…Within two hours of being stabbed, I thought so…Most interesting…What? Repeat that for me in English, Harris…Hemlock…But that means she was killed three times!'

*

Allinson pulled on the ringer by the fireplace. Almost instantly, the butler, Ambrose, arrived.

'You rang, Superintendent.' He was from cockney stock. Nevertheless, he carried himself with that refined air that only men of his occupation seem to possess.

'Yes, Ambrose. What was on the menu for last night's celebration?'

'Coquille St Jacques, 'ole stuffed quail with Madeira sauce, creamed spinach, h'asparagus, h'and game chips, followed by Charlotte De Bananes. Cheese h'and figs.'

'I'll send one of the uniforms down to the kitchen to retrieve the remains.'

'That is h'impossible, Superintendent.'

'Why?'

'They 'ave h'already been disposed of, Superintendent. I'm h'afraid 'amish finished the meal for 'is breakfast.'

Dread settled on the superintendent's shoulders, like a murder of crows settling in an old oak tree.

'"Amish"?' he repeated.

'Miss Balantine's h'Aberdeen Terrier, Superintendent.'

'What do you know about hemlock, Monroe?' asked Allinson.

'Not much, sir, why?' replied Monroe.

'She was poisoned with it last night.'

'What? Was it in the drinks, sir?'

'The butler prepared White Ladies, distributed them on a silver salver and let the guests help themselves.'

'He could have spiked one and guided it in her direction, sir.'

'Are you seriously suggesting the butler did it?'

'But how then?'

'Harris hasn't finished with his tests. We might have a better idea later today.'

'If you think about it,' said Monroe, 'Lady Sisely would have planned the meal with the cook days in advance.'

'It's the cook now, is it? And how did she not poison everyone else?'

'The butler placed the poisoned food in front of Isabelle.'

'The butler and the cook are in it together, are they? Really, Monroe?'

*

Patrice Lombard reclined on the soft sofa like an engorged sea lion. His balding head reflected a modicum of light from the nearby window, while his colourful smoking jacket hid a bulging stomach. He took a moment to suck on the cigarette holder before answering the superintendent. Allinson's nostrils rejected the overpowering scent of liquorish.

'I met my dear sweet Isabelle six months ago. We were introduced by Lady Georgette Fenwick-Ffield. Do you know her? Lovely person. Very much her own woman. Isabelle was a vision and perfectly suited to my designs. We came to an arrangement, and she agreed to appear as a mannequin for me. Quite a coup on my part, a society girl agreeing to be in my frocks.

'We agreed to get married a week ago, and told the family last night.' He flicked a speck of dust from his trouser leg.

'Really?'

'Nothing official yet, but the family knew and appeared to approve. We were going to announce it in The Times after her birthday, when Lady Sisely could arrange a more formal gathering.'

'Really?'

'Why do you keep saying that, Superintendent?'

'It's just that, well, you're—'

'Older, my dear? Yes, but only by seven years; we actually got on like a house on fire. We were the best of chums and told each other everything, no secrets between us.'

'Everything?'

'Yes, why?'

'What do you know about her and M.M.?'

'Oh, him? He became a little infatuated with dear Isabelle, it bored her. When it ended, he demanded the letters were returned. It entertained her to see him vexed at her refusal.

'Morty says you don't believe it to be suicide. Perhaps you suspect *him*? Well, be careful, Superintendent; he's a man I'd rather not cross.'

'Tell me more about your friendship with Isabelle.'

Patrice stood and paced the room, resting the elbow of his smoking hand in the other palm.

'Despite what people may think about our differences, Superintendent, we were very fond of each other. I'd go so far as to use the word "love". Not all that flowers and hearts nonsense, but true friendship and respect, a love of the other's company. She felt safe with me, as I did with her.

'She wanted to put some of her inheritance into something she could be proud of. I was all for it, of course. Business partners would have been fine by me. The money would help me expand, and she had some marvellous ideas: a certain look, perfume, even men's attire. Marriage was a necessary condition of her business proposal.'

He stood in front of the mirror over the mantle and adjusted his cravat before running a hand over his oiled hair. When he turned to face Allinson, his eyes had taken on a watery reddish quality. He lifted his chin and said, 'So you see, I had no reason to see her dead; quite the opposite in fact.' Then he left in a swirl of silk and smoke.

*

Doctor Harris arrived just after eleven that morning. He removed his hat, left his overlong overcoat with Ambrose and was shown into the library.

'Hallo, Harris. What brings you here?'

'I'm the bearer of bad news.'

'What is it now?' Allinson flopped into the chair behind the dominant desk and fiddled with the ink blotter.

'The Balantine girl seems to have taken a rather larger dose of sleeping powder than one would normally expect. Touch and go as to whether or not it would've been enough to kill her, but definitely enough to put her into a very deep sleep,' said the doctor, settling himself in to the sofa recently vacated by Patrice.

'But, if she was unwell, might not she have taken more to sleep through it?'

'Not necessary. The cachets are dosed to knock someone out for eight hours. I'd say she'd had about one and a half of these. A suicide usually puts two or more in their water and quietly waits for oblivion.'

'So now someone's tampered with her sleeping powders.'

'Yes. When you combine this with the hemlock, I think you'll find you have two different attempted murders. Anyone administering hemlock would know it is deadly with no antidote. Anyone tampering with her sleeping draught, with murder in mind, would just have doubled it up. It's just not a good enough attempt. Of course, if the same person wanted her to die slowly from hemlock poisoning without making a fuss, they might have tried to send her to sleep with an increased dose of sleeping powder. Furthermore, is it the same person who stabbed her and is that the same person who tried to make it look like suicide? She must have made a lot of enemies in her short life.'

'It's no joking matter, Doctor.'

'No, old son, it isn't, and I don't envy you trying to untangle it all.'

'Tell me all about hemlock.'

'Socrates was the real expert. Basically, after the initial symptoms of stomach cramp, headache, and nausea, the body begins to shut down. Numbness and paralysis gradually take hold of every part the body. Victims lose the use of their limbs, then their voice. Blindness occurs in most cases, but the brain remains aware of everything right up until death. All very painful.'

'How long does it take to die?' asked Allinson.

'Six to eight hours. In her case, I guess the former because of her size.'

'But why didn't she ring for help when things got bad for her? She'd have been able to hobble or call out. She hadn't even made an attempt to reach the pull cord.'

'You're forgetting the cachet. She'd taken it and knocked herself out. Even if the pain had woken her, the paralysis would have had a good hold of her.'

'But how did the stuff get in her?'

'Now that I can help with. As we know, they had quail last night, and quails have a natural immunity to hemlock seeds. However, the flesh remains poisonous if eaten. Whoever killed her must have had access to a bird and hemlock seeds. Then, they carefully kept it apart from the others, cooked it separately and ensured it was laid in front of the correct person.'

'Well, I'll be a monkey's uncle.'

'Yes, it looks like the cook and the butler did it.'

*

Ten minutes later, the butler and the cook were led away in handcuffs by Detective Sergeant Monroe. Within the hour, he had returned to the Mayfair house on Kemble Street, having overseen their incarceration at the local Police Station.

'Let's get something to eat, Monroe. Compare notes and let them stew for a while,' said Allinson.

They found a tavern on the other side of Regent Street, down a dark lane where a beer and a pie could be bought without bankrupting hardworking police officials. The bare floorboards carried years of dubious stains. The landlord carried the misshapen countenance of a man who'd worked his way up through street fights and bare-knuckle boxing bouts to the heady height of landlord of one of the best drinking establishments in Soho. Wearing a leather apron and high collar, he reminded Allinson of a butcher — perhaps that would explain the stains; better not investigate them too closely. The booth they sat in afforded enough privacy for them to talk without interruption.

'Fill me in on your chat with Timothy and Madeline,' said Allinson.

'Timothy didn't have much to add to the story, sir. He and Mortimer have been friends since school, and he spent the occasional summer vac here in town with the family.'

'Vac?'

'His word, not mine, sir. Vacation, you know, holiday.'

'Yes, carry on.'

'Anyways, it turns out he was engaged to Isabelle a year or so ago.'

'Really?' said Allinson, through a mouthful of beef and oyster pie.

'Yes, but I don't think it was too serious. He didn't seem that cut up about it. And when I was talking with Madeline, who is a friend of Jennifer's but *not*, she said on more than one occasion, a friend of Isabelle's, I found out about the lovely Isabelle's cruel side. She has, in the past, taken Jennifer's admirers simply because she could. And she, Isabelle I mean, only got engaged to Timothy to see Mortimer jealous. Anyways, the whole thing lasted a matter of days, and it appears that Mortimer and Timothy are back on friendly terms.'

'Jennifer expressed a fondness for Mortimer this morning,' said Allinson, rubbing the back of his neck again.

'What was she like, sir?'

'A strange one. I'll never get used to women wearing trousers, Monroe. But, like her mother, aloof and superior.'

'They're all like that, if you ask me,' said Monroe.

'She's clearly intelligent,' Allinson continued as if uninterrupted. 'Of course, she gets that from her father. She was brusque and to the point, even had her movements for the whole day and night written out for me. Declared herself sick and tired of Isabelle's spoilt and manipulative ways.'

'Motive for murder?'

'I'm not sure.'

'So, to recap, we have a butler and a cook who poisoned Isabelle, but no motive,' began Monroe.

'A cousin who could be riled by her but has no incentive to kill her as he is to inherit his own fortune,' Allinson continued, using his fingers to count off each of the suspects. 'A friend of the family who was engaged to her but appears to have no lingering feelings of affection. A friend of the half-sister who detested Isabelle with no motive to kill her. And a half-sister whose feelings verge on hatred but has no opportunity to kill, because, like the other youngsters, she is at the Café de Paris watching Cole Porter.'

'I wouldn't call Patrice Lombard a youngster, sir.'

'No, but I think Patrice genuinely cared for her, probably more than any of the others. Besides, if he only wanted to marry her for her money, he had every reason for her to live.'

'Sounds about right, sir,' agreed Monroe.

'Finally, we have Sir Michael Melrose, who has reason to be vexed with her as she wouldn't give his love letters back, but he has the girl's father as his alibi.'

'He did have ten minutes, sir.'

'Yes, he did, but do you have any idea how much blood there is when you plunge a knife into a person's chest? He'd need to clean himself up, maybe change his shirt and jacket; he'd need more than ten minutes.'

'Don't forget the mother either, sir. She has no alibi, but she had taken a sedative, as was her usual routine, and consequently was almost impossible to wake.' Monroe completed the list as he finished his pale ale.

Monroe proceeded to light a cigarette while Allinson scooped the remaining sauce up with bread, both clearly lost in thought at the complexity of the case.

'Café de Paris is only five minutes on foot, sir. It is possible for one of them to slip out, run back to Kemble Street, stab the victim, and run back to the club in fifteen minutes,' said Monroe.

'It's possible, I'll grant you, but they'd need longer than fifteen minutes. They'd need to clean themselves up.'

'And, sir, we only have Lady Sisely's word that she took the sedative.'

'Yes, the thought had occurred to me too.'

'You also said Jennifer was fond of Mortimer, sir.'

'Yes, her manner changed. She became, I don't know, more feminine when his name came up during the course of the interview. Perhaps she thought the path wasn't open to her because Isabelle could easily manipulate Mortimer's feelings. She didn't want to chance it until Isabelle was out of the way.'

*

Allinson and Monroe arrived back at the police station before two o'clock.

'The dog died, sir,' said the desk sergeant.

'What?'

'The murder at Kemble Street—the dog died, little black thing. Young Williams brought it in as evidence,' the desk sergeant explained.

'Very well. Ask Harris to take a look at it, would you?'

As they moved off, Monroe said, 'That puts the butler and the cook in the clear then.'

'What do you mean?'

'Well, they don't have a motive, and if they knew the quail was poisoned, they wouldn't have given the leftovers to the dog, would they? No one would do that, sir.'

'We haven't found their motive yet, and not everyone likes dogs, Monroe. Perhaps it was a blind to fool us into thinking they didn't know about the hemlock.'

'I hadn't thought of that, sir.'

'Get back to the house, snoop around for a bit. Ask questions, find the murder weapon. Anything. I'll join you in a few hours.'

*

Monroe arrived back at Kemble Street to find two of the house guests attempting to leave and the uniform on duty trying desperately to impede their passage to the waiting cab.

'Here, Monroe, tell this buffoon to let us go,' said Timothy Sinclair. His pale features had taken on the look of Mount Etna about to erupt.

'You have no right to keep us here,' said Madeline. 'After all, you've arrested the servants. I knew it couldn't be anyone in our set, Timothy.'

'Let them go, Constable. I'm sure they won't mind letting me know where they will be for the next few days.'

Timothy straightened his jacket and trotted down the steps to hold the door of the car open for Madeline.

'Madeline has invited me to stay at her parents' place in the country. We're not staying here a moment longer.'

The door slammed shut and the little car chugged away, spraying the air with black fumes. The constable raised an eyebrow and said, 'Manners is manners, sir, no matter what class you is.'

'I know, Jones, I know,' Monroe replied and made his way inside.

The house had had many departures in the last twelve hours or so — two guests, a personage of great standing, two servants in handcuffs, a corpse on a stretcher, and a dead dog in a hat box — and now it felt hollow. He made his way to the library, the unofficial base of the investigation. Reginald Balantine promptly refused entry with a wave of his hand, not even bothering to pause in his conversation with whomever it was on the other end of the telephone. Apparently, commerce and business wait for no man, certainly not a daughter's death.

Monroe needed time to think, so made his way to the breakfast room, only to be asked to leave. Lady Sisely had not yet been interviewed, but he would gladly leave her to Superintendent Allinson.

In search of a quiet place to think and not feel like he was intruding, he proceeded downstairs to the basement kitchen. It was a large open space, with a stained and warped wooden table for all the servants to sit around. No doubt, the servants that remained were busy about their daily duties, and the basement for the time being was deserted.

The fireplace looked like it might have been cosy in a household at peace. He sat in the rocking chair and stared at the ash in the grate, mulling over recent events and the characters he'd encountered. It was quiet and peaceful and ideally suited to contemplation, if only his slow brain would work.

A draft shifted the ash and with it came the distant echo of voices carried by ancient brickwork. He sank to his knees and held his head to the opening.

'But…were…gone…' a man's voice.

'Yes…long…really…' a woman's voice.

'Thirty…its…time…ask…'

'What…will…do…'

'…don't …o…fond…her.'

'But…love…oo…yes…the…is…us now…'

The voices stopped abruptly and Monroe's eavesdropping session ended. He recorded the partial conversation as best he could in his notebook, and then tried working out where in the house the conversation had originated. He then spent twenty minutes checking the rooms he thought might share the same chimney, but Monroe was disappointed to find that side of the house devoid of family and guests.

*

Superintendent Allinson had interviewed the butler and cook for more than an hour. The cook had cried but said nothing of value. Ambrose, the butler, said, 'H'I h'am very sorry h'I cannot be h'of h'any further h'asistance, Superintendent.' And of course, he denied having anything to do with hemlock. "Emlock. Wot's 'emlock?'

Deciding to let them stew for a while longer, the superintendent thought it time to pay a visit to Sir Michael.

He had to wait for the great man to meet him in the public lobby of the War Office. Being in one of the greatest symbols of power in the world made him more than a little nervous. People in these places had little concern for one murder; they were too busy planning mass murder on a global scale. He had to remind himself that Scotland Yard was the great symbol of justice. Wrongs would be righted; he had nothing to feel inferior about.

'I don't have long, Allinson. Try to be quick, will you?' said Sir Michael by way of greeting.

'Yes, sir. Erm, is there anywhere more private we could talk?'

'Can't take you upstairs, you haven't any clearance.' A little reminder of how unimportant Allinson was in the great scheme of things. 'Let's take a walk outside. Nothing more private than being out and about with great British public, is there?'

Allinson didn't like to contradict the man, so he remained quiet until they were among the dappled shade of the trees of Whitehall Gardens. Sir Michael chose a bench and smiled as he invited Allinson to sit next to him.

'I hear this is what the secret service types do? Sit in public places to play their games,' said Sir Michael.

'Really?'

'So what is your opening move, Allinson?'

Allinson removed the letters from his coat pocket and laid them on the seat between them both.

'What are those?' Sir Michael asked, with hardly a glance at them.

'They are letters of an intimate nature that *you* wrote to Isabelle Balantine.'

'Nonsense. If that is the best you can do, our conversation is at an end — as is your career, Superintendent.'

'They have your initials.'

'It can't have escaped even someone of your intellect, that I share my initials with one other member of the household, as well as probably a thousand other men.'

'The nature and wording of the letters lends itself to a man used to authority. Marsh is not that sort of man. And our handwriting experts will easily establish that your handwriting is a match for these letters.'

'I'll refuse to give a sample.'

'This is a murder investigation, Sir Michael, and if I may say, I think I have won this round. Your refusal implies involvement.'

'Not as dim as you make out, are you? Very well, let us speak candidly, as all men should. Isabelle and I had a brief dalliance. We would meet for luncheon and, once or twice…you know.'

'So you searched her room on the night of her death looking for these,' said Allinson, returning the letters to his inside pocket.

'At about eleven, I went up for my briefcase, which contained papers that Reginald and I were going to go through one more time, before agreeing and signing, the details of which I cannot discuss with you. The room I had been allocated was next to Isabelle's. I took the opportunity of an almost empty house to see if I could persuade the girl to return them.

'There was no reply to my tapping at her door, so I tried the handle and entered. Light from the landing fell across the bed. She had a small knife sticking out of the chest. I was frozen for a few seconds, then — despicable as it may seem to you, Superintendent — I searched the room. I didn't want the letters to be found by anyone, especially the police. I am only a man, Superintendent, and I'm fully aware of my weaknesses. Panic took over.'

'Did you remove the knife?'

'Ah, well, you see, I covered the body with the bed covers, to try to prevent the girl being discovered before I could leave the house.'

'Really?'

'It sounds ridiculous, but as I said, I was panicking. With the cover over her, her chest was bulging, so I pulled the knife free using some clothing of hers to keep my hands clean. Then, I put the bed covers over her, hurried to my room and hid the knife and her bloody underclothes in the briefcase I intended to take down to Reginald.'

'I don't think that you did panic. You're a man of action, Sir Michael, and more importantly, one of intelligence. What was the real reason for removing the murder weapon?'

'I don't know...'

'The truth, Sir Michael.'

'If you must know, I was trying to protect Lady Sisely.'

'Now, why would you want to do that?'

'Well, she and I have been friends for a few years. My assumption was that she had somehow found the letters and killed the girl in a fit of rage — *crime passionnel* the frogs call it—using her own letter knife.'

'You recognised the murder weapon as belonging to Lady Sisely?'

'Yes.'

'So you removed the letter knife to protect your jealous lover.'

'Friend, Superintendent. I don't expect to repeat it again,' Sir Michael said with a steely edge.

'Have it your way, *friend*. What happened next?'

'I went downstairs to conclude the meeting. I made a fuss about my secretary not supplying the right papers and intended to leave. But Reginald was in a good mood, what with the girl's engagement and with the department agreeing to meet his payment demands, plus bonuses. He enticed me to a drink or two. He said signing paperwork could wait. He was happy. I felt for the man; his joy was about to be ruined in a most horrendous way.'

'But, at midnight, a shot rang out through the house,' urged Allinson.

'Yes. I can't say what I thought, except that I reacted as any real man might. We both ran from the library. I don't know why, but Reginald turned the other way at the top of the stairs, evidently thinking the shot had come from his wife's room. But I called out before he got there. We both stood at Isabelle's door; we could see smoke still rising from the gun.'

'But you must have suspected Lady Sisely of this shooting?'

'Well, yes, obviously. The house was practically empty, whom else could it have been?'

'I'm still trying to figure that out,' Allinson was forced to admit. 'What did you do with the knife?'

'After I left that night, I dropped it in the Thames, and I burnt the bloody clothing and papers when I got home.'

'You'll need to come back to The Yard to make a formal statement.'

'We could keep this between ourselves?'

'You need to make a statement, and I need to arrest you for attempting to pervert the course of justice, interfering with a crime scene, for not reporting a murder and as an accessory after the fact. You may want to bring your solicitor along.'

'Is this really necessary?'

'This isn't a game for spies, Sir Michael. It's murder.'

'Well, may I tie up some loose ends here first, some security matters? I promise to be with you by seven o'clock this evening. You have my word as a gentleman.'

'Very well,' said Allinson with a slight nod of his head.

*

'Lady Sisely, we need somewhere we can talk in private,' said Allinson upon his return to the house on Kemble Street. She was coming down the stairs, like an ageing vision from a bygone era.

'Don't be ridiculous. I obviously have nothing to say to you, I was sleeping and had to be roused from my slumber.'

'Very well, I'll just get the constable to take you down to The Yard for formal interrogation.'

'I shall be complaining to the assistant commissioner,' she said and led the way to the breakfast room.

Clasping her hands beneath her bosom, Lady Sisely stood tall and straight against the windows, her silhouette accentuated by bustles and corsetry long since consigned to the annals of fashion history.

'Well, get on with it,' she ordered.

At that moment, Monroe tapped at the door and walked in.

'Excuse me, sir. May I come in?'

'Certainly, take notes.' Then to Lady Sisely, he said, 'I've been talking with Sir Michael.'

'Good for you. He can be quite entertaining for an old bore.'

'He tells me you and he are *friends*.'

'That is stretching a point, Superintendent. I have only met the man a handful of times.'

'Perhaps, but I see no other reason why he would risk going to the gallows, if not for friendship or love or to protect a woman's honour.'

'The gallows?'

'He admits to certain events.'

She sat heavily on a stiff upright William Morris chair. Allinson expected her to draw a fan from her sleeve or fall into a faint. Neither happened. She took a minute to recompose herself and said, 'I think you're lying, Superintendent.'

'I'll tell you what I think, Mrs Balantine. You discovered love letters from Sir Michael to your step-daughter. Imagine, Monroe, what might go through the mind of this suspect if she had found those letters. "How dare he?" she might think. This man whom she had dared to love, who was better in class than her low-born industrialist husband. How dare he become involved with the dazzling Isabelle, socialite and talk of the gossip columns?

'Did you have plans and desires to be with him someday? Whatever your fantasies, you made definite plans to kill Isabelle and muddy the waters as much as possible. First, you tampered with her sleeping draught to make things easier for you later on. Why you didn't just double the dose, I don't know; maybe you wanted to look into her eyes as you ran her through with the knife.'

'Knife?'

'Yes, knife, Lady Sisely, your letter knife,' he said, raising his voice. 'She is sleepy and drugged and a blade is a silent killer. After you'd killed her, you had time to clean yourself up and prepare for bed. You went back to her room at midnight and placed a small pistol in the palm of her hand, pointed it at her head and pulled the trigger. And then you quickly ran back to your bedroom and feigned sleepiness. It was a crude attempt to confuse us.'

'Letter knife? But it went missing days ago.'

'You deny stabbing and shooting the girl?'

'No, I mean yes.'

'Lady Sisely, I am arresting you for the murder of Isabelle Balantine and attempting to pervert the course of justice. You may want to change into something a little more suited to a night or two in the cells. Monroe and I will wait here while you make arrangements.'

She nodded her head, once again the picture of Victorian discipline, and sailed from the room.

'Something you might be interested in, sir,' Monroe said.

Hearing this, Lady Sisely stopped outside the breakfast room, with the door slightly ajar, and for the first time in her life eavesdropped on a private conversation.

'I overheard something when I was in the basement, sir. The chimneys carry the sounds of conversation. I only caught bits of it. But imagine these notes without the gaps.'

'Show me.'

'But _you_ were...gone...' man's voice

'Yes, _but not very_ long, _not_ really...' woman's voice

'Thirty _minutes is a long_ time _if you_ ask _me_.' man's voice

'What will _you_ do _now?_' woman's voice

'I don't know, I was fond of her.' man's voice

'But I love you...yes I do. The way is clear for us now.' Woman's voice

'Who was it, Monroe?'

'The only woman it could have been was Jennifer, as Madeline left earlier today taking Timothy to the country.'

'You let two suspects leave, Monroe?'

'I couldn't stop them. But I know where they're going, and if they flee then they're guilty of something, sir. Anyways, Jennifer could only have been having a conversation with Patrice or Mortimer. My money's on Mortimer.'

'Mine too,' agreed Allinson. 'Patrice is not the sort of man women normally go after, nor he they, I'll wager. Jennifer, as I said earlier, softened when talking about Mortimer. He and she had practically been brought up together and his loyalties may well be in turmoil.

'It's perfectly possible that Jennifer left the Café de Paris,' Allinson continued, 'came back here, and stabbed Isabelle with her mother's letter knife. Why? Maybe spite or jealousy, or some other woman's emotion, so as to clear the way for her and Mortimer. Then, she cleaned herself up and returned to the nightclub, probably disposing of her blood-stained clothes on the way. Those manly clothes all look the same to me; they'd be easy enough to change without anyone noticing.

'However, Mortimer was the only one to notice her missing. If Patrice had noticed an absence, I'm sure he would have told us. After all, he's had all that cash in reach, he must be feeling cheesed off and cheated.'

Having heard enough, Lady Sisely made haste to her room.

'Mortimer must have confronted Jennifer, and you've overheard part of the conversation. Good work. We'll talk to him, get the full story.'

*

'We need to talk, Mr Marsh,' said Allinson.

'Righto, what about?' Mortimer replied, taking a sip of clear liquid from a cocktail glass.

'You lied to me about the night of your cousin's death. You noticed Jennifer missing when you were dancing. What time did you notice her missing and for how long was she gone?'

'Now look here, Inspector, old Morty has a code you know.' He pulled himself up, not so much by the laces as by the lapels, and took on the stance of a great orator about to go into debate. 'Oh yes, he does, and part of that code is faith and trust and wot-not. There's no way I could ever —'

'You had better tell me everything you know or you'll find yourself in very deep water.'

'Dash it all, Inspector, that's not fair.'

'Superintendent, please.'

'Same thing, isn't it?' Marsh said, with a perplexed look on his already chagrined face.

'The time you noticed Jennifer missing, Mr Marsh.'

'You're a persistent blister, I must say. Well, if you must know, it was not long after ten o'clock, and for not more than half an hour, I think.'

'And when you questioned her, what did she say she was doing?'

'She said she wanted to talk to Isabelle, to reason with her or some such nonsense; no one could reason with Isabelle when her mind was made up about something. She told me she hadn't stabbed cousin Izzy, and could never do such a thing, and I believe her.'

'Monroe, find Miss Balantine and bring her here. Find a member of staff to ask Lady Sisely to meet us in the hallway too.' When Monroe had left the room, he said, 'The thing is, Mr Marsh, no one in the house knew she was stabbed. It was assumed by everyone that we were investigating a shooting.'

'Don't talk complete bilge, Allinson…' He rolled his eyes as the ha'penny finally dropped and then clicked his thumb and finger together for added effect. 'Oh, I see, you mean she knew before she should've known. The rascal.'

*

'A maid is fetching Lady Sisely now, sir,' said Monroe as he led Jennifer Balantine down the stairs.

'We are going to have a word down the station, miss,' said Allinson.

'Look here, old thing, these coves think you did Izzy in. Did you?'

'Don't be ridiculous, Mortimer. They've worked it all out. I suppose he gave me away?' she said, tilting her head in Mortimer's direction.

'In a manner of speaking, miss.'

'She was a Jezabel, and I'm glad I killed her. The world is a better place without her.'

'There's a car waiting if —'

At that moment, a scream broke through the household and a maid staggered along the landing to the top of the stairs. Monroe and Allinson raced up the stairs two at a time, Monroe pausing to settle the maid. Allinson carried on to Lady Sisely's rooms. He found her in a shallow bath, in her underclothes, blood sprayed up the green and white tiles from deep cuts along her wrists. A small bone-handled kitchen knife lay at the side of the bath.

Allinson felt for a pulse, as a matter of procedure, but it was quite clear that Lady Sisely was beyond help. Her body had already taken on the pallor of the recently deceased.

Monroe arrived at the bathroom door. 'This was on the bed, sir.'

'Call for an ambulance,' Allinson said and sighed as he began to read:

I am responsible for Isabelle's death; my reasons for doing so are my own.

I first stabbed her, and then shot her to confuse the police, but the Inspector has done his job too well.

Forgive me, Reginald, but I cannot go through the public humiliation of a trial.

S

*

Assistant Commissioner Percival Wilkins lit his pipe and threw the match on the fire. He had a fire every evening, even in high summer. Allinson suspected he liked to see people sweat.

'It's a mess, Allinson, a bloody mess.'

'It appears that way, sir. But Lady Sisely's suicide is just another attempt to muddy the waters.'

'How?'

'Jennifer stabbed Isabelle with Lady Sisely's letter knife. She is the one who ended the girl's life. She admitted it. Lady Sisely planned to kill Isabelle, by tampering with her cachet and then putting a bullet in her head to make it look like suicide. But she ended up shooting a dead body because Jennifer had already killed Isabelle.

'Having somehow found out we were finally on the right track with Jennifer, Lady Sisely writes the note and makes the ultimate sacrifice to save her daughter—I suspect Mr Balantine is aware of her suicidal thoughts. Now I don't know who the jury will believe, but Jennifer Balantine has to be tried as a murderess.'

'Impossible. It will mean Sir Michael giving evidence. He's too important to be mixed up in a thing like this. There's a war coming, everyone knows it.'

'But he is mixed up in it. It's his fault for toying with the emotions of women.'

'Pah! Women should control themselves.'

'Sir —'

'Be quiet, I'm thinking. What about the hemlock? Didn't the butler and cook do it?'

'No, sir. They have no motive and no connection other than as servants. They were upset at the death of a member of the household, but genuinely distraught when the dog died. The cook cried for hours. They wouldn't have let the animal die. They simply cared for it too much.'

'So it was an accident. What does Harris say?'

'It's plausible that the quail had eaten hemlock seed in the wild and that the bird's flesh then became poisonous, resulting in the accidental poisoning of Isabelle Balantine. It could've killed anyone around the table.'

'Good, that's it then. An accident, no reason to come to trial.'

'The doctor's report says life was stopped by the rapid and sudden insertion of a six inch blade to the victim's chest.'

'But she was going to die anyway. And we have a written confession from Sisely.'

'Yes. But the inquest, sir.'

'The inquest will report exactly what I want it to report. We have nothing further to talk about.'

'But, sir —'

'Not another word. You are in danger of demotion, Allinson.'

*

'Jennifer should be tried and hanged, Monroe, but the A.C. won't have it,' Allinson said.

'There was too much death in that house anyways, sir,' replied Monroe, rubbing the back of his neck and inadvertently mimicking his superior.

'What do you mean?'

'I mean all those attempts on Isabelle's life, any one of which could have been successful. Then Hamish and Lady S.'

'She should still be tried.'

'And death walked among us too.'

'What are you talking about, Monroe?' asked Allinson.

'Mortimer. They all called him Morty. Sounds like the French for death — Mort.'

*

Evening Chronicle July 24th, 1936

Isabelle Balantine Murdered
The inquest into the death of Isabelle Balantine, has returned a verdict of murder.

The same inquest returned a verdict of suicide for Lady Sisely Balantine, who killed herself after killing her step-daughter while temporarily of unsound mind.

1962

(First published in Love by Black Hare Press.)

The whole world loves her. And I love her, too.

Everyone loves her — except perhaps the movie studios.

She has episodes of, shall we say, weakness.

If it weren't for our high profiles, we would never have been introduced. If it weren't for our high profiles, we might be happy together.

However, she threatens to talk, to tell the world of our love.

Plans were already afoot when she sang *Happy Birthday.*

A gangster has everything arranged. Hoover has made sure no one talks.

She's special, the public will always love her.

But it's more important that Americans love me.

Second Date

(Published in Bad Romance by Black Hare Press.)

Paris, 1985

For their first date, Julian had chosen an expensive restaurant. It was exquisite.

For their second date, she suggested the Jules Verne on the second level of the Eiffel Tower. Men threw longing glances in her direction and women envious ones. She was used to people looking at her and knew how to draw their attention; fortunately, she also knew how to blend into the scenery. However, right now she wanted to be seen. Being six feet tall in four-inch heels helped. Striking looks and cold blue eyes ensured people wouldn't forget her in a hurry. She wore a faux fur but preferred the real thing.

Julian was a gentleman. He stood when she excused herself. He ordered the right wine for each dish, and he treated the staff with respect. He kept the conversation neutral, staying away from topics of business and politics. They had a lot in common—a love of travel and old TV programmes—and he made her laugh. It was such a shame he would be dead before the night was over.

Given a choice, she would have picked a more secluded spot. It's easy to kill a man in the privacy of his own home, but Romanov was paying good money, very good money, and besides, it was unwise to refuse him his little indulgences. Romanov wanted Julian to die on the Eiffel Tower. Still, he must have been losing his marbles to think it would be possible to kill in such a public place and get away with it.

Her plan was simple. Lure Julian to the top under the pretence that she had never been there. In return, she promised—with heavy sexual innuendo—to satisfy his every need and succumb to his every desire. She would offer him a line of top quality coke to cement their forthcoming union.

The cocaine, of course, was cut with a not-so-healthy dose of cyanide and would ensure a quick but painful death. Then, as he lay dying, she would head to the rest room at a sedate but brisk pace, turn the reversible coat inside out, take the wig off, shake her hair out, remove the coloured contact lenses, unscrew the special heels and hopefully be on the Jardins du Trocadéro before anyone noticed the dead lawyer at the top of the most famous tower in the world. Tricky, but it was what Romanov wanted.

It was close to midnight when they got to the top. Fortunately, not many sightseers came up at night, especially at this time of year. The wind buffeting the tower took one's breath away. Finding a spot where they could shelter from the wind, she took a moment to marvel at the beauty of the great city by night.

'Come over here, Julian. I want to kiss you.'

He clung to the iron frame by the elevator. She was sure he was about to bottle it and said, 'Keep your eyes on me. Just look at me. That's it, Big Boy. Keep coming.'

She put her arms around him, drawing him into a tight embrace and then looked down into his face. His forehead glistened with a fine sheen of perspiration. She kissed him long and sensually. After all, if a man is about to die, he might as well die happy.

'There. Wasn't that worth it?'

He smiled, his lips now shining with some of her red lipstick, and nodded.

'Fancy a line?' she said, opening her clutch and waving a little paper sachet under his nose. He smiled again as she formed the fine powder into a thin line on the mirror of her compact.

She offered him a rolled up two-hundred franc note.

'Ladies first,' he said.

'I couldn't possibly.'

'I thought so.' He took a step back from her. 'How much is Romanov paying you?'

Her mouth opened a fraction as she tried to take in the full meaning of the words. How had he known? She didn't even have a back-up weapon with her. The alternative—beating him to death with her bare hands—was not only messy, but her only option if she was not to become one of Romanov's targets herself.

'I'll double it,' he continued, unaware of her fist clenched in readiness to strike, 'if you turn your unique skills on Romanov. Kill him and you'll be doing me and my associates a tremendous favour. How about it?'

She smiled and let the wind take the poison.

'This might be the beginning of a beautiful relationship,' she said and kissed him again.

1963

(Published in Love by Black Hare Press.)

Strange, I thought I could live without her. But her image is everywhere. The films will always be there. There was no one like her.

I dream about her more than ever, taunting me with her breathy voice and come to bed eyes. But now those eyes are dead and worms fall from her pale lips.

I thought I might be able to cope with the guilt, but I cannot go on anymore.

Everything is in place. My assassination will be the greatest cover up in history.

The American public will always remember my sacrifice.

They will always love me.

The Bunker

(First Appeared in World War IV by Zombie Pirate Publishing.)

The stasis bunker was a relic from the third Great War, 2051 - 2053. My father said they built things to last back then. Not like today, when everything is so ecologically friendly it can be returned to its natural components easier and quicker than ever before.

The bunker was already in the garden, half buried as was intended and half overgrown with weeds and rubble, when my parents had bought the house. So, it was a surprise when they discovered it and cleared it out of all the rubbish that accumulates in old unused spaces.

Mum wanted to tear it down, but Dad said it would make a good storage room. That was years ago, when I was a toddler and my sister wasn't around.

When things started to go wrong between Earth and Mars, Dad said it would be worth testing the bunker to see if it still worked. He said the way the Yanks were going on like they owned the whole planet, he wouldn't be surprised if Mars sent a few warheads in our direction and then all Hell would break loose. Mum cried and said talk like that shouldn't happen at the dinner table, but Dad said we should all take an interest in politics, even if it is the politics of splitters trying to make a better life for themselves.

In due course, Dad tested the individual stasis chambers and found two out of four to be working. He even tested them on the dog, who froze in mid bark for twenty-four hours. We were there the next day, when the timer reached zero, to see him continue his barking and jump off the bed as if no time had elapsed. It was just a game for him.

The news via the inweb—that little chip we were all given at birth, that connected us to everything else—was that some Martian ambassador bloke had been assassinated and Dad went into full blown panic mode.

'Things like this have started world wars before,' he said.

'Really, when?' I asked

'Oh, a long time ago. Hundreds of years ago.'

He took me to the stasis bunker to show me how it all worked.

'You're a big boy now and if anything should happen to me and your mother, or if we're not here, you need to be man enough to take control. Do you understand?'

'Yes, Dad,' I said nodding.

'Good lad. First you need to close the bunker door. After the door is shut, you need to put the bunker out of phase. Phasing will protect the structure against everything except a direct hit from a warhead, and that isn't likely out here in the sticks. Only major cities will be targeted.'

'But you will be here, Dad, won't you?'

'Of course, this is just in case I'm not. To put the bunker out of phase, enter the code. 19042099. Your sister's birthday. Okay?'

'19042099,' I repeated.

'Then you're going to need to put the sleep capsules into stasis mode. Make sure your sister is in her capsule first, and that the lid is correctly shut, like so,' he said demonstrating how the lid lowered to create an airtight seal, 'and simply enter the code again. Then press "stasis". The countdown timer will start. One hundred years should be enough to give the radiation and fallout time to clear and for nature to take over again.

'If there is a malfunction, the stasis pod will come out of stasis early and you or your sister will be able to release the lid from the inside. If you wake early, you have to make a decision as to whether to release your sister too. Pay attention to the read out, at least fifty years has to have passed for the environment to be even tolerably safe. If less time than that has passed, then I would suggest—and this will be very difficult for you—I suggest you leave and try to make a life for yourself elsewhere.

'The more time that has passed between the bombs falling, and you or your sister's emergence into the world, the more chance you will have to survive.'

'What will it be like?' I asked.

'Don't interrupt!' he snapped. Then he wiped his forehead with the sleeve of his shirt and continued. 'Sorry Pete, just pay attention. This pod, that we tested on Timmy, and the one opposite are both working. The other two closest to the entrance are beyond my abilities to repair. I've arranged for a specialist, but it will be weeks before he can do the job. In the meantime, we must double up, but if your mum and me aren't here, then take one capsule each.'

'But you will be here,' I said.

'Just get to the bunker as quick as you can. Phase it and when you're ready go into stasis.'

'But you will be here, won't you?'

I was desperate for reassurance that we wouldn't be left alone. I couldn't believe the things he was saying and it only got worse.

'If you and your sister are to survive, you'll need protection. This is an old stun laser; it's the best I could get. Don't dick around with it. It will send thirty-thousand watts at a target.'

He attached the laser to a charger in the far wall. That end of the bunker had lots of storage cabinets with tinned and dried food. Then he drew a thin sharp knife from one of the drawers.

'This is an old knife that used to belong to one of your ancestors. He was in the army, I think. Your great-grandfather always kept it in great condition. It slit the throat of a great German called Nazi once. All I really know is that this might save your life one day, so take care of it. And this one is for your sister, it's a little ankle knife. Strap it to her leg before you send her in to stasis. Do you understand?'

'Yes, Dad.'

'I hope the longer we're in stasis, the less need there will be for violence. In a world fragmented by war many individuals will strive to gain the upper hand and take power. As time moves on, I hope society will stabilise. It will be easier to survive if we are not a part of that initial struggle. Do you understand?'

'Yes Dad, but—'

'I haven't finished, Pete. Do not trust anyone. In a dangerous situation, the likes of which I have no idea of yet, trust must be earned. Do not give your food or your weapons to anyone. Always have them ready and do not be afraid to use them. Do you understand?'

'Yes, Dad.'

'I don't think you do, Pete. You may arrive in a world where the survivors are so starved they'll eat other people.'

'Dad, you're scaring me.'

'Good. When you meet someone new, have your hand on the laser or the knife and be ready to kill.'

'But, Dad.'

'Right, that's it. One of the chickens needs slaughtering; you should have learnt to do this a long time ago. Let's go.'

We had a chicken coop near the house. We weren't farmers or anything like that, just a bit green. We had a vegetable patch too, growing carrots and parsnips. He reached into the coop and, after a bit of feather flying and squawking, pulled a chicken out, its wings flapping like crazy.

'Of course, the traditional way to kill a chicken is simply to twist its neck, but I want you to get used to using that knife to kill. It's what it was designed for. So go on, cut the bird's head off.'

'But Dad, what good's a knife against lasers and god knows what sort of guns will be around in a hundred years?'

'When those bombs start falling, nothing survives. Nothing, Pete. Buildings are flattened, metal is melted, people vanish in the blink of an eye and mountains tumble as if they never existed. Only something out of phase will have a chance of surviving. I'm going to find everything I can that might be useful and store it in the bunker. Your great uncle Jim might have old shooting guns he could give us.

'Now, kill the bloody chicken.'

His red eyes told me how upsetting he found all this. His hands shook as he held the chicken out for me to slaughter. I thought he might have gone insane as I stepped forward and raised the blade. The chicken had calmed down a little, perhaps accepting its fate. I tried to steady my hand as I touched the sharp edge of the knife to its throat.

'Do I have to, Dad?'

'Do it,' he snapped.

So, I did it, warm blood spurting on to my face and hands. As I ran back to the house crying, I heard Mum shouting at Dad. I puked into the toilet bowl. It took hours to wash the blood off.

Later that day, I saw my dad plucking the bird.

'He means well, he's just worried about us,' Mum said later, 'and I'm worried about him. I'll try to get him to see a doctor tomorrow. I'm so sorry he made you do that, Pete. Are you okay?'

Lying on my bed, with my back to her, I couldn't think of anything to say. She left me to my uneasy sleep.

*

The next day the sirens went off. The inweb in my head became so loud with the noise, I thought I might faint. My sister and I were alone in the house, as my father was at the doctors with my mother. I had to carry my sister to the bunker — her inweb safety protocols had malfunctioned — she must have been in agony. Timmy trotted along next to us, his normal exuberant self somewhat deflated. I think he knew what was happening. The world was about to burn.

I locked the door, phased the bunker, and settled down to wait for my parents. The viewing portal gave me a view down to our house. The minutes ticked by, and then they came bursting through the back door, Dad dragging Mum by the hand. She had lost a shoe. I could see him yelling at her to run faster. But the garden must have been a hundred feet long. My finger floated over the open button for the bunker door. I knew I would have to wait till the last minute before I let them in. Even then if the timing were wrong, I might not have time to phase the bunker again.

Halfway along the garden, Dad slipped and fell. Mum was trying to lift him. She was trying to drag him to his feet, but he froze, and my mum followed his gaze to the sky. She stopped trying, and simply knelt with him. Each of them hanging to the other. She crossed herself, and I could see her lips moving as she said a prayer.

Then everything went white.

Less than two minutes later I could see again, and I wish to God I hadn't looked. Everything was gone; our house, our garden, our parents. The ground bled red and boiling blood. The heavens looked like a living bruise. The sky, dark green with purple and black clouds, moving so fast it looked like time had been sped up.

I was too shocked to do anything but watch. I had never known silence like it. Sound could not penetrate the bunker and the inweb was gone. Nothing was there. No messages, no news updates, no recordings of family events. The images of our entire family all the way back to the turn of the twenty first century were simply gone, as if they had never existed.

No one could ever feel as alone as I did then. Eventually, I went back to Joanne, whom I had laid in one of the stasis chambers. She was still unconscious. Timmy lay alongside her, he looked up at me, his big eyes looking sadder than ever, and I knew he knew what had happened. I found the knife my dad had said to strap to her leg and did as instructed. Timmy licked my hand and I stroked his ears. Then I lowered the chamber door and entered the code. The display began its countdown –

Years	days	hours	mins	secs
99	364	23	59	59

I took my own knife to my chamber in case I needed it the minute I came to, lay down and activated the stasis with a press of a button.

And then I lowered my hand. I thought 'Oh God, it's not working and I'm gonna die in here, 'cause I sure as shit can't go out into that hell beyond the viewer.'

I nearly entered the code again, but something felt strange. I looked over at Joanne's chamber only to see the lid up. It gave me such a start, that I sat upright and hit my head on the chamber door. I fumbled for the release mechanism and staggered over to her pod. She was gone, as was Timmy.

The countdown clock said she had twenty-five years left in hibernation. It must have malfunctioned and released her early. My own clock read zero. This was so strange; one hundred years had passed for me in the blink of an eye.

Some empty tins lay strewn on the worktop, rodents having striped them clean long ago. A faded note from Joanne was pinned under one of the tins.

Der Pety

    Me and Timmy hav to go now
    Luv Joany

If I had thought I was alone earlier, I was mistaken.

The door was open, and sunlight poured through. I cautiously stepped out on to lush green grass. A cherry tree grew in the middle of what should have been our garden, in the place I imagined where our parents had knelt. I decided that I must find my sister. I didn't know how, or where, but I had to try. She had to be somewhere, didn't she?

If she had lived, she would be about thirty-five years old. My little sister would be older than me. She might even have children of her own.

I started walking.

Broken

(First published in Monsters by Black Hare Press.)

In his mind's eye he saw a young man's face, but whenever he caught his reflection in a stream, he would wonder whose face he wore now.

His hands came from another too, a manual worker by the look of them. Why was the stitching so rough?

Because one leg was shorter than the other, each leg being from different men, he would forever have a limp. Did not the madman care for the creature that would have to walk upon them?

And the less said about what should have been in his britches, the better.

He could still cry.

The Affair of The Missing Tiara

(Originally published in The Inner Circle Writers' Magazine as a three-part serial. It appears here, for the first time, as one complete story.)

Part One

The house could be seen from more than three miles away. Even on a day like today in October when rain seemed to be the predominant weather condition, it would have been possible to see the gargantuan structure from the heavens in one of those beastly flying machines.

The Lagonda, following the winding drive, dipped and rose over small hills and flew past a copse of woods at a speed likely to give Malcolm Campbell the shakes. They passed a small church, where the wedding ceremony would take place in twenty-four hours. A flock of sheep meandered onto the road, and Mortimer slammed his foot on the brake causing his passenger to give a tiny squeal of excited pleasure. She then rebuked the driver in her firmest tones, 'Oh, Morty. Do drive thenthibly. You nearly hurt one of the poor little lambth.' Those with the required level of astuteness will no doubt notice a distinct lack of rigidity in her firmest tones.

Mortimer looked from her to the sheep which somehow was at eye level.

'Baaa,' said the sheep.

Then he looked back to his passenger.

'Do drive along, Morty. You're thcaring the theep,' she instructed.

'And how am I meant to do that? I'm stuck in the middle of a herd of the beasts.'

The shepherd, a man used to travelling at more sedate speed than a flying Lagonda, pushed a few of his flock aside and shook his head at the bonnet of the red dragon that had disturbed his meander through the working day.

'I say,' called Mortimer over the braying animals.

The shepherd turned his head slowly at the call. They say dog owners always look like their dogs. It must be doubly so for a man who spends his whole day with cloven-hoofed ruminants. He chewed on something unseen in large circular movements of the jaw.

'Yar.'

'Any chance you could move a few of your pets aside? We've a wedding to get to.'

'Yar,' said the shepherd again, and turned his head back to the bonnet. He touched the shiny metal with the tip of his finger.

'What's wrong with him?' Mortimer said to the passenger.

'What'th wrong with who?'

Mortimer, never one to find himself in the top half of the class, had the sudden feeling of being the only one in the room who knew the answer to life's greatest question, 'Who will romp home the winner of the Derby?' It was as clear as the pretty little nose on the pretty little thing next to him, that today he was for the first time in his entire life a genius. A man of knowledge and esteem. He could take on the world and give it (that is, the world) the benefit of his encyclopaedic knowledge. Wise men would consult him, leaders would seek his council. He was the coming man, if only he could figure out how to communicate with the blister currently leaning on his transport.

He revved the engine. A deep rumbling roused the expert idler.

'Yar,' he said.

'Would you mind trying to clear a path?'

He looked to his passenger for support. She was busy making cow eyes at a sheep. The shepherd took a step forward and leaned on the door frame. He chewed at Mortimer.

'I say, Constance. You ask him to move the sheep. I don't think he understands me.'

'Me, Morty?'

'Yes you, Constance.' Mortimer gripped the steering wheel tight enough to turn his knuckles white.

'But you're the man.'

'Please try,' he said with a tight smile, and then added, 'for me.'

'Okay, Morty. For you.' Her large, innocent eyes smiled at the shepherd as he turned his slow chew in her direction.

'Pleathe move your lovely lambthth out of the way, tho we can vithit hith grathe for the wedding of hith lovely daughter to my bwother, Timothy.'

The shepherd looked at Mortimer. Mortimer shrugged his shoulders. The shepherd moved away from the car and tapped one of the sheep with his crook. Soon the flock were following the shepherd.

'Eathy,' she said. 'You have to learn to be nithe to theth people, Morty.'

'I was nice.'

'Never mind that now. Tell me how you tholved the cathe of your couthin'th howible murder.'

'I didn't solve it, Connie. But I was, you know, important. The police wouldn't have had a clue without my help.'

'How did Ithabelle die?'

'Yes. Um, rather complicated that one. She was sort of stabbed and shot and poisoned all at the same time.'

'Golly!'

*

Mortimer, ever the gentlemen, hopped over the car door and scooted around to open the passenger side. He held the hand of Constance by the fingertips as she demurely twisted and then rose from the seat.

'Thank you, Morty, but they have a man for that thort of thing. Ah, there he ith now.' A butler and a footman were descending the steps.

'Miss Sinclair, Mr Marsh,' said the butler, as he took control of the car door with a look that brooked no argument. Mortimer stepped away and watched as the footman unloaded the case clasped to the rack on the back of the car, before reaching into the backseat for the other three items of luggage.

'That's me old kitbag. Where am I to be billeted?' he asked, indicating the first and smallest of the cases.

'You are in the oriental room, Miss Sinclair,' the butler replied with a stiff nod of his head in her direction. 'Mr Marsh is to occupy the orange room.'

A scream similar to that of a baby elephant discovering a gorilla in its normally safe enclosure at London Zoo, erupted from the top of the steps. Mortimer turned to see a blur as Connie swept up the steps to be engulfed in the multi-layered white robes of the daughter of the house, the honourable Milly what's-herself.

'I'll just take the motor 'round to the stable.'

When no one responded, he flopped into the driving seat in a dark mood and roared the engine for the entire mile it took to get to said stable yard. However had he agreed to this? A wedding of all things. It was his firmest believe that weddings were for those who had given up on life. Guests who attended them were joyous, when really they should have been envious. Envious of the happy couple, their youth, and a whole life ahead of them. The fatheads actually getting married had given up on all the fun they could have been having with their chums. Any man fool enough to be tricked into the situation deserved all that was coming, which would probably mean attending more weddings and wishing they were still young enough not to be married.

Marriage was for chumps!

As he made his slow way back to the hall, he pulled a silver cigarette case from his jacket pocket, tapped one of the sticks on the lid and then lit it with a silver lighter his cousin had given him not long before her murder.

Things had been difficult since her death, and some of the crowd had withdrawn their hospitality. They were friendly enough when he said hallo to them down the Twenty-Two Club. But he was rather lacking in social invitations since her demise at the hands of her step-mother — or was it her half-sister? He still wasn't sure.

Timothy Sinclair, who had always been quick off the blocks when it came to falling in love with flibbertigibbet girls, had taken pity on him and gone around to see him with the good news.

'Come to the wedding, old bean. Be good for you to get away from Town for a spot of country air, don-cha-know?'

'I don't want country air. I am replete with town air. What do I want country air for? If you ask me, country air is overrated and best left to those who were meant to breathe it, otters and stags and what-not.'

'Calm down, Morty,' said Timothy.

'Well I mean, country air, really.'

'And you know Milly. She'd love to see you there,' Timothy continued.

'Mildred Oliver? Horsey type? Tall Girl? Need a mounting block to look her in the eye, don't you?'

'Not really,' said Timothy, a little too shortly. But Morty was in full flow and failed to see the intense look that taken over the normally docile features of his friend.

'Oh come on, Timo, she has to duck when walking under Marble Arch,' said Mortimer, with a little chuckle and a mime which involved raising his hands above his head. Timothy by this point had turned a rather interesting shade of beetroot. He could restrain himself no longer and grasped Mortimer by the lapels, 'Kindly refrain from making such comments about my fiancée, Marsh, or I shall no longer try to show any concern for your well-being. Quite the opposite in fact.'

'Just a joke,' said Mortimer as he dusted himself down and straightened his tie.

'Do you want to spend a few days in the country or not?' asked Timothy through clenched teeth.

'Thank you, Timo, but no.'

'Good, you won't mind collecting the sibling from our parents' place. Mater and pater have gone down already. So I promised you'd get her to Esserington Hall safely.'

'I just said I didn't want to go. I don't want to wave someone I consider a chum off on a voyage he's never likely to return from.'

'You have a knack of insulting a fellow, do you know that, Morty?'

'And you have a knack for promising my services to your pill of a sister. Why can't she travel down with you?' Mortimer Marsh, determined to defend his right to not go to the country, stood straighter.

'It's a surprise for Milly. They came out together and haven't seen each other in some time. Connie's idea, she thought it might be fun to surprise Milly. And you get to enjoy all that abundant country air while making new friends who won't mind that you were involved in a murder.'

'You were there too. Hasn't done you any harm.'

'I was a guest. This is your house, isn't it?'

'Well, actually —'

'Good, see you tomorrow then, and don't forget the wedding present. Fortnum's have the list.' And with that, Timothy left Morty standing with his mouth open and his eyes wide.

And so, much to his chagrin, Morty found himself in the country, taking in the air (leave it to the sheep), elaborately wrapped F&M box in hand (costing nearly half his monthly allowance), trudging back to the house and about to witness the imminent departure of a chum to the land of marriage.

As he arrived back at the imposing front door which stood twenty-five feet high and reflected the sun in hundreds of glass panels, a small black cab came to halt.

From its interior stepped forth a vision of beauty the likes of which he had never seen before. Morty had a keen eye for an attractive ankle and lower leg. Unfortunately, he had lost count of the amount of times he'd been disappointed by the emergence of an attractive appendage from stationary automobiles, only to be followed by a body and features that would make John Sullivan think twice about starting an argument.

However, the dish currently emerging would make Venus insist on a bit more rouge, before Botticelli applied the finishing touch. This stranger exuded confidence and womanliness like no one else he'd ever met before, and he'd seen Marlene Dietrich perform at The Café de Paris. Good Lord, what would this one be like to talk to? But if he were honest, talking was the last thing he wanted to do with her. Simply being in close proximity would be enough.

'What ho!' he said, as he trotted down the steps. 'Here for the nuptials, what? Let me help you with your bag. They normally have a chap for this sort of thing, don-cha-know?'

Before the vision could respond, Timothy burst forth from the doors at the top of the steps.

'Morty, there you are! Thank God. We need to talk.'

'What ho! Timo. What's ruffled your what's-it?'

'There's been a theft. Milly's diamond tiara has been stolen.'

Part Two

'Hallo, everyone's in the drawing room. Go on up,' said Timothy to the recent arrival.

'Well actually —' she began.

Those two words were such sweet music to Morty's ears, he could now die a happy man, although he would prefer to hear a few more of her words for a few more years. What was all that guff about marriage being for chumps that had been filling his brain box recently? He could readily see the appeal now. His eyes had been opened, the way forward was as clear as day.

'Morty, we need to talk,' insisted Timothy trying to turn Morty away from the object of his attention.

'Now look here —' began Morty, fully intending to not have this delicious moment sullied by Timothy in a funk.

'Stop dithering, you fat-head,' said Timothy, this time stepping between Morty and the vision of complete womanliness.

'No, Timo. As your butler and what-not haven't done their shoelaces up yet, let alone crouched on the starting blocks,' said Morty, 'I am going to assist this lovely guest of yours, and I reiterate the phrase "Your Guest", with her luggage. Old Morty has a co —'

'Please don't mention that blasted code,' snapped Timothy.

Morty stepped around Timothy asking, 'May I take your thingummy for you, Miss…' and paused long enough for the lady to reply, 'Highsmith, Julia Highsmith.'

'How do you do, Miss Highsmith?' he said, smoothly gaining any ground he may have lost by his interfering pill of a friend. With swift aplomb and his quick wit he had scuppered the plans of the evil blister before they had come to fruition. He felt like one of those movie star Johnnies, Clarke Grant or Cary Gable. Yes, he was in fine fettle, indeed. And he'd have the vision all to himself soon enough.

As they walked at a sedate pace up the steps, Miss Highsmith said, 'I'm actually here to catalogue the library. Bring it into the twentieth century. I didn't realise there was a celebration taking place.' Morty could feel Timo heating up behind him, but he only had eyes for Miss Julia Highsmith. Timo — and Timo's problems — could wait, for he was with an angel and he was about to enter heaven.

'You know your mouth is open, don't you?' said the angel.

He closed it rather faster than intended and caught his tongue between his teeth.

At the top of the steps, Sloane arrived to carry out the duty for which, no doubt, he was well remunerated. Morty was left standing, tending to a bleeding tongue with hand on cheek. Miss Highsmith actually smiled at him as she passed through the great doors.

'Now, will you help me, Morty?' said a high-pitched voice behind him.

'Do you know, Timo, you're just about the most irritating blighter I know?' he replied.

They started to walk around the house and Timothy started to tell the tale he had been desperate to tell.

'Milly's diamond tiara has been stolen, Morty, and I need you to get it back.'

'Why don't you call the police? It is their normal line of work. Mine is not hunting down priceless pieces of jewellery.'

'We can't get the police involved. It's not the done thing to go accusing one of your guests of theft, is it? Besides, it's not like there's been a murder.'

Morty stopped and delivered one of his blackest looks at the docile features of his friend.

'Sorry. Forgot and all that,' said Timo, 'but the thing is, Morty. I know who took it.'

'Well there you go then. Just go and ask for it back.'

'I can't do that, she's not supposed to know I know.'

'Of course. Cat burglars of high society don't normally go around advertising the fact. Hang on, how do *you* know who took it?'

'It was Connie,' said Timothy, kicking a pebble that had inadvertently wandered into his path.

'Connie? Why? When? She's only just got here, I know, I brought her and I haven't even had time to take off me driving gloves and have a sharpener. How in the blazes did she manage it?'

'The thing is, she has this habit of taking things that don't belong to her. She must have swiped it while they were squealing and being all girly up in Milly's room, you know what women are like. I could go and demand it back from her, but then I would be admitting that I know, and if I do that, I'll have to tell the old man, and he would have her committed or something. She doesn't mean it, she just likes pretty shiny things.

'But more importantly, if Milly finds out it was Connie that took her grandmother's tiara, she will call the wedding off. But if the tiara isn't found, then she won't be able to wear the veil tomorrow and the wedding is definitely off. Do you see my predicament, Morty?'

'I certainly do, old top. But, if you ask me, you have the perfect excuse to call off this arrangement to the giantess.'

It was Timothy's turn to deliver his blackest look.

'Sorry, but I still don't see why it's my problem too?' argued Morty.

'You are my only friend in all this. The only one I can turn too. I need your help.'

'I see.'

'Just go to her room tonight, when we're all at dinner. Have a look around (she usually hides them under the bed), find it, then hide it in your own room and return it to me during the night. Easy.'

'If it's that easy, why don't you do it?' Mortimer had been coerced into these situations before. They usually ended up with a visit to the headmaster and six of the best. That time Pinky Pinkerton had persuaded him to steal the key to the science lab while everyone else was still inside with a concoction of Pinky's manufacture — something to do with ammonium sulphide or some such rubbish — still smarted.

'I can't be seen leaving the table the night before my wedding. The in-laws will think I'm getting cold feet.'

'Fine, fine. I'll do it, but you owe me, Timo,' agreed Morty, against his better judgement.

'Thanks Morty. Come on, I'll give you a tour of the shack and point out all the salient rooms, what?'

'Fine, and while you're doing it, you can tell me all about Miss Highsmith.'

Part Three

Twenty guests have been arranged around a table which runs the length of the room unimaginatively called The Room of Light. One whole wall, made entirely of glass, gives a view of unrivalled spectacle over the flowing hills and downs. Well, it would have, if it hadn't been the evening. A seven-course meal was to be presented to the assembled peers who were to celebrate the marriage on this fine autumnal night. Another one hundred and thirty were to arrive tomorrow for the actual wedding. It was considered a small affair by high society standards. Ornate candelabras glinted in the light. Crystal glasses tinkled. Silver scraped on china.

Conversation murmured, sometimes harsh, 'What does she see in him? He has no prospects, does he?' a voice heavy with haughtiness travelled easily to the ears of the bride's mother.

'She calls it love, Lady Montdore.'

'Oh dear. She'll learn.'

Sometimes innocent, 'My roomth covered in Chinethe wallpaper. Why ith it called The Oriental Room?'

And sometimes inane, 'It was funny at the time. You had to be there really,' said Morty to the vicar sitting next to him.

In truth he was rather nervous about the task ahead of him, and the thought of making polite chit-chat with a bunch of strangers made his stomach churn — butter would be the result if milk had been poured in. The house was quite possibly the largest he'd ever stayed in, and he'd visited a few. At the top of the wide and imposing stairway, three corridors led to three different wings. He'd already misplaced his own room twice that afternoon. How he was supposed to find the dratted Connie's room he didn't quite know.

Then he'd had the bright idea of finding the lovely Julia Highsmith. It was an approach of two-fold brilliance. First, just spending some time with her and listening to her voice would be a pleasant way to spend the afternoon. Secondly, he hoped to persuade her to help in his quest to ensure true love reigned in the hearts and minds of men and giantesses, by assisting him in returning the item in question to its rightful owner. He eventually found her in the grand library where she sat amid texts and scrolls that she said were from the late Middle Ages.

'Golly! Did they all have a problem with time keeping?' he said and then went on to explain his situation. She replied that she was only a visitor in the household and felt the required skill set for such a task fell far outside her remit as a librarian.

'That's a no, is it?'

'Yes, it is Mr Marsh. Now if you really don't mind?' she said, turning her head back to her scrolls, leaving Morty feeling like a man who'd collected his winnings, ordered celebratory drinks and picked out a new blazer, only to find his wallet had been pinched.

He looked along the table to Timothy, who in turn looked up at his bride-to-be, sitting next to him. Timothy said something, she scowled at him. Timothy looked down the length of the table to Morty and gave a questioning look and a nod of the head which said in no uncertain terms, 'Move Morty, you've a priceless tiara to recover.' Morty looked down at his consommé, and then back at Timothy with a look that said, 'I've barely started the soup, you blighter.' Timothy replied with, 'Move or you'll be wearing the foul-tasting fluid.'

Morty made his excuses and left the gathering. No one paid him any heed, except the vicar who seemed more than pleased to be left alone with the young librarian on his left.

'Left, right or straight on? Einy, meeny, miny, mo…' he tapped his lips with his figures as he tried to recall the route Timothy had taken him on when he first arrived. Five minutes later, he found himself trying the door to Connie's temporary accommodation, only to find it was a linen room. The girl occupying herself with the task of rotating the bedsheets was not surprised to see a guest of the wedding party looking for the room of another guest.

'What ho!' said Morty having recovered from the shock of Connie apparently sleeping in a laundry room. 'Any idea where Connie Sinclair is boarded these days?'

'Turn right at the top o' the stairs, sir. Seventh door on the left — The Oriental Room,' she replied, thinking how unfair the world was. She daren't even imagine what might happen to her if a young gentleman was found in her room.

Having found the correct sleeping quarters, our reluctant hero was greeted with a scene of utter devastation, or perhaps she always left her room with clothes thrown all over the floor, suitcases upended and drawers emptied of their contents? Morty thought this unlikely. Things did not bode well for the forthcoming nuptials.

*

Mr Sloane, the butler of Esserington Hall, was a man who did everything by-the-book. He took a very dim view on the workings and rituals of the house being done in a way which did not conform with his idea of how a house should be run. Morty could tell all this by the way he moved, and the way he looked at Morty as if he was the sort of guest they were not used to having at such a great house. With a great amount of trepidation, Morty interrupted Sloane after he had exited The Room of Light.

'I say Sloane, old thing,' he said, dabbing at his forehead with a handkerchief.

'Sir.'

'I wonder, would you mind asking Timo to come out and have a word with me?'

'Sir?'

'Look, I know it's not the done thing and all that. But I really do need to talk with him. And it's the sort of talk best not overheard by lords of the realm and what-not.'

'Sir,' said Sloane as he returned to The Room of Light.

Morty sat on a leather fender seat by a blazing fire, burning with enough force to heat a hospital for a week. Sloane returned with a vexed-looking Timo in attendance.

'If you would come with me, Mr Sinclair, Mr Marsh.' Sloane then escorted them to the billiard room.

'Where have you been? How long can it take to swipe a little thing like a tiara?' demanded Timothy.

'It's gone, Timo.' Straight to the point, no point in dilly-dallying.

'What do you mean, gone? If you've messed this up for me —'

'Now don't be like that. It wasn't my fault. I found your sister's room, eventually. Only someone else had beaten me to it. Turned the room upside down. I had a look around and all that, but I think it's been stolen.'

Timothy flopped into a leather chair by the fire. Having found the drinks cabinet, Morty poured two belters. He passed one to his friend.

'But I promised I'd get it back for her,' said Timo.

'I know, old thing. We have to think, who could it be? Which one of your wedding guests could do this?'

'You realise the people we've got in there don't go in for petty burglary, don't you? They're all above suspicion.'

'The servants then?'

'It's possible I suppose, but what would any of them know about tiaras? Did you tell anyone about it?'

100

'Oh dear,' said Morty. When he had been very young, and his parents had still been alive, they had taken him to the circus. His one clear memory was of the clown who got everything wrong. He tripped over his own feet, his trousers fell down, he was kicked up the backside by other not-so-friendly clowns, and he was the one finally drenched in water. Morty now knew what it felt like to be that clown.

'Julia Highsmith,' he said, with head lowered into his hands.

'You fat-head, Morty. She left the table ten minutes ago, shortly before you returned.'

'But she is such a divine creature. She can't have done this, can she?' But even as he asked the question, he knew the answer. It could be no one else.

'Oh! She was a clever one,' said Timo, pacing up and down the room, 'Inveigling her way into a house when plenty of aristos would be here, all done up in their best sparklers. You are a complete liability, Morty.' Morty spurred on by the hurtful words, gathered himself together by the lapels and prepared to do all that was necessary to restore the honour of the Marshes.

'Never let it be said that Mortimer Marsh isn't the sort of chap to let a friend down, and then do nothing to rectify the posish,' he said, draining the glass and then dashing from the room to the stables, to ensure the miscreant could not break for it in one of the guests' automobiles. She had after all arrived by taxi-cab and would need transport to escape. His quick thinking would be sure to save the day.

By the time he arrived at the stables, out of breath and gasping for air, he was cursing the architect for putting such an important building so far away from the main abode. He heard the red dragon, his beloved Lagonda before he saw it. Horses brayed at the demonic sound of six cylinders spewing fire from its exhausts. It tore passed him, spraying muck and pebbles in its wake, forcing him to dive out of the way.

There was nothing for it, he would have to borrow one of the other cars and give chase. Two Bentleys parked side by side gave him little hope, but needs must. He passed over the blower knowing it would be too much to handle and opted for the older roadster. It coughed into life at the second press of the starter motor and he felt the beast give a deep rumble that might have woken the gods. All was not lost.

It seemed to take forever to get rolling, but he passed the chapel at nearly forty miles an hour, desperately wishing he had a pair of goggles, for the wind at this speed made it difficult to keep his eyes open. He hoped no sheep were wandering about. He could see the lights of his quarry and fancied he was gaining ground, even though the Lagonda should be able to touch ninety miles an hour on a straight road.

'Come on you old relic,' he shouted, as he urged his steed to even greater speeds, the pistons making such a noise as to send nesting birds to the heavens in giant flocks. His only ambition to retrieve the loot, the smell of heated oil concerned him not.

He turned sharply onto the main road with a squeal of burning rubber. One of the thin spheres popped. He barely noticed as his attention was taken — just for a moment — by flames licking through the grilles above the running board.

Minutes later, it became clear Julia was heading for the train station. He screeched to a halt, pleased to see his own car in a relatively unharmed condition.

Sprinting onto the platform, he heard the shrill whistle and saw the lovely, and daring, Julia Highsmith being helped aboard by a guard. The train was moving off and had already gathered quite a head of steam. Morty, all thought of safety long ago blown away by a Bentley convertible doing nearly fifty miles an hour, jumped for the departing train and was hauled aboard by two boy scouts who would dine out on this for the next two weeks.

The scouts followed the stranger as he quickly dashed from compartment to compartment, politely apologising to each occupant as it became clear the object of his recklessness was not in residence.

A guard tried to calm the advance of the heroes, only to be told, 'Don't be such an ass, I'm on the trail of an expert jewel thief, aren't I boys?'

'Yes, sir,' they chimed in unison.

'Well, let's be at him then, sir,' said the guard, and three became four.

They caught up with her as she entered the Pullman car. Five flying figures dashed through the car scattering apologies left and right. Eventually, Julia, having run out of carriages, was trapped by the ageing guard, and a scout troop led by a wide-eyed, filthy, soot-stained playboy with more courage than brain power. Her only option was to jump. She flung the door wide open. Fortunately for Julia, the train was travelling at a slower pace as it rounded an embankment. Now or never.

'Good-bye, Morty,' she said with a smile.

'No, Julia don't...'

As she was about to leap, one of the boy scouts ran forward to block her way. She deftly pushed him aside and took her chance with gravity.

Morty and the guard braved the buffeting wind in an attempt to see if she was alive, but she was lost in the darkness.

'Sorry, sir,' said the guard as he pulled the door closed.

'Well, that's that, I suppose,' said Morty. 'She fooled the lot of us and because of me, my friend will not be getting married. If yours truly wasn't a social pariah before, he shall certainly be one now.'

The boy scout picked himself off the floor.

'Was this what you was after, sir?' he asked. 'Me mam says I shouldn't be doing the dipping now I'm a scout. But as it was a good turn an all that, I don't think she'll mind, do you?'

He held in his hands a glittering tiara likely to make everyone's day, even if it was a little bent out of shape.

A Soldier's Honour

(First published in Angels by Black Hare Press.)

We were separated from our battalion and had wandered for half a day, until a French girl gave us sanctuary in her father's farmhouse for the night.

It was the way my comrade looked at her out of the corner of his eye, as she laid bread and cheese before us, which alarmed me.

She wouldn't be safe while we remained under her roof.

Hearing him creep from the room we shared, I followed. Whatever innocence our merciful angel had, was about to be lost forever.

He died quickly before harm was done.

Then she pointed the pistol at me.

Sins of The Father

(My first published story. It appeared in Vortex by Clarendon House in 2018. During the 2020 lockdown, Sins was read and performed by actors via Zoom conference, watched by people from their own homes. The production by BookStreamz is available to view at <u>https://vimeo.com/432756822</u>)

I will tell you everything, but please let me tell it my own way. I won't leave anything out.

I met her in a public house in Hammersmith. The Eagle, I think, a little pub with a big music scene. Every London pub had a music scene in 1977. I'd gone to see one of those bands that spawned so many other great singers and groups, but have, in the fullness of time, faded from memory. Only true music devotees would be able to recall their energy and inspiration. Punks said pub rock bands were dead, but I still liked their sound.

Not many will remember the pub either; it's probably part of a chain now with plastic menus and wheelchair access. Back then, with its stained glass windows and faded golden filigree plasterwork, carpet that stuck to your feet, atmosphere thick with smoke, and the ceiling stained with nicotine, it was a home from home. The old woman sitting at the other end of the bar, drinking port and lemon, saw everything, and said nothing—a landlady never to get on the wrong side of. The girls behind the bar called her Mother, although she couldn't possibly have been Mother to them all. The tiny stage in one corner of the pub had just enough room for the four-piece band to stand on. I sat on a red leather stool at a small wooden table. If I reached out, I could touch the guitarist.

That night, I was there with a housemate who went by the name of Scud. You had to call him Scud, he got agitated when you called him Martin. Overweight, with a round face already scarred from the abuse he'd given his many whiteheads and spots as a teenager, Scud complained incessantly about the music.

'This is so fuckin' shit. I knew we should've gone to see The Slits.'

'We're here now, try to enjoy yourself.'

As I watch my one-time friend harrumph back towards the bar, a sulk clearly imminent, I see the ridiculous figure of a fat, spotty eighteen year old in tight tartan and leather, with a blue mohawk going limp at the end of its seven-inch spikes.

We looked very different; he was embracing the emerging punk scene, while I was clinging to the glam of a few years earlier. I had given up on glitter, but mascara, thick and black, was essential to my look back then. My hair was shoulder length and shaggy like a west coast Eagle, and my complexion, although not perfect, was not ruined in the same way as Scud's. I was also stick-thin, my student grant not enough to get the beers in and eat regular meals.

The room was crowded and smoky, and I knew Mother was watching us; mainly my friend, but me too because I was with him.

A girl flopped down beside me in the seat Scud had vacated moments earlier. A very pretty girl with green eyes, a touch of punk about her, red lipstick, and a deliciously pale face with a cigarette in a holder.

'Music's shit, init?'

'I've already had that conversation.'

We were shouting over the noise, leaning in to hear each other. She smelled of Charlie, that ubiquitous and leathery scent that so many women chose to wear.

'Who's your friend?'

'Martin, I mean Scud.'

'Think he'll go for me?'

'He wanted to see The Slits, so probably, yeah.' I was trying to be cool without much success.

'Ha. Funny. What about you?'

I took a long look at her. She was attractive, like a reject from a Hammer film. There was a chance she might have been a prostitute, but she wasn't trashy enough and, although young, I knew the working girls around there would usually start a conversion with the price. She crossed her shapely legs, revealing more thigh. Ripped fishnets were the thing that year.

'We only just met, perhaps we should get to know each other.'

'Fine, I'll be at The Hope and Anchor tomorrow night.'

Then she was off, intercepting Scud on his way back to our table. She plucked a drink from his hand, took a large sip, and winked at him. He changed course, and I was left on my own to watch her flirt with him. Ten minutes later, they were leaving. She was leading him by the hand.

I was bubbling with jealousy, and I didn't even know her name. How often does it happen? An attractive girl more or less offers herself to you—idiot, Mike, you're an idiot—and she's gone off with *him*, the ugly one. Yes, I really was conceited enough to think that. Please bear in mind I was only seventeen. Mind you, she had given me first refusal.

But all was not lost.

The Hope and Anchor. Tomorrow night.

*

Bands played in the basement at the Hope and Anchor. A confined, claustrophobic place that made for an intimidating first visit. The band was loud, a punk outfit, and not my sort of thing. But I had a date, of sorts. The room was crowded, and there was nowhere to sit as every last piece of furniture had been removed. It was a mad, jostling, bouncing mass of crazed, sweaty flesh. The singer was spitting into the crowd, the crowd were spitting back.

My stomach churned; I was glad to be at the back of the room away from the main action.

I tried not to make eye contact with anyone. The increasing feeling of danger and knot in my stomach warned me I was out of my comfort zone. I also began to suspect I shouldn't have worn bell bottoms and a Snoopy t-shirt. Going to meet a pretty girl who was a bit avant-garde while dressed like a twelve-year-old boy; I felt like such a fool.

She was standing at the back of the room, with Scud. Shit. I should have left then; my life would have been different, I'm sure of it.

'Watchya,' she said.

'Hello,' I said to her before turning to him. 'All right, Scud?' I lifted my chin in greeting.

'All right,' he said. What he was really saying was *piss off*.

Standing next to Scud, she appeared much taller than the previous night. She smirked down at him.

'Run along, Martin, your friend and I have business to talk about.'

'But what about us?' he protested.

'I told you, there is no *us*. A failed fumble in a car park does not make us an item, darling. Now, go and jump about with your little friends.' She was cruel, and yet my heart jumped at her words.

She kissed me on the cheek, leaving a red smudge, and led me away from Scud. He had been omitted just like that.

'He won't like being called Martin,' I said

'Tough tits, shit stinks.'

She smiled at me. My heart melted.

I asked if she wanted a drink, to which she answered, 'Bah, it's piss in here. I'm sure they water it down. None of this lot would know. They're all speeding their nuts off.' She swept her arm in a wide arc, indicating the pogoing fools up by the stage.

We leaned against the rear wall. Should I have got myself a drink? I didn't know; it was difficult to say what would have impressed her.

'I don't know your name,' I said.

'Are you sure you want to, Mike?'

She knew my name. I felt flattered, but I also knew how easy it would've been to get such simple information from Scud. None the less, she had me at a disadvantage.

'Yes.'

'Tell you what…help me out with a little something, and I'll tell you my name and anything else you want to know about me.'

'Okay. You're on. What do you want?'

At that moment, I would have happily crawled over burning coals just to hear her speak.

'You sure? It'll be different, but fun…maybe a bit embarrassing. Still want to help?'

'Yeah.'

'See him over there, the little man on his own who looks about as out of place here as you do.'

'Yeah.'

'He's the manager of the band. Nice man with a wife and child at home.'

I looked sideways at her, where was this going?

'How do you know?'

'I like to know things about people. Now, listen. He's a nice man who likes nice young boys, understand?'

'So…'

'So, make friends with him and ask if he can find somewhere quiet for you to talk where you won't be interrupted.'

'Hang on a minute,' I said, 'you've got the wrong idea about me. I thought you and me could—'

'Don't worry, I'll rescue you.'

'Why?'

'You'll see. Trust me.'

I was worried. Despite what my father would always say about men who wear makeup being poofters and pansies, I was not that way inclined. Just an inexperienced boy trying to find a place in the big city.

'Get me a drink then.' I was annoyed with her. For what, I wasn't quite sure. She was playing a game with me, that much I knew, and although I didn't know the rules, I was excited. Why? I didn't have the answer for that either.

She came back with a lager and a whisky, both for me.

'Pint o' piss and some Dutch courage,' she said.

I necked the scotch and went forward to my destiny.

It was ridiculously easy. In a matter of minutes, he was showing me into the manager's office on the pretext of an impromptu audition.

He stroked my hair and said kind words about my youth and beauty. He promised a proper audition with a band if I only relaxed and took my t-shirt off. I did, but I was sweating—where was she? Was the joke to be on me? Just how cruel could she be?

He ran his fingers over my chest, chasing goose pimples as I shivered. He put his arms around me and slid his fingers under my belt at the top of my buttocks. To my amazement, I found myself becoming aroused. This shouldn't be happening. I was straight, I knew I was. It might have been raging hormones in combination with the closeness of another human being.

He was looking into my eyes, waiting for my kiss. Just as I was thinking I might have to either go through with it or storm out of the room, the door burst open. A camera flash illuminated the doorway, stinging my eyes, leaving a lightning strike afterimage.

The little man began to rant 'How dare you? This is private,' then he started to call for help. I started to dress.

'Be quiet,' Polly shouted from the doorway. 'No one can hear you over that poor excuse for a band. Now, I'd hate for this to get in the papers, ducky. Twenty quid and I can keep it out of the news.' She was shaking the Polaroid the way people used to.

'I'm not paying you a penny, sweetheart. Blackmail is illegal. I shall get my lawyers.'

'Not blackmail. I'm looking after your best interests, for a fee.'

'We live in enlightened times, you stupid cow. No one will care. In fact, it might even be good for the band.'

'Now you are bluffing. I'm sure the wife will care very much. Twenty quid *now*, or the papers find out about your fifteen-year-old friend here.'

I was stunned; it had all happened so fast. But Fifteen? He'd lost and he knew it. He threw the notes at me, calling me a whore and her a blackmailing bitch.

We ran out holding hands, her laughing and me oh so relieved to be with her. She was dangerous and amazing, beautiful and smart, and I was smitten. I had tricked the little man. I was enjoying being with her and I wanted more.

We went to China Town and feasted. I hadn't eaten so well in months. As promised, she told me about herself. Polly, as I found out, was a couple of years older than me, and her parents were relieved when she moved out. She had always been a great disappointment to them ever since the nuns refused to have her back.

Polly had a room in Notting Hill. Today, one associates Notting Hill with the carnival, the stylish, and Hugh Grant. But, back then, house after dilapidated house still bore the marks of war, each in need of serious repair or to be torn down entirely—they were all owned by Rackman-type landlords. Feral cats and children roamed aimlessly around the streets, and over-flowing metal bins lined the litter-strewn slum area.

Bob Marley was stirring it up through the floorboards from the room above while we made love until the early hours.

In the morning, she thanked me for being brave, for trusting her with her plan, and asked me if I wanted to do it again.

I told her I loved her and that I would do anything.

Two months later, we were married at a Catholic church in the suburbs. Some might say a quick wedding, but she had something on the priest.

Polly liked to know things about people, I asked how she found things out. In response, she tapped her nose and said she kept her ear to the ground and her eyes wide open. I'm sure people might ask why she decided to partner with me in her small scams. The simple truth is that I don't know. She was clever enough and brave enough to get everything she needed on her own, and I wasn't exactly Giant Haystacks, so I couldn't offer much in the way of protection. I think she needed someone to know her secret. She needed someone to show off to, someone to impress. I supported her wholeheartedly in the beginning, although I only played the role of a fifteen-year-old boy once more after the band manager incident.

We went to gigs most nights, everything from big venues to small pubs. She barely drank, but Polly—like old Mother—watched everything; a husband slipping a wedding band into a pocket before he went to chat to a girl, money exchanged for plastic baggies. And she wasn't afraid to ask for money to keeping her mouth shut. She was cocky in her approach to business, but it didn't always work. She took a severe slapping one night. When I stepped in to protect her, I had my fingers broken and couldn't eat solid food for a month. Things had to change.

She turned her talents to band management, focusing on one band in particular. Gathering her evidence beforehand and approaching the band during a break in one of their sets, she asked if they wanted fresh representation; someone who would really look after their interests without trying to get into any of their knickers.

'I wouldn't mind you tryin', love,' said the lead singer, reaching a hand around her waist.

'If you're not going to take the offer seriously, then you can stick with the perv. He's tried it on with each of you, hasn't he?' she said as she moved his hand away.

The singer looked like she had slapped his face. He stood taller and shared an embarrassed, knowing look with his fellow bandmates. Trying to recover the situation he asked, 'Who else you manage? I don't wanna sign up with a bint who knows nothin' 'bout nothin'.'

'Billy and the Bad Girls,' she replied. Of course, this was a lie.

'They any good?' asked the singer. The drummer was nodding, twiddling his sticks.

'Could be, but you could be better. But only if you take me seriously. Call me *love* again or think of me as just a pair of tits and your dumped. Call me Polly, act like a gentleman and not an adolescent twat, and you'll do well. Promise.'

His bandmates nodded their agreement. He held out a hand to Polly. They shook.

'But you'll have trouble getting Old Roy to let us go. Want us to have a word?' asked the singer.

'Leave the business side of things to me. Don't worry your pretty little head.'

Soon after she coerced the manager into releasing them, she had her evidence.

We rented a small office, where I answered the phone. She changed the band's name and image. Out were the wannabe punks, and in were the groomed and suited. Very romantic. A keyboard player joined, all previous songs were either softened or dropped. Gigs were arranged all over the capital. She worked them hard. If they went further afield, I went with them, but it was rare; London was where it was at.

She knew of a journalist with the NME and invited him to see the band now they were a tighter unit.

'They're okay, but nothing special, Polly. They look a bit too clean. Know what I mean?'

'They're the next big thing…and shall I tell you why?'

'Go on, enlighten me.'

'No one minds if you're a coke head, in fact, it's to be expected you being a hack in a music rag,' she said, 'but sucking it off the cocks of rent boys for six pence a time might give you a bad name.' The journalist looked around, checking to see if anyone had heard. 'I want a fabulous write up for my band. I want you to suggest they're better than the Beatles and The Stones served up together on sliced bread. The lead singer is a bastard love child of Jim Morrison and Tom Jones. Know what I mean?'

It was indeed a good write up, and it wasn't the last piece of praise her pet correspondent produced. Bigger and better gigs came in. An album was released, which sold well thanks to a favour owed to her by someone at the BBC. More bands came to her as the 'best choice' in music management. We got a bigger office with shiny glass desks and plush, cream coloured Axminster on the floor. We employed a secretary. We acquired even more bands, all of whom went on to do even more gigs and release even more albums—some sold well, others not so well. All the while, Polly collected her secrets. For her, secrets were priceless, her most precious commodity.

Rock and pop stars were renowned for being naughty boys and girls and people expected as much, so their secrets didn't hold much bargaining power for Polly. But the real headache came from all the solicitors involved in the many layers of the complex music industry. Talented liars—all of them—and far too many for Polly's liking.

A year or two later, public relations merged with and eventually replaced music management. We opened our doors to radio DJs and TV presenters, comedians, and newsreaders. We acted as their agents, managers, and representatives.

It had all moved so fast, thanks to Maggie Thatcher's Britain, and we were operating completely above board; secrets weren't a necessity anymore, but Polly still valued the information. People paid for information, but more importantly, they paid to keep it out of the papers.

A few weeks into a new signing, the conversation would go something like this…

'We are here for you, to get your name out and about, get you the right work, create the right image. Agreed?' Polly would begin.

'Yes, absolutely,' the talent would say.

'Would you agree that keeping negative aspects of your life out of the news would benefit your image?'

'Yes, but I'm clean as a whistle, Polly darling.'

'If we're going to work together, we need honesty. For instance, it is well known you like a little visit to a certain massage parlour down Soho way.'

'Nonsense'

'No point trying to hide it. My job is to know everything about you so I can present your best image while hiding your, shall we say, less favourable qualities. If you must use these places, try to be more discreet. If anyone gives you trouble, send them my way. Better still, tell me everything about them and the problem. I can, in most cases, stop the news getting out, but it can be very expensive keeping bad news out of the papers.'

We soon had a small team to help run the public lives of our celebrities: we organised public appearances and the opening of supermarkets and hospitals; newspaper articles and magazine interviews had to be scheduled; parties had to be organised and attended. Our lifestyle was hectic.

We were flying high, but every now and then, a secret revealed itself. Usually because the talent refused to pay, or because they actually wanted the news to come out. Someone's poison or vice then had to be protected. We hired private investigators to dig up the darkest secrets on all our clients. Polly would even use nuggets of information to entice existing clients to dish the dirt on friends and colleagues. And, of course, it was all in the name of protecting their interests. It was all very seedy, and I was losing interest in it.

I had grown weary of our business, and if I'm completely honest, it wasn't really mine. It was her baby and it almost ran itself, so I had less and less to do with it as time moved on. I had a growing cocaine habit, which very quickly became my main source of comfort.

Early one evening, it all came to a head when we had a meeting with a client. We greeted each other and made ourselves comfortable on big white sofas. Polly and I on one, a united front, and he, the client, sprawled on another. Polly, immaculate as ever in a black trouser suit, he in white tracksuit.

'The grapevine tells me you're considering other representation,' said Polly.

'Well, Poll, you know how it is. This other lot say they can get me more TV exposure.'

'Yes, I do know how it is. More than you think. You remember a little conversation we had all those years ago when you first came to us? The one about openness and trust?'

'I've a vague memory but I've nothing to hide. Why do you ask?' he said. He pulled on a chunky cigar.

'My job, our job, is more about what the public don't know about our clients than what they do know. We work very hard to keep it that way.'

'What are you on about? I've nothing to hide…I said already.' Impatient anger quickly replaced avuncular joviality.

'Fourteen-year-old girls. Eleven-year-old boys. Rent boys. Children. The star-struck teenyboppers. The sick and infirm. You don't care, do you? You abuse your position and you attack the kids.'

'Now look here, darling, I don't know where you heard this sordid filth, but say another word and you'll be hearing from my solicitor.' Pointing the cigar at Polly, he stood to leave, his face glowing red.

She slid an envelope forward.

'Take a look at these before you leave.'

With a trembling hand, he slid half a dozen black and white photographs off the coffee table.

'Like I said, we have to keep some information out of the press. If you leave, which you are perfectly entitled to do, I can't guarantee that will happen.'

'You're a bitch.'

'Maybe so, plenty have described me as such, but unlike some, I'm certainly not a molester of children.'

'What do you want?' He sat again.

'Nothing, but I have had a new contract drawn up. Sign here and here.'

He signed it, as she knew he would, and then stamped his cigar into the carpet before storming out of the office.

I was aghast. I had no idea we were covering up such grotesque behaviour. Drugs and married women, yes, but children? Good God Almighty.

It was the most viscous row we'd ever had. We had, in the course of both our professional and private lives, had the occasional spat or dispute over minor things, but hardly ever with raised voices. Now, I raged at her; how could we be mixed up with anything like that? She accused me of being a self-obsessed addict and of spending all our cash on filth. As the argument progressed and our slurs and accusations became more and more personal, it became apparent my feelings of love for her were no longer existent. I only loved the life, the glamour, the drugs, and the money.

In a sudden revelation, it became clear I hadn't earned any of it. With her cunning and brazen attitude, she had built a successful enterprise. I was just the partner. One she didn't need. A deadweight.

'I'm out. We'll divorce, then you can run the company any way you want. I want nothing to do with *it* or *you* ever again.'

She replied with a hard slap across my face; violence for the first time. I slumped down on a chair, holding my stinging face. It hurt more deeply when she said, 'I'd divorce you in a flash, but we made a vow in front of God. I can't go against the Almighty. This marriage is for life.'

'What? You never even go to church!'

'Beside the point. Leave if you want, but you won't get a thing from me, least of all a divorce.'

I was stunned. No attempt at appeasement or reconciliation? Just a 'no', based on a flimsy excuse. It was 1985, people got divorced all the time.

The corners of her lips twisted in that cruel, signature smirk of hers. I was being treated the way Scud had been all those years before. I was her pet, to be dismissed only when she was ready.

The chair tumbled backwards as I lunged at her. She lashed out, her fingernails drawing blood—I still have a faint scar along my left jaw, under my beard. We rolled on the floor. I was bearing down with my weight, hands around her throat. She slapped at my chest, my face, and my arms. Someone grabbed me by the shoulder, I lashed backwards and heard them stumble and fall. It was enough to bring me back to my senses and I sat back, breathless. Polly was pulling away from underneath me, gasping, clutching at her neck.

Taking in gulps of air between each word she said, 'I…will… never…divorce…you.'

Her outright cruelty and innate need to control everyone and everything were beyond rational sense. But who was I to talk? I had just tried to kill her.

We stared at each other, waiting for the other to react first. I turned away and stood before pouring myself a drink. That's when I remembered someone grabbing my shoulder. Looking behind me, I saw, lying prone with her head on the marble hearth, Polly's secretary.

'Oh shit, Daisy.' I said, barely a whisper.

Polly joined me. We both looked on in horror as an expanding pool of blood spread over the marble and the surrounding carpet. I touched Daisy's neck, the way they do in films. No pulse.

'You stupid man.' Her words full of hate and venom.

Instead of pulling together to conjure up a plan or at least get our story straight for the police, she was on the attack. I'd had enough.

'You're good at covering things up, Polly. You deal with it,' I said as I pushed past her.

*

Could I have a drink of water, please? There's more to tell, I haven't finished yet. Thank you.

I went to our apartment on Half Moon Street, retrieved my passport, and picked up a thousand pounds in cash before travelling by tube to Gatwick. Early the next morning, I was in Northern Ireland. I had family in the south I'd never met; only vague memories of blurred photographs my mother had displayed on the mantelpiece.

Crossing the border was simpler than I imagined, given the troubles of the time. A truck driver in a cafe agreed to carry me through the checkpoint, for a small fee. My stomach flip-flopped as we approached the armed guards. I was sure I was going to puke; I must have been as white as a sheet by then. My driver assured me not to worry, saying he was always crossing over and that they only looked for bombs, guns, and terrorists. 'Sure we're fine, please God,' he said. He took me to Dublin, his final destination, where I stayed the night in a B&B overlooking The Liffy.

Lying in the bed that night, I tried to rationalise the sudden turn of events in my life. In my sensible head, I knew I shouldn't have run, but I justified my actions by blaming Polly. More than anything, it was her I was running from. If she had agreed to a divorce, we wouldn't have been brawling and Daisy wouldn't have tried to intervene. It was her fault; *everything* was her fault.

I considered the possibility that I may have been having a breakdown. I couldn't understand why the police hadn't caught up with me. The question had been spinning around and around in my head, keeping me from any meaningful sleep.

Buying the plane ticket had been the most nerve-racking experience. I had expected to be pounced on as soon as I showed my passport or seized as I got off the plane in Belfast. I had to wonder what scheme Polly would employ to explain her dead secretary.

Half a day on a bus to Cork, and then a taxi to the small town of Brandine where my mother had been born. I found, within a day, cousins and extended family that remembered her. Some still wrote to her, and she wrote back, sometimes with news of her son and how proud she was of him. My shame surfaced with tears as I appealed to their better nature and our family connection for help.

I must have looked a fright in unwashed clothes, with a couple of days of beard growth, and tired red eyes sunken into the shadows of my pale face. I couldn't let my mother see me like this, not until I was better. The life I was leading, I told them, was tearing me apart and I dealt with the stress by overindulging in drink and drugs. My wife, I also told them, coped much better, but I needed time away from her too. I threw myself on their mercy and asked that I be the one to tell my mother where I was when I was ready.

These complete strangers accepted me and my deception into their lives with unquestioning friendliness.

An Uncle Pat and Aunt Mary put me up in small box room. I didn't venture from that room for two days, except to take care of nature's necessities. I slept, and when I wasn't sleeping, I wept. I cried for my stupidity, my anger, and my lies. I wept for Polly, not the woman of today, but the girl I had once loved. She had always been dangerous, it was part of her appeal, but her avaricious collecting of secrets had destroyed the joy she used to have and accentuated the dark, cruel side of her nature. And I wept for Daisy. Poor, blameless, not quite the brightest Daisy, who suffered the misfortune of working late on the night her employers tried to kill each other. Twenty years old and engaged to be married to a football player with Tottenham Hotspur.

Uncle Pat took me on as a kind of apprentice gardener. It felt good to get my hands dirty and do some honest graft. We worked in many gardens, large and small, doing everything from basic garden tidying to a bit of tree surgery. After two months of clean living and hard graft, my face and arms had taken on a natural tan, and the stubble I'd arrived with had grown to bushy proportions. I barely recognised the man in the mirror anymore.

One day, while we were packing up our tools, Uncle Pat asked what I was really running from.

'I can't tell you, Pat. But I can't go back…not to her or the world I once knew.'

'Ye should go to the confessional. You know what they say 'confession is good for the soul'.'

I remained silent, horrified that tears were once again brimming. Pat was one of those men who never showed emotion. Everything could be laughed at, but he surprised me.

'Do ye need help, son?'

'What do you mean?'

'Help…ye know…maybe a new whatchya-ma-call-it.'

'Identity?'

'The very word, a passport.'

'It would help, but they will catch up with me sooner or later.'

'The Garda?'

I nodded my reply and wiped my eyes with my t-shirt.

'Leave it to me, son. Sure, it can't be that difficult.'

Pat made arrangements through some people who knew other people, who knew 'those kinds' of people. The price was arranged and I supplied him with a passport photo. Several weeks later, Pat took me to a pub way up in the hills. An old white building, which may once have been a farmhouse. It would be a drive for anyone to visit on a night out, so I doubt they were ever busy because I didn't see a single house within walking distance. Inside, the fire roared and, as I expected, it was empty of customers. Pat sat at one end of the bar, which was situated in the middle of a long, thin room, and picked up a Gaelic paper before telling me to sit as far away as possible at one of several small tables so he wouldn't be able to overhear.

Two men came in, and the barmaid made herself scarce. They sat opposite me, I wondered if I should offer them a drink.

'Ye the one?' asked the taller of the two. He was the only one who spoke. It seemed the other's sole purpose was to look menacing, although he really wasn't needed; the talker was clearly a man with whom not to tangle.

'The one what?'

'Five hundred pounds, have ye got it?'

'How do I know I can trust—'

'Stop right there, son, before someone is insulted. Do ye want this here passport or don't ye?'

'Yes, of course.'

'Five hundred pounds.'

We exchanged envelopes, then the leader dropped his bombshell.

'That's only part payment, of course. What ye have in yer package there is a complete identity. A birth certificate, British passport and a National Insurance number, all of them the genuine article. A passport and birth certificate are easy enough to get hold of, but a National Insurance number takes a little more cunning, ye hear me?'

'Now hang on—'

124

'Yer to deliver something, and if ye don't, we'll find ye and put a bullet in yer thick English head.'

'I want nothing to do with it,' I tried to protest, but my throat was quickly drying up.

'Fine then. Give back the papers, we keep the money and yer man over there delivers for us instead. And ye still get the bullet. Certain individuals have taken risks to get us to this here point tonight. Now it's time to return the favour.'

'What? This is crazy.'

'Just who do ye think we are? The Sally Army? Now what's it to be?'

Failing to see any other options, I nodded my acquiescence.

The quite one remained inside while the leader took me to the car they had pulled up in. He handed me a backpack from the boot. Inside was a small package about the size and shape of hardback book, wrapped in brown paper.

'I want this package delivered to an address in Belfast by ten o'clock tomorrow night. Everything ye need to know is in here,' he said, tapping the bag.

'What is it?'

'Now that is a stupid question, son.'

'I can't…I didn't expect all this.'

'Fine.' He pulled a handgun—from where I don't know, it was too dark to see properly—and rested the muzzle against my forehead.

'I'm sorry. I'll do it…I'll do it!' My quivering legs lost all ability to hold me up, and I fell to my knees in a puddle of mud behind a pub I didn't know the name of. With the gun still pointed between my eyes, I had no time to think. He pulled the trigger. I lost all control as the dull sound of metal on metal reverberated through my head. Seconds passed. I was still alive.

'Tis that easy, son. Now deliver the damn package.'

I heard the doors of a car click open and slam closed before the same car drove away at a sedate speed, leaving me to be helped to my feet by Uncle Pat.

'Did you know? Do you know what they want me to do?' I asked, panting.

'No. And I don't want know to either.'

'Fucking hell, I've been so fucking stupid. What can I do?'

'Ye have to do what they want, Mike. I'm sorry, I really am.'

'The police…I'll go to the police.'

He shook his head. 'It won't change anything. Just make things worse. Yer'll be a police informer, yer'll drop me in it, yer'll reveal whatever it is yer running from and they'll still get ye. Even in prison.'

I was leaning against Pat's truck, wiping vomit from my chin with a tissue. I tried to straighten up and face my future like a man, but my legs wouldn't let me. Instead, I tumbled into the passenger seat and cried like a baby. Pat started the car, and we slowly trundled away.

'Can you give me a lift, Pat, to somewhere near the border? A quiet place where I can cross without fear of patrols.'

'Sure.'

We exchanged few words during the journey. Five hours later, he stopped at the edge of a small town, I forget the name now, and we both stepped out of the car.

'Yer a mile or so from the border here. Tis hilly, boggy, and still dark, but a clear night. Head north, that's away from yer moon tonight. Ye'll be in the UK by the time the sun comes up.'

'I won't see you again, Pat. Probably best, don't you think?'

'Aye, son.'

He thrust a ten pound note into my hand and hugged me. 'Don't be silly,' I said, trying to return the money. He quickly turned away, dropped back into the car, and drove away before I could say goodbye.

By daybreak, I was cold, filthy, and terrified. At midday, I stopped at a pub and ordered a scotch, drained it, and made use of the gents. I was surprised they served me. I washed my face and hands as best I could, but my clothes were filthy and I stank to high heaven.

My fears were numerous, and all centred around the package. What would happen if it got wet? Would it detonate? Or would it fail to detonate? What would happen to me if that happened? I was more terrified I'd end up giving it a quick shake and it would explode, taking me with it.

Shit, how did I get into this situation? Was I really contemplating this? A bomb, for Christ's sake. The instructions were to post it through the letterbox of a private house. I knew nothing about the recipient; he might have a family, or worse, children might die. Oh fuck.

I chose to do the only brave thing I ever did in my whole miserable life. I chose to warn Mr Sinclair—whoever he may have been—but I didn't want to write on the package directly for fear of detonating it, so I stuck a yellow note to it instead.

DO NOT OPEN
CALL THE POLICE

A man with a van gave me lift into the city and dropped me near a large market, which was coming to the end of its trading day. With my remaining money, I bought cheap jeans and a new t-shirt, changed in a public toilet, and threw the ripped, filthy clothes away. I decided to keep my donkey jacket.

I clutched the bag to me in an attempted to protect it. Why was I trying to protect this evil device? My morals felt twisted beyond reason. I wished for Polly then; she would know what to do. I also wished I'd not been so soft headed, as my dad might have said.

Having been a part of it, a facilitator, I knew the kind of things the rich and famous got up to. With our help, they made money, and with the money they made, they indulged their vices. Why had I been so stupid? Not all vices are equal, a small voice in my head argued.

I gripped the bag tighter as I tried to hang on to my sanity. It would be over soon.

By five in the afternoon, I was there, dog tired and scared witless, my feet sore and blistered. The target house was in a row of mansion-like houses, in what I can only assume was one of the more affluent areas. It was too early and still light; I didn't want to be seen delivering the package. In a nearby park, I rested on a bench and sleep eventually overcame me.

An hour or so later, with my head still on the backpack, I was awoken by two police officers.

'On yer way, son, no dossing down here.'

'Sorry.'

I stood and started to walk away, rubbing my eyes.

'Don't forget this now.' One of them was holding the backpack out to me.

'Yeah, thanks. Sorry.'

I walked the streets, my legs like jelly, my stomach churning, my thoughts in a whirl. *Don't do it, just walk away. Throw it in the river. You can't be part of this, Mike.*

Walking by the river, I contemplated chucking it all in, myself included. Why not just open the package? I asked myself. I can't, I'm a coward, I replied.

At just before ten o'clock, I returned to the house, which was now in darkness. Twenty-four hours ago, I had been safe, but now, I had a deadly package in my shaking hands and I was climbing the short flight of steps to the door of a house I had no business being outside of. I took the yellow sticky off and crumpled it into a pocket, my cowardice finally getting the better of me. What would happen to me if they found out I'd warned him?

It took me several attempts to line up the package with the slot. I didn't let it fall on the other side because I was worried it might detonate. The spring-loaded letter box, thankfully, held the package in place.

Then, I ran on stumbling feet as far and as fast as I could, stopping only to retch as my body tried to eliminate the evil I had done. Exhaustion finally took hold, and I collapsed down by the docks into a restless sleep.

Woken by the sun a few hours later, I proceeded to wander through the day, watching news on TVs in shop windows and picking up papers from park benches or bins, all the while avoiding patrols.

Later, I found a shelter for the homeless, which offered soup, a bread roll, and a camp bed for the night. Luxury. My anxiety levels rose as I waited for news of my terrible deed.

The next morning, I walked back to Mr Sinclair's house. All seemed normal; the house still stood, no piles of rubble or debris from a recent blast, and no cordoned off areas or sirens wailing. Perhaps Mr Sinclair was cautious and had called for the police anyway?

I hadn't eaten since the soup and bread of last night's supper, and I had no money to buy anything. Although I knew I would have to start getting back on my feet again, I resigned myself to the fact that I was destined for another night in the homeless shelter.

As I walked in through the front door, I took in its name: Safe Haven. I recognised some of the volunteers from the night before, but this time a visiting priest was moving around the room, sitting and chatting with the lost and forlorn of the town. He came over to my bed.

'Hello, my name's Father Kelly. What's yours?'

I turned my back on him without answering. I didn't know who I was. I hadn't even looked at the ID I'd gone through Hell to get.

I stayed in Belfast for three more days, sleeping rough and begging. I needed to be somewhere safe but had no idea where to find it. I also wanted out of Belfast with its tales of destruction, and its war that was more secret than the evidence of patrols, barriers, and checkpoints led you to believe. Leaving early, I headed west. I had barely eaten in a week so lifting my feet was difficult, let alone my thumb to cadge a lift with. A car eventually stopped, a small, rusty Ford Cortina.

'Hello again. I'm going up near Coleraine. Give you a lift?' said Father Kelly.

'Thank you.'

We travelled in silence, apart from my rumbling stomach. Rooting around in the door compartment, Father Kelly then handed something to me and said, 'It's a bit melted, but you're more than welcome to it.' He was holding a Marathon in his left hand.

'Sure?'

'Sure, I'm sure.'

'Thanks,' I said, snatching it from his kind hands and almost finishing the bar in one mouthful. 'Sorry,' I mumbled through a mouthful of chocolate and peanut.

'Never mind, that stuff is no good for me anyways. Where ye going?' he asked.

'Anywhere, I don't care.'

'Fine, I could do with the company.'

But I'd fallen asleep again and wasn't much company for the priest.

When I woke, I was in a single bed and looking at a small crucifix on the wall opposite. Father Kelly was just coming into the room.

'Hello, Thomas, how are you? I couldn't wake you when we got back to my parish, so we let you sleep here. Are you ready to eat?'

I was famished and accepted with a smile and a nod.

'Good. See you downstairs in ten. Your clothes are on the chair there.' He pointed across to the chair by the window.

Following the smell, I found the small kitchen. A bowl of stew was steaming, and Father Kelly was pouring tea from a large brown pot. Sliced white bread with a thin layer of butter on it lay piled high on a plate.

'Thank you,' I said as I sat opposite the kindest man in the world. I studied him as I ate. He was older than me by at least thirty years, and he was totally grey, even his eyes. We ate in silence after he gave a short thanks to God for the meal. I joined in with the 'Amen' and meant it with all my heart. When we'd finished, he leaned back and lit a cigarette.

'I won't pry, but I had to look in your bag to find out your name.' He placed my documents next to a mug of tea.

'S'okay.'

'How long have you been sleeping rough?'

I thought he'd said he wouldn't pry?

'Couple of days. I had to come north and found myself bereft of funds.'

'Well, we could try to help you get home again?'

'NO…um…no, thank you. I must try to get along on my own.'

'Well, if you're sure.'

'Tell me something, Father. I don't know why I'm asking… you're not going to say anything negative.'

'Ask it anyway, I might surprise you.'

'Is confession really good for the soul?'

He paused; his silence full of peace. 'It depends on the person. Some don't ever want to confess, others want to be seen to confess without seeking redemption, while the person who seeks true forgiveness through confession can be happier in the knowledge that a better life awaits their soul.'

'It sounds too simple.'

'I have to be somewhere soon, but we can talk about it later if you like?'

'Yes, I'd like that very much.'

Father Kelly left me alone for more than an hour, trusting a stranger with his meagre possessions. I contemplated recent events; had the documents for Thomas Williams, my new identity, really been worth all I had gone through to get them? I even reasoned with myself that the package might not have been a bomb, only a package that had to be hand delivered. Surely a bomb could be sent through the post? This item, whatever it was, needed the personal touch. I'd had no option at the time but to follow through; after all, my life was in danger. The Father returned to find me still sitting at his kitchen table.

'Now, what shall we talk about?' he asked.

That was when Father Kelly and Thomas Williams became friends. I helped around the garden and the house. He arranged work for me in the surrounding area, gardening and doing other odd jobs that, if I'm honest, I wasn't very good at. He vouched for me and I moved into a small flat. I started to help during mass, becoming more involved in church activities and the wider community in general. We spent many hours discussing the nature of God and goodness, theology and philosophy, faith and doubt.

It dawned on me that I'd met Father Kelly at this time in my life for a specific reason. My need to serve the community was a growing itch I couldn't ignore, and I felt the pull of the church more with every passing day. This was my calling.

Father Kelly and I went to see the bishop. Only when the bishop was certain of my genuine intention did I enter the seminary, where I spent the next five years studying and praying, leaving with a degree in theology.

I was first a deacon for six months with my old friend, Father Kelly. Once ordained, I was sent to Africa as a curate, where I spent three years in a small town with a whitewashed church and a bell tower. Despite the people's intense love of God, one didn't have to travel far to see the remnants of ancient witchdoctor rituals. I can't criticise these practises; my own faith is rooted in superstition. Didn't the Christians highjack pagan feast days and festivals? I'm enough of a realist to accept the truth.

I returned to Ireland to perform the funeral service when my friend and first mentor died, and ended up staying for seven years.

Life was better than ever, and with faith and God by my side, I felt courage that I'd never had in my previous life. I requested a placement in England, the land of my birth, and was sent to Birmingham where I had some of the greatest challenges of my ecclesiastic career.

Religious tension in the city was on the rise, myself and fellow spiritual leaders strove hard to bring the communities together out of a basic desire for love, respect, and acceptance. I am of the view that it is our differences that make us all so interesting.

Everywhere I had the pleasure to preach and pray, I encouraged love and acceptance, to be a better human being, not just for the glory of God and a better life beyond this, but more importantly, for the benefit of our friends, neighbours, and brothers here and now in this realm. Bitterness, cruelty, hate, spite, secrets, and lies only lead to unhappiness in our own souls and lives.

I moved here three years ago and now have the custodianship of a small Norman church with lots of character. The town is packed with lords and ladies, artists and posers. A council estate sits on one side of my church, with a private estate sold for development on the other. A melting pot for the lost, the temperamental, the rich, the poor, and seasonal visitors.

I have always done my best for all my congregations, their souls especially, and I'd all but forgotten the person I used to be. My world was turned around by one good man and his belief in the human spirit and God Almighty. I tried to emulate Father Kelly in every action; I wanted to make him proud.

It was while I was in the confessional one Saturday evening, hearing the secrets of my parishioners—the peeping toms, the petty thieves, and the potty mouths—when I heard her voice again. A touch of cut glass, now scratched with a lifetime of smoking. But I recognised it all the same.

'Forgive me, Father, for I have sinned. It has been thirty years since my last confession.'

'The Lord forgives all.' I tried to remain neutral, but I'm sure my voice cracked. The mesh between confessor and priest limits what is seen each way, but I recognised her silhouette.

'Really? Are you able to forgive me in the Lord's name... considering I'm still your wife?'

'You're not here to confess, Polly. Return in an hour when I'll be finished here. We can talk openly.'

'No, we'll talk now, you hypocritical bastard.' Her voice raised, no longer reverential as is expected in the confessional.

'Control yourself. For now, these people need me. An hour, Polly.'

The confessional door was almost ripped from its frame as she stormed away. For the rest of the hour, I listened patiently as the good people of my congregation unburdened their souls. But I didn't hear much.

An hour later, kneeling before the alter and asking the Lord for strength, I heard her approaching steps in unison with the tap of a cane. She knelt beside me.

'I should apologise. Let's try to be civil,' I said.

Then, I looked at her, aged now with fine lines and carrying more weight, which gave her an extra chin. Her eyes still beautiful, but now with heavy dark circles.

'How have you been?' she asked. I thought I heard a sarcastic tone. She continued. 'I never expected to see you as part of the cassock brigade...you were always so sceptical.'

'I have found happiness. What about you? Happy?' I knew the answer before I asked it.

'No. I always hated you.'

'Oh, Polly, we were happy once.'

'You left me to deal with Daisy. I did, too. A little pig farm, not far from here actually.'

I crossed myself and said a silent prayer for Daisy's soul, and mine.

'I missed you, you selfish bastard. You were my only friend.'

'I was the only one you could trust. Everyone else was wary of you.'

We were quiet for a minute. She sat back on a pew and I joined her.

'The police?' I asked.

'As far as they're concerned, she went missing and never returned home. Coincidently, it was the same night you disappeared, so the police put two and two together and got two lovers. They didn't try very hard, you were just two people who'd done a runner. Everyone was laughing at me. 'Poor Polly, her husband left her for the bimbo secretary."

'I'm sorry, but—'

'You ran and left me to cover it up.'

In the silence that followed, she struck a match and lit a cigarette.

'And then there was Yewtree.' The famous investigation of children who claimed to have been molested by famous personalities. 'They were rigorous in their investigation. I was lucky not to receive a custodial sentence, but the business was ruined.'

'I'm sorry.'

'So you should be. I might have changed if you'd stayed around, Mike.' That name sounded so foreign to my failing ears. 'I might've listened to you.'

'I think I remember one or two conversations about that. You'd never have changed Polly. You're a one-woman wonder, doing everything your own way.'

More silence. I looked up at Christ on the cross, seeing in detail the chipped and flaked paint around the wound to his chest. My whole world seemed to focus on the detail.

'What are you doing here, Polly? Let's leave the past where it belongs and part as friends.'

'Bollocks to the past. Do your parishioners know you're married? Do they know what you did? Do they know who you really are?'

'Of course not.'

'You're a fraud, a lying, cowardly fraud.' She stood, pointing down at me, her hand shaking as she raged. Spittle landed on my face.

'Polly, please be calm.'

'Do you know, when I found where you were, *what* you were, I thought I might try a bit of the old blackmail. See what I could get from you.'

'Polly…' I began to plead, for calm if nothing else.

'But then I thought fuck it, just kill the cunt.'

I was still seated when she lunged at me, unsheathing a thin stiletto from the cane. I barely managed to grab the wrist of the knife-wielding hand before the blade plunged towards my chest. I was sliding sideways on the polished wooden pew as she continued to bear down on me. A few seconds later, we toppled to the floor. She on top, the thin blade ripping my robes.

We began to roll, each of us trying to get the upper hand. I swear I only wanted to disarm her, but that's when I felt the gush of warm blood over my hands.

I knelt back, the thin blade still embedded in her chest, staring at my hands and then back at her as she went through her death throws. Blood spurted from the fatal wound in her chest and spread over the ancient stone floor; I was soon kneeling in it. So much blood.

I held her head on my knees and tried to comfort her. Blood bubbled from her mouth and her legs started to shudder, the final vestiges of life draining away. Complete stillness soon followed. I'd like to say there was understanding or peace in her eyes at the end, but all I saw was malice.

I took my stole from my pocket and placed it around my neck, bloodying it in the process. I forgave her in the name of God. Who would forgive me?

I don't know how long I knelt there. The silence of the empty, holy place echoed in my head, intruding on my grief. Long moments passed as I looked down at the only woman I'd ever loved. My tears fell like rivers and mingled with her black blood. I kissed her lips and closed her eyes.

Hero

(First published in Unravel by Black Hare Press.)

Where were all the superheroes when you needed them?

Tommy held his hand to his throbbing stomach.

In the films, Batman would have turned up in the nick of time.

Instead it was just him, two armed thugs and a scarred girl.

He couldn't let them do what they wanted to do.

His fingers were sticky now.

In comics, a superhero with healing powers would arrive now.

But he'd done enough with the rusty piping and they had run off.

The girl held him, phone pressed to her ear by shaking hand.

'My hero,' she whispered.

He closed his eyes.

The Waiting Room

(First round competition entry for The Inner Circle Writers' Magazine.)

She was elegant, in a way one does not expect to see in these modern times. That would make sense, for she was a lady who must have experienced eighty years. The sound of the zip pulling her much-loved wax jacket closed, announced her entrance into the waiting room.

'I have to come back in three weeks,' she said to the man sitting quietly studying the crossword. Her voice reinforced the opinion forming in the minds of the other patients who looked her way; despite her advanced years, she was a force of nature.

Whereas she was elegant, he was well-fed. He grunted as he stood, rolled his newspaper into a rough tube and wedged it between arm and ample body. His stomach made an awkward barrier his head had to cross, as he leaned forward to kiss her tilting cheek. He may have been younger than her, but the older one becomes, the less important these things are.

'Really, why?' His voice could only be described as theatrical. In another life he may well have been a great actor, for he surely knew the whole world was a stage and the three other people present were his audience.

'Because I haven't been cleaning my teeth properly, dear.'

'BLOODY HELL! Your mouth is full of decayed teeth and my soul of decayed ambitions,' he misquoted, making the little boy sitting next to his mother giggle. The women shushed her son and the old man winked at him.

'You will have to pay, dear,' she said, when they stood before the reception desk a few minutes later.

'Why? They're your teeth.'

'Don't be difficult, dear. I paid last time if you remember. You had X-rays.'

'Did I?'

'Yes.'

'What on?'

'Your teeth.'

'Really, I don't remember.'

'I do.'

'That will be seventy pounds please,' said the receptionist.

'What? I'll have to sell a kidney.' He slid a card into the handheld machine. 'Didn't dentists used to do a bit of surgery in the old days? Perhaps she'll take part exchange? Will you ask her for me?'

The receptionist smiled, but said nothing. It was obvious that she didn't know what to say beyond the expected responses of the role she had to play.

'Don't make a fuss, dear.' Then addressing the girl behind the desk, the force of nature said, 'I should like to make an appointment for three weeks' time. Do you think you can manage that?'

The time and date were set, and the appointment card handed to the woman who slipped it into an ancient crocodile handbag.

As he held the door open for his wife, he said, 'Life is short, my love, and we are but brief specks of dust in the long years of this lonely planet.

'Let us eat cake!'

No one heard her response as the door clicked into its closed position.

Three weeks later she returned, dressed entirely in black; she carried herself with impeccable dignity and perfect poise.

Elegance personified, even alone.

He Watched

(First published in Beyond by Black Hare Press.)

He said he would wait an eternity.

While he waited, he watched.

Every night he watched his wife as she put the child to bed. After showering, she would rub her body with fragrant oils. He ached for one more hit of her scent.

When the time came and she had put the book down, he would watch over her dreams.

Sometimes, he sat on the edge of the bed and tried to touch her as he used to when he had still been warm.

After years of this torture, she met someone new and he could watch no longer.

Kruz

(First published in Deep Space by Black Hare Press.)

Sirens wailed their death cry throughout the destroyer; in the cantina, the rec room, the dorms, the private cabins, the hangers and along all the corridors. Emergency lighting cast every available surface in a harsh red glow that flashed on and off at regular two second intervals. A thump went through the fabric of the destroyer, causing well-trained personnel to stagger a little, as the 1000 kilo Ion Canon roared its deadly answer at the incoming swarm of fighters.

Crew members ran hither and thither hurrying to their stations. Pilots slid helmets over their heads and buttoned-down gloves to their flight suits. Engineers made last minute preparations to the coffin-shaped ships. The joylessly nicknamed Undertakers were twenty feet long with a compartment moulded to take a regular-sized human. Once attached to oxygen and synced with the onboard computer, the pilot controlled everything at the speed of thought. The ship's computer relayed all information to the human's brain as the pilot made snap decisions. The Undertakers could turn on a pin head, shoot high impact ionised energy bolts from three guns, two of which were directional and the third fixed and always rear facing. Sensors gave the pilot a perfect 360 degree field of vision. Seth knew he was lucky; in the old days pilots had to rely on H.U.D. only. When hooked up, he would be fully integrated with the ship's software.

Seth Kruz took a moment before hopping into his coffin. Nine elongated skulls were etched onto the exterior; one more to make Ace. The average kill rate for a first Luna-month long mission in an

Undertaker was seven. His wing commander had reminded him of this fact only an hour ago but desire to see more skulls decorating his ship forced Seth to take wilder risks. He laid a kiss with his fingers on the hull of his bird and then settled into the moulded compartment. The domed magna-glass hood slid into place and he positioned the self-connecting catheter so it could do what it had to do. With the oxygen mask over his mouth, fine tendrils found their way up his nostrils making contact with the nano-jack at the front of his brain. That weird moment where his body became the Undertaker was never an easy sensation.

'Welcome back, Seth.' The voice was comically old school. Why they couldn't give him some sort of sultry space siren, he didn't know. After all, if you're patterned for life (and that life might be very short lived) with someone so intimately then you might as well fancy their voice.

'I know what you are thinking, Seth.'

'Sorry, Anis. Engage anti-grav, let's get among it.'

'Engaging.'

Seth joined the steady flow of other Undertakers and a few seconds later had rushed into space through the hanger doors and was speeding towards his first target. He was determined to make Ace before he died. The Igor craft didn't stand a chance. Seth fired early causing the star-shaped ship to veer, fortunately for Seth, into the path of his follow-up burst. The craft was ripped apart in a silent explosion that his Undertaker emerged from half a light-second later. He spun the ship around, his rear gun firing wildly, which earned him a warning from command. Two seconds later, Anis was confirming the same command module had registered his tenth solo kill. If he made it out of this conflagration alive, he could wear the much-sought-after silk scarf. If he died, his family would receive it along with his medal. He took pursuit of his next target, which appeared to be leaving the main fray. It dodged his bursts with ease. Anis warned him to stick with the squad. He told Anis this was more important, but he didn't know why. The Igor was heading for the domed command module of the Royal Earth Corp Destroyer, *Churchill*, and Seth let rip with more short bursts of hot Ion. Damn, this Igor was good; spinning and dodging with something close to preternatural skill. Seth's bolts bounced off the command deflectors as the Igor evaded. To starboard an Igor bomber rose, it too on a slow but steady course for the command module.

Faster, Anis. They're going for the CM.

I would not advise—

Just do it.

He felt a gentle increase in g-force and let rip yet another burst. What the fuck was wrong? That Igor should have been dust seconds ago. Clearly, the Igor was going to ram the CM, which would undoubtedly weaken the deflector shields, and then the bomber would drop her payload. With a jolt, Seth realised he was focusing on the wrong ship. He let the Igor slip from his sights and manoeuvred the Undertaker into a revolving spin that arched around the bomber in a complete 360, all three of his guns engaged and dangerously close to overheating. If that happened, he would be out of the fight for a full minute while they cooled. His original target hit the command module defences and he saw the energy grid spark and fizzle as it died. He reversed course so that he settled under the bomber, evading the beams that came his way from the mega-machine with a swinging swaying motion. As the bay doors opened, he managed to squeeze a single shot into the hold. The bomber went up like a new millennium party, throwing him further from the fight and scattering debris in every conceivable direction.

Seth soon returned to stand guard while the repair engineers diverted power back to the CM deflectors. With a sigh of relief, he took off for the eye of the battle as the power grid shimmered and came back online.

Later in the dorm, his wing commander ripped a strip off him for not sticking with the rest of the squadron. Then she hung the coveted white scarf around his neck and shook his hand. Seth blushed but happily accepted the congratulations and gentle ribbing of his squad mates. Then they had a moment's silence for three fallen comrades, before welcoming new recruits.

Alcohol was forbidden for servicemen, but there was always someone who can get hold of illicit homebrew, and he shared a nip of something with more spirit than Christmas with Magda as they sat on his bunk. She had flame-red hair, and a body her flight suit always presented as sheer perfection. Magda was due for leave in three days and had made her Ace a week earlier, which was when they had first kissed. They were the only two in the squadron to have hit the mark so far. Joy filled his heart as he lingered in the moment; he was an Ace pilot, still buzzing from the battle and sharing homebrew liquor with a beautiful woman. Whether Seth got his leave was still in the hands of the gods, but right now he was flying high. It wasn't long before they had drawn the privacy curtain.

*

That is how he pictured it in his mind's eye as he sat daydreaming on the rocky outcrop, makeshift fishing rod in hand. In actual fact, he had come out of the hanger, taken his tenth Igor and, in his jubilation, had dashed off after another, ignoring his wing commander's instructions to keep formation. He had destroyed the bomber, but the close proximity of the blast had sent him and Anis reeling. Something snapped in their connection and she was dead to him from that moment onwards. The tendrils withdrew from his frontal cortex, his catheter disengaged, and he couldn't see as he usually could when connected with her. Through the magna-glass panel, stars swirled in a never-ending, tumbling darkness that made him want to upchuck. The Undertaker was running on emergency power and following a deep basic programme that could not be overwritten or destroyed.

In such an event, the capsule guided the pilot to the nearest habitable landmass. All well and good, providing said landmass was within the thirty minutes of however fast they happened to be travelling, as that was all the emergency oxygen an Undertaker carried.

The crash landing had been about the scariest thing he had ever endured. The heat of entry had remoulded the front section of the Undertaker. Small braking paddles had extended along the length of the ship, slowing it to a speed that wouldn't rip the parachute apart. But not before circling the small planetoid several times, night and day blurred as his crotch damped and his bowels loosened. It was made all the more terrifying as he was facing away from the surface and had no idea if he was about to strike a mountain at Mach 4. The chute eventually deployed, changing his world view to inverse vertical. The sea he splashed into was small, not much more than a lake, and by the time he had bobbed back to the surface, he was relieved to be floating right side up and was able to slide the magna-glass back before unbuckling and then vomiting into the water. He used his helmet as a makeshift paddle to guide the dead Undertaker to the nearest landmass as the sun rose in the distance.

Several hours later, he was trying to drag his dead ship as far up the orange sand of the beach as he could. But tiredness and shock had robbed him of strength, and he was forced to leave his partner partially submerged on the shoreline. Then grabbing the emergency ration packs and med kit, he headed inland.

When the tide came in, Anis was completely submerged, but right now her silver shone. He was beyond tears for his lost partner.

He scratched at the skin beneath his beard. Feeling a tug on the line, he drew it in—nothing. He cast again and said a prayer to the ancients that someone would find him soon.

Still, it was as pleasant a planetoid as one could hope for. The sea was pale blue and reflected the sun's rays in millions of tiny shards of broken light on its surface. He hadn't ventured too far into the forests except to find a water source, which he was lucky enough to find on his third day. The days were warm, and because the nights were short the temperature did not seem to drop into the unbearable zone. The planet the moon orbited looked grey and was probably devoid of life.

A streak of fiery space debris crashed into the sea about a mile away, disturbing the waters and ruining Seth's chances of catching anything for the day. It wasn't the first time a meteorite had crashed down, but it was the first time a rock had floated back to the surface. Therefore, it must have been man-made or, heaven help him, an enemy ship.

The chances of surviving that kind of impact would be rare, but the ship might have useful supplies. It took a day and night for the star-shaped ship to float ashore and Seth covered several miles of coastline to converge with the pod. With his gun drawn, he cautiously approached the five-pointed star of an Igor craft. As with his own Undertaker, a clear panel let him see the creature he had been programmed to hate for as long as he could remember.

Like humans, it had four limbs and walked on two powerful hind legs. Images from school showed the creatures running on all fours like dogs. They had four rough claws and had been known to rip a man's intestines out in one sweep. Ground troops who went into combat wore ultra-dense reinforced armour, but even so, they were powerful creatures.

It must have been dead. Brown blood decorated the inside of the clear panel. Part of its face was cut and bruised and covered with dried blood. A quick look around the exterior revealed some sort of handle contraption. He holstered his gun in order to use both hands to twist the handle anti-clockwise. With a sucking motion, the vacuum broke. He jumped backwards drawing his gun again. As a pilot, Seth's hand-to-hand combat skills were limited. Should the creature somehow still be alive, Seth would probably die.

After several minutes of inactivity, he approached the escape pod again. A stench came from inside. Stench was probably too strong a word, but it was a high pungent aroma. He raised the gun, double-checked the settings, *kill it just to be sure, Seth.* The creature opened one eye. Seth brought his other hand to steady the first. This was different from killing the enemy from afar in the midst of battle. The eye was so human. In the propaganda they always had yellow devil cat's eyes.

'It's just a dirty Igor. Pull the trigger on the bastard,' he said aloud.

'Help.' The guttural gravelly word shook him to his core. He hadn't expected that. The eye blinked and the dark blue mottled skin shimmered, becoming a muddy yellow colour.

'Don't do that.'

The creature croaked several words in its mother tongue before finishing with a human word: 'Please.'

Seth stepped away from the ship, lowering his pistol. He took a sip from his water canister. Should he help it? How do you help a thing like that? Could he trust it? Better to kill it, isn't it?

He stepped back. Its eye focused on him.

'You are my prisoner. Do you understand?'

Part of its mouth rose, and again the skin shifted its colour range, becoming dark orange.

'Yes,' it said.

Seth dribbled water between the Igor's lips. It sighed.

The Igor's harness was still locked in place, so he hit the release button in the centre of the creature's chest and stepped back. When the Igor did not move, he returned.

'Can you move?'

He looked the creature over. Its flight suit appeared to be intact. Bones were probably not broken.

'Come on. Get out.' He indicated with the pistol for the Igor to exit the craft and then stepped away, the gun pointing at the creature's head. The heat of the sun soaked his back wet with sweat.

Slowly, the Igor rose, with one hand held against its long head. Once out of the craft, it sank to its knees. Like Seth, some sort of pistol was holstered at the Igor's waist. Keeping his gun levelled at the alien's head, he circled behind and drew the gun from its place at the creature's side.

'Thank you for not destroying me, hu-man.'

'I still might. Where are you injured?'

'My cranium. My thoughts are unclear. One of my visual orbs is dysfunctional.'

'You're blind?'

'Only in one orb. It will not be much of a hindrance.'

The creature needed to rest often on the journey back to Seth's cave. However, two cycles later, Seth had brought the creature to the creek where fresh running water tinkled over glossy pebbles. It drank and washed its wounds.

'How come you speak our language?'

'We are taught to understand the enemy. It makes us more efficient hunters. But do not worry, I will not harm you, hu-man. You may put your weapon away.'

'I don't think so, Igor.'

The alien's flesh turned bright red, 'We are Igorensee. I am the fifth offspring of the second prince. Show me some respect, hu-man.'

'You're just a filthy Igor.'

'I can still use these to rip your cranium from your torso, hu-man,' it said raising the claws of its right paw, 'and could have at any time. You are tired and suffering from high stress fatigue as well as hormone depletion. We appear to be alone on this planetoid. It would be best to put our differences aside to increase our chances of survival.'

'Shut up.'

'I will not harm you.'

'Shut up.'

The Igor, constrained with wild vines, rested inside the cave while Seth stood guard outside. Despite his attempts to stay alert he could not fight tiredness, and eventually, succumbing to exhaustion, he dropped off to sleep while sitting near the fire.

Seth woke as the sun rose, to see the Igor walking up the slope with a small dead creature hanging from its belt.

Seth, in a state of panic, pushed himself backwards and went for his pistol only to find it missing.

'Give me back my gun, you filthy Igor.'

'My moniker is Dreptusi,' it said withdrawing the pistol from an inside pocket. 'I hope you realise I could have dispatched you easily while you slept. I said I would not hurt you, and I did not.'

Dreptusi threw the pistol at Seth's feet. He snatched it up and pointed it at the Igor with hands that shook. Seth and Dreptusi looked into each other's eyes. The Igor remained calm and unarmed. Seth pulled the trigger.

'I have removed the power pack, hu-man. The pistol is dysfunctional.'

'Give it to me.'

'Not until you realise that I will not hurt you. On the journey from my craft I could have ripped you open. When you slept, I could have killed you with your own weapon. I did not have to return here. But it is always best in survival situations to work with others.'

Seth's head dropped and the pistol clattered to the dusty ground.

'I hate your kind, Igor. I should have killed you.'

'If it is any consolation, I hate hu-mans too. Your skin does not show emotion and the smell that comes off you is enough to put me off my food. But we are here now.'

'What have you got there?' Seth asked, bending to pick the gun up, but he still didn't holster it.

'First-meal if you wish to share it with me.'

'Did you catch it?' Seth asked fearing it might be what the oldies called 'road kill'.

'Of course. We are good hunters.'

Dreptusi drew a knife from his boots and quickly skinned the animal and placed it over the hot embers of the fire on a wooden skewer and spit.

'I didn't know you had a knife.'

'I know,' Dreptusi said. 'Do you want to take it from me?'

Seth shook his head and piled up more wood on the fire. 'We need more heat to cook it.'

When they had ripped the animal apart and shared the meat, leaving nothing but sucked dry bones, Dreptusi asked, 'How long have you been here, hu-man?'

'A little over three weeks. Do you know how long that is?'

'Twenty-one revolutions of your home world. Did your ship not send out a distress beacon?'

'No. Did yours?'

'I am not sure. I was unresponsive. What are your plans?'

'Today, like most days, I'm going to collect wood for the fire and then I'll fish.'

'Here is your power pack, hu-man, you may put your gun away. I will hunt, you can be sure that we will feast well tonight.'

'Bring water back too.'

'Do not presume to tell me what to do, hu-man.' The Igor's flesh flashed bright red as it stalked away.

They each returned to the dying embers of the fire as the sun was setting. They ate the fish and some of the meat Dreptusi had caught, saving the rest of the cooked food for a quick breakfast in the morning.

'I have set traps and will check them in the morrow.'

'Perhaps you could show me how they work.'

'Yes, I will do that, hu-man.'

'You don't have to keep calling me that. My name is Seth. Seth Kruz, pilot first class, Amber 606 squadron assigned to the R.E.C Destroyer, *Churchill*.'

'It is an honour to meet a fellow warrior. I am also a pilot. You may call me Drep. My rank and position do not translate well in your language, but we are of about equal status.'

'Apart from you being the offspring of a prince.'

Drep's skin flickered orange and pale green. For a moment Seth thought he had upset the Igor then it revealed yellowed jagged teeth and nodded its long head. He was laughing or at least amused.

*

Three weeks into the uneasy truce they made an expedition to recover their ships from the water. At low tide, Seth's Undertaker was partially buried and they worked tirelessly to expose enough of it to try to drag it farther up the beach. They smiled at each other as they pulled their feet from the grasping, sucking wet sand. All amusement came to a sudden halt when Seth found he couldn't drag his foot free, so he shifted his weight to the other. In seconds he was up to his knees. The sand had a hold of him and he was sinking fast.

'Drep! Help!'

Immediately seeing the danger of the situation, Drep gave instruction, 'Don't struggle. Lie flat.'

'What?'

'Trust me. I will try to save you, but lie flat and stop struggling. The more you fight the more it has you.'

Seth fought every instinct and forced himself to calm down as he bent forwards at the waist, laying his torso along the grabbing sand.

'The tide must be turning. I will free your legs but do not struggle. If it gets hold of me, we both die.'

Drep went to work clawing the sand away from Seth's right leg, but as soon as he removed a handful of wet sand more replaced it. The minutes dragged by as his powerful claws scooped and threw, scooped and threw.

'Hurry up.'

'I am trying, Seth. I think the limb is coming free.' Drep panted. 'It is a matter of introducing as much air as possible.' Suddenly, the leg had room to manoeuvre and Drep eased it free with that same sucking sound, which wasn't so funny anymore.

'Be still. I still have the other leg to free.'

As the tide lapped against Seth's face, his other leg came free, and Drep instructed Seth to stay as flat as possible to the sand while they used their elbows and knees to push and pull themselves to dryer, more stable, land. When they reached the tree line, they lay on their backs gasping for breath.

'Thank you, Drep. You didn't have to do that.'

'Yes, I did.' He pointed at Seth's lower legs. 'In my haste to free you I have cut your limbs with my claws, I am sorry. Will your med-kit suffice?'

'They're just scratches,' Seth said, after inspecting the cuts. From his prone position, he held a hand out to Drep. 'Thanks, I owe you.'

The next day they found Drep's escape capsule on firmer sand. Using vines, they dragged it to the tree line where they could help themselves to spare parts at their leisure. Over the coming months, it was soon stripped to its bare bones as they used it along with wood and vines to improve the shelter that the cave provided.

*

About six months into their isolation, as they ate their evening meal, Drep pointed at the night sky.

'It looks like another craft is about to crash-land.'

Seth looked up from his wooden platter with the remains of fish on it and watched as the night sky was lit by a long streak of burning space debris.

'Might be a meteor?'

'Might be another hu-man. What will happen to me then?'

'And if it's one of your lot, then I'll be your prisoner.'

Drep stood up saying, 'Let us set out now. If someone is onboard, they may need our help. I will ensure you are treated fairly.'

Seth pulled his boots on and checked the power-pack in his sidearm. Enough juice to defend himself.

The sun had risen before they found the crater the craft had made as it ploughed into the wooded area a mile or so inland from one of the beaches. Seth's fears that it was an Igor ship were confirmed when they came across the body of an Igor that had evidently crawled from the ship. One of its forelimbs was completely severed and it lay in a pool of thick dark blood. As Drep knelt beside the body examining the insignia on the uniform, Seth drew his pistol. He was taking no chances.

'There are more, probably still in the craft.'

'More?'

'Yes. This is a diplomat. He would have had at least a pilot.'

Smoke billowed from the crater a few hundred yards from the dead Igorensee. The craft was larger, designed to carry several beings in relative comfort. Drep indicated that it resembled a Royal transportation vessel. They stepped inside; Seth on guard waiting for ambush; Drep calling out in his guttural mother tongue. A sound came from the front, possibly the pilot's cabin. Seth spun, his gun at the ready. Drep snatched the weapon from his hands in a quick movement that surprised and startled Seth.

'No one will hurt you while you are with me. Make sure you do likewise, or I might forget our truce,' Drep said, his mottled skin a fierce red.

The pilot still strapped into his seat was clearly dead with what appeared to be a small tree trunk buried in his torso. Drep searched the rest of the ship moving slowly towards the rear. It appeared empty. Seth was considering what might be salvageable when Drep called to him. He ran to a second cabin to find Drep kneeling over a figure slumped in a chair, hidden from view. It gurgled in reply to something Drep said. Clearly alive, but by the thinnest of threads.

Drep, his skin turning a dark blue looked at Seth and said, 'The princess is ready.'

'Princess? What is she ready for?'

'The birthing.'

'The what? You mean she's pregnant.'

'Yes. There is little hope for the parent, but the offspring might still live. I will attempt an emergency delivery. Help me get her from the seat.'

As Drep began to unbuckle and lift the female, Seth said, 'But a baby. We can't look after a baby.'

'Would you try to help one of your own?'

'Of course, but —'

'What? Is it different?' Spittle flecked his red chin. His eyes darkened to a yellow. 'Fine hu-man. Go. Leave us. I will take responsibility for my own.'

He turned his back on Seth and heaved the dying princess from the chair and laid her along the aisle. He reached into his boot and drew his knife, then looked up a Seth. 'I do not need you. Leave.'

Seth stepped outside, equal feelings of revulsion, remorse and regret overwhelmed him. Breathing was difficult. He'd developed a certain respect for Drep, but with a child to care for, the Igors would both become baggage. From now on, it would be up to Seth to do everything. It might be better if he made his own way from this point onwards. The planetoid was large enough for them not to interact with each other.

However, Seth recognised that Drep was right; he *would* have tried to save a human baby. And knowing the Igor as he did, he believed Drep would have behaved with more humanity if the situation had been reversed. He wiped his eyes with his thumb and returned to the interior.

The female's stomach was cut wide open.

Drep, his skin as pale as imitation ivory, cradled a tiny bloody version of the mother in his arms.

'She died. I had to act quickly. They both died.'

'Let me try,' Seth said.

Taking the child, he checked its airways, poked his fingers inside the mouth and released some gloopy liquid. Then holding the newborn upside down by the legs said, 'Trust me.' He swung the baby in a gentle arc, forwards, then backwards, forwards and backwards again. Then he sat in one of the chairs, rested the still-unmoving child on his knees and vigorously rubbed its chest for a minute, then swung again and returned to a seated position to massage the chest. He checked the airways. Cleared more gloop. Massaged the chest.

The youngling spluttered.

Drep, a look on his face that showed more than any multi-coloured skin display, quickly took the robe from the dead mother, wrapped it around the youngling, then tucked the bundle inside his own jacket, fastening it tight for the trek back to their cave.

He grasped Seth by the shoulder. No words were necessary.

Hours after the youngling was dragged into the universe, Drep managed to fashion a harness from vines and fabric from the interior of the crashed craft. The child was carried on the Igor's back throughout the day. He did all the tasks he had previously done, but with the youngling secured to his back. Drep would wash the youngling in the sea and feed him with regurgitated food — the one thing Seth could not watch. Drep named the youngling Kemptruti and consented to allowing Seth to call him Kemp.

A few days later, Drep approached Seth as he sat on his favourite outcrop with his lucky fishing rod in hand.

'My Levelling approaches,' he said.

'What is your Levelling?'

'We go through The Levelling several times in a lifetime. It is too soon for me, but with the close proximity of the youngling and no female, my chemistry is altering sooner than expected.'

'Levelling? I still don't understand.'

'The Levelling. We alter sex. Scientists think we took this evolutionary path to ensure the race will always survive. It has produced a very fair society unlike —'

'Never mind all that. You change sex?'

'Yes. I will be in pain for some time. You will need to care for Kemptruti for two, possibly three weeks.'

'Fine.' Seth turned his attention back to the sea. He knew it. They were beginning to be a burden. 'Do you need anything?'

'Only privacy.'

Minutes passed. Drep sat next to Seth, dangling his legs over the rocky edge, the youngling secure in his harness.

'What? I said I'd help.'

'The youngling needs two parents, Seth. In a few months he will begin to form words and recognise our features.

'I need to be this youngling's parent and intend to take the place of his birthing parent. I would be honoured if you would be his second parent.'

Seth, his mouth dropping open, stared into the Igor's eyes.

'You've got to be joking. Me. But what do I know about bringing up one of your lot?'

'Perhaps it is time you learnt?'

Drep stood and began the hike back to the cave.

Seth gave a sigh, realising he had little choice in the matter, then called back to Drep, 'Where I come from, he would call me "Dad".'

Drep bared his teeth as his skin blossomed into shades of violet. Seth hoped that was a good a sign.

*

As the years passed, the cave entrance expanded, transforming into a wooden-roofed structure allowing the three of them to rest in relative safety and comfort. Their diet of meat and fish was supplemented with fruit and some roots. A small patch of soil was dedicated to the attempt at growing flavoured roots. They kept a large bird, which Kemp called Brydi, that laid an egg every other day cycle.

When Kemp was only five years old, Drep returned from an expedition to the far side of their island. He—for he'd gone through another painful Levelling, becoming once again male— had been gone for a week, confident that Kemp would be safe with Seth. His skin was fixed in a pale grey shade and his eye was unable to focus. Sweat ran in rivulets down his face, and a smell came off him reminding Seth of a dead dog he had come across when he was a child.

Drep recounted the story in between states of semi-consciousness. He had been bitten by an insect-like creature with a red dot in the centre of its cranium. He had to tell them, warn them of the foot-long creature that lived in the marshes on the far side of the island. With his last words, he told Kemp that it was important to do as Seth said and to remember the lessons he had been taught about his home world. Seth nodded, letting the warrior-prince know he would not let the boy down. Kemp clung to his parent's body as Dreptusi of Susinatra exhaled his last breath.

Together, the youngling and the human removed Drep's clothes and washed his body, before casting it adrift on a raft which they set alight. As the sun set, Drep's body was consumed first by flame and then by water.

When Kemp was about ten years old, he went through The Levelling and for three weeks, groaned and screamed in agony as the sexual parts and internal workings transformed into their female counterparts. Physically she had changed little — same face, same body shape — but her masculinity was missing. Seth, although having witnessed the transformation with Drep, felt a deep sense of helplessness during the change. The child was in extreme agony and called out night and day, clutching at his stomach while curled in a ball. All he could do was hold the youngling close when her screams woke the night birds, and wash the sweat from her face with sea sponges they had collected together.

'You're almost as big as Drep, you should start wearing his clothing. We kept them back for a reason,' Seth said, once the pain of The Levelling had finally eased.

'Yes, Dad.'

It was strange seeing Kemp in clothes. For years she had lived in skirts made from leaves and bark. But now she looked like a warrior.

'Drep would be very proud.'

'Thank you, Dad. Why do you cry?'

'I was just thinking, that's all.'

It wasn't long after this when the ships arrived. Star-shaped ships. After more than ten years, there wasn't much left of his uniform, but Seth pulled his boots on and the scarf Drep had made from bleached palm leaves. He removed his pistol — why he still carried it he wasn't quite sure; the power pack had died years before. Then he strode out to meet the landing party as they disembarked from their carrier, with his hands held high to show he was unarmed. Kemp followed a little way behind doing her best to be brave.

He must remind the enemy that he was a serving member of the Royal Earth Corp.

Thirty killing machines armed to the teeth with sidearms, blades and assault rifles lined up in front of him. From the carrier trundled a star-shaped all-terrain tank, its cannon positioned on him.

Perhaps he should have hidden, continued the war as a lone attacker, taking them by surprise, eliminating them one at a time. Deep down, he knew that was a pointless task. He and Kemp were barely managing to survive as it was. And what would he do with her? She was one of theirs, he couldn't let her know he intended to kill her people—not her Dad. If he let her go to them, they would know that he could be hiding, biding his time. They would find him in a matter of days. And besides, he was tired. He needed to rest; he needed an end to this struggling life, even if it was as a prisoner of war.

The commander stepped forward; his troops levelled their guns at Seth. Seth's knees itched on the inside. The fight had gone out of him. Nonetheless, he came to attention, raising his right arm in the age-old salute. 'Seth Kruz, pilot first class, Amber 606 squadron assigned to the Royal Earth Corp Destroyer, *Churchill.*'

'Release your hostage,' the commander ordered.

'She is not my prisoner. Her name is Kemptruti, offspring of Dreptusi. A princess of the royal household, Susinatra.' It was a white lie, but he had never found the right time to tell Kemp the complete truth about her biological parentage.

The commander spoke its long-worded natural tongue towards Kemp. She reached for Seth's hand, sending confidence through every cell in his body, but more importantly filling his heart with love. In return, he squeezed her paw, sending reassuring warmth, and she stood taller. Seth loved her as any father would love his own.

'Kemptruti does not know much of her native language. Her parent died when she was very young.'

'Are you responsible for the death of a prince of the royal household?'

'No, his death was a tragic accident.'

'On your knees, you will die for the atrocities and assassination of Prince Dreptusi.'

Seth remained standing. 'Drep's death was an accident. He was my friend, my ally.'

The commander stepped forwards, his skin so red as to be nearly purple, and raised his gun.

'So be it. Death is all any hu-man deserves.'

'No. You cannot do that.' Kemp stepped in front of Seth.

'Stand away, Kemptruti of Susinatra. All hu-man vermin must die.'

'No. He deserves gratitude and the respect of a warrior. Am I of the royal line? Does the name of my parent grant me privileges?'

'If you are royalty, yes. But only if you are.' The colour of his skin returned to a pale orange.

'Then please take my father onboard and treat him with respect. He tells me the war has lasted for more than fifty years. Our friendship may well be the beginning of the end of the war.'

The commander's skin quickly flashed red, he took a step closer and backhanded the youngling across the face. She fell to her knees and Seth pulled her close to him. The commander's voice dropped an octave as his face darkened to midnight.

'Father? A member of the royal household would never degrade themselves in such a way. There will never be any peace. Not until their kind has been eliminated from the galaxy. And those who say we should forgive them, or trust them, are no better than the filthy hu-mans who infect everything they touch.'

The Igor commander placed his gun against her head, 'No. Not her!' Seth cried out, as the single projectile made its deadly course first through her head and then his chest.

He cradled her lifeless form, trying to hold her to this realm, while his own lifeblood ebbed away in spurts and judders. For the first time in years his body convulsed, not with the cold but with sorrow and fear.

He is in school, the children repeating the teacher's words, 'Igors are vermin.'

He is at the academy looking at an Undertaker for the first time.

He is kissing Magda.
He is shaking Drep's paw.
He is teaching Kemp to swim, to hunt, to cook.
He dies.

The Last Life

(First Appeared in Angels by Black Hare Press.)

The Guardian of The Dead sent Clay, his trusted deputy, into the world.

Clay's task was to ensure the delivery of the last life.

In a world fraught with disease and darkness, he found her by a glistening stream.

With an innocent smile, she offered him plump fruit from the last surviving tree.

He accepted the offering, before carrying out his master's wish, for he was an obedient servant.

Then, weeping for lost beauty, he destroyed his scythe, before sprinkling one of his crushed ribs over her remains.

Clay waited for forty days and forty nights.

The magic didn't work.

I, Dragon

(First appeared in Dragon Bone Soup.)

You are the first person I have seen in several human generations. I suppose, like the others, you seek knowledge and wisdom from the ancient days. Very well, let us start at the beginning.

*

In my mind, I see the mare clearing a space, before laying her eggs and then covering them over with earth and leaving them to their fate. Obviously, I don't remember much but I know I must have been one of the first to hatch. A combination of hunger, panic and natural aggression force the first hatchlings to kill the late arrivals. In a clutch of half a dozen eggs, no more than two hatchlings will live. The scholar in me resents the brutality of this emergence into the world, while simultaneously realising there is nothing to be done about it — it is nature's way and besides, it was a long time ago.

I myself must have fathered hatchlings that fought and scratched and gouged and ate their siblings just to survive those first few hours.

A young dragon grows quickly and within a few months is half the size of its fully-grown self. It gets through a lot of meat, and usually isn't too picky about the quality. Moving from small things that crawl in the earth to rats, then foxes and goats, the fast metabolism of a growing dragon soon requires a cow or a horse a day. When traversing the globe, long distance journeys over the sea can be tedious, a quick dip and dive with dolphins is a very pleasant way to cool off. Seafood was never really to my taste, but I used to know one who lived on nothing but.

Our immense size can warn the lower beasts of our approach, which is why the gods gave us flame; to kill, and coincidentally, cook our food from afar. Humans and elves also made tasty morsels.

We are solitary by nature but occasional interaction with other dragons is necessary. I met a mean mare with green and gold scales. She called herself Goldjade and said our offspring would be glorious. When I first saw her on the horizon, rising like Phoenix, I thought the sun had given birth to a son. We danced in the sky and dove to the ocean depths. Eventually, after much drawing of blood, we lay exhausted and spent. Then she turned on me with her flame, which was something I wasn't expecting. From that moment on, we were drawn to each other every thirty or forty years when her season arrived. I would hear her call from across the continent and be powerless to resist. However, I had learned not to hang around and took flight when we were both satisfied. In all the times we copulated she never asked my name. But we were bound to each other like magnets and I never mated with any mare other than Goldjade, even after she died during the last battle of the Dark Wars.

The Dark Wars spanned more than a hundred years. At first, the dragons were not concerned with these trifles of mortals. The elves were leading a stand against an evil warlord, who had gathered a vast army, which included the dead raised by dark magicians. His aim was to rid the land of goodness in order for the Dark Goddess to walk the land once again. Thousands of years earlier, she had raised her own army in an unsuccessful attempt to destroy The Overgod. Consequently, she was banished to her own dark but limited realm.

I said earlier we aren't sociable. When dragons meet, blood is nearly always spilled. Even our lovemaking is violent. So, when an old scarred dragon called to me while I slept, my hackles rose at his impertinence. He sat calmly before me at the base of my mountain and said, 'Let us not battle, young one.'

'Who are you? Why are you here if not to challenge me?'

'I am Greystaff. I would like to talk. The mortals put great store by it.'

'Mortals? Are you feeble-minded?'

'There is a reason why I am so old. Do not try my patience, young one.'

I leapt at him, inhaling and triggering my ignition muscle. But he was fast and laced my underside with his own acid breath, which is rare amongst our kind. The humans have a phrase that is fitting, 'Take the wind from your sails'. I landed in a thunderous heap while he glided away unscathed.

Greystaff returned a little while later and with powerful magic (another rarity among dragons) healed my badly burned lower legs, although to this day the scales are dull.

I was wary of this ancient and powerful one, but we talked. He was concerned about the evil of the mortal warlord. A balance that had always existed was swaying and depleting the land of love and peace. These were words I did not fully comprehend. Greystaff explained that in all things there is balance; night and day, males and females, good and evil.

The evil elements of the mortals were overwhelming those of goodness. There was a very real chance they would destroy the world, leaving us, the higher beings, with no sources of food. All living things needed the lower beings to survive. If the Dark Queen walked the land, it would soon become a barren landscape.

We spent several days in each other's company. It is the most time I had ever spent with another dragon. He told stories of the ancient times.

Greystaff planned to make an alliance with some of the mortals who were fighting for peace and had already sought three other dragons who had agreed to join the cause. We were all to meet on the northern continent in a very short time. But it would only succeed if we could agree not to fight each other. The destruction it might cause the mortals would be more detrimental than beneficial. It is difficult for creatures who are normally territorial to find themselves in close proximity to others of their kind. For the safety of the mortals, we spent most of our time alone and away from each other.

The first battle didn't last long. Thousands of humans, elves and dwarves, on foot, camel and unicorn with machines for throwing flaming balls of wood, lined up against more humans, dark elves, orcs, and the living dead. I took to my wings and my four brothers followed, we dispersed the ranks of the enemy with flame and acid before even one arrow had been launched.

Greystaff was our organiser, co-ordinating our movements, ensuring we were always on hand to support the mortal cause. The battles were short; the enemy taken by surprise was left reeling, rapidly losing ground. Soon, more of my kind made their presence known by joining the ranks of righteousness.

And then, as Greystaff had predicted, the enemy struck with their own dragons. These dragons were ridden, if you can believe such a thing, by dark-elf mages and human lancers. Hexes and curses sparkled all around, while the lancers dived at us, fast and furious, from all directions. Now we had to soar and swoop beyond the reach of the devils. Those dragons ridden by dark-elves were not eager to engage in mid-air battle, keen only to protect their riders who could attack from beyond the reach of our flames.

Fortune was on my side that day. I claimed two dark-elves and crippled a big black feathered dragon who crashed into a deep chasm, her wings on fire.

In total we lost six dragons, but none so important or as noble as Greystaff, who went the way of all living things that day. It appears that I had learned the meaning of love for I was immensely upset and thought the ache in my heart would break it.

I prayed for the misery of his passing to end. I threw myself into the battles with more wrath and anger than I ever had before. I earned the moniker 'Redfury'. In truth I wanted my life to end and was determined to take as many of the enemy with me as was possible. Fury and hate were all I lived for.

The skies blackened with our numbers as more of my kind joined the war. Dragons on both sides took to the sky with riders, although I and a handful of others refused the humiliation of that. Falling dragons would destroy whole platoons of ground troops, indiscriminate of side or allegiance.

The culmination of these wars ended when I went claw to claw with my mate. Yes, Goldjade had joined the ranks of the enemy. I hadn't seen her in nearly fifty years, but I still recognised her scent while in the middle of a tussle with a small brown dragon. Knowing she was close by, I buried my mouth against the back of his neck and engaged my ignition muscle. He fell like a stone and made the waters of the lake he fell into boil as he died. Despite the brimstone and fire going on in the sky and on the ground, the only scent that mattered was hers. We crashed into each other and I felt the heat of my loins rise, as her rider fell. She clawed at my back and tempted me with lustful words. I wanted her, but she wanted my death more. She was about to ignite when I broke free and swooped away from her. My own fire glanced harmlessly off her scales as she dived for me again in a rage. We were in an embrace falling fast to the ground. We broke apart, my feet grazing treetops and pulling pines free as I caught an updraft just in time. So intent was she on destroying me that she didn't notice the lancer. He was aiming for me but skewered her with the fifteen-foot long pole as she turned me this way and that. It burst out of her chest ripping her away from me. The lancer, clearly nonplussed at having destroyed one of his own, shook her dying body free. I watched as she fell, end over end, for nearly a minute before crashing into the enemy base camp. She landed on the tent from whence the Dark Warlord oversaw the battle. He died in the explosion along with his offspring, his generals and his aides. His dark mages and necromancers were also wiped out by Goldjade's fireball. In turn the mages who were boosting the power of the dark riders channelled the flames and the riders turned into instant bombs, killing or maiming their steeds.

That was the end of the Dark Wars. Much jubilant rejoicing occurred, and the long road to rebuilding could start, but I went away to recover and lick my wounds. The two people I knew better than any others had died within a few years of each other. Many of our kind died in those wars. I had no idea of our numbers before the war, but they were dramatically depleted in the name of peace.

I had seen too much death in that short period of my life and in truth liked it far too much. I was good at killing. However, I had grown to respect the short-lived mortals, their tenacity and their ingenuity. I have not fed on them in a thousand years or more. Wild animals are my mainstay these days. Not farmed; it takes the mortals great effort and it is unfair of us to deprive them of their food.

I see very few dragons these days and fear I may be the last. Our natural aggression, a tendency to monogamy and the great culling of the Dark Wars have made it difficult for our numbers to recover. The last time I saw a dragon was on the distant horizon more than a hundred years ago, and we discretely avoided each other. As the years progressed, the dwarves retreated deeper beneath the ground. And the elves, they destroyed each other many hundreds of years ago in their own blood-feud wars.

Not long ago, a prince of a distant land hunted me down, thinking to beard me in my lair and skewer me with a rusty diamond-encrusted sword. I pinned him to the ground with one of my fore-claws. When quizzed, he said he needed my scales to prove his love and devotion to a princess. I asked if he was prepared to kill a hero of the Dark Wars for love and he said those wars were just myths. So, I told him about Greystaff and Goldjade and the evil warlord, and of night battles that lit the heavens and spies who choked on their own poison, and of deceit and revenge, and also of love and loss. When I had said everything there was to say, I gave him a freshly shed scale. He returned soon after, older and greyer, with two young males in tow. He had wed the princess and now brought his sons to hear the lessons of the past. I never saw myself as a teacher, but as I had no other dragon to tell the stories to, I gave my memories freely to the humans who sought me out, as Greystaff had with me when we had first become friends. I would look forward to their company and dreaded the lonely years in between.

And now I am older than Greystaff. Human-made dragons streak through the sky and invisible magic in the air interferes with my wings making them ache whenever I take to the air. I am forced to cling to this mountain and survive on goat and eagles.

I am happy you have made the arduous journey to find me, human. I fear my last day approaches. Will you keep me company until my end comes?

His Love

(First published in Love by Black Hare Press.)

God was not pleased.

He could read the hearts of men, but angels were a mystery.

Why did this angel persist in whining?

'De-wing him and send him down,' He ordered the Seraphim.

*

Falling like a fiery stone, the angel crashed into the Earth with enough force to leave a crater.

Someone held a pitcher to his lips.

'Come, there is a place where all The Lord's exiles can live in peace, without fear of reprisal for refusing His selfish demands.'

'But, He loves all His creations.'

'This isn't love,' Lucifer said, rubbing healing balm onto the burnt flesh.

April Violets

(First published in Rapture by Clarendon House. More recently, April Violets featured in the webzine, Setu and had the honour of being the first story read by Dave Gregory for Sweetycat Press on their YouTube channel.)

It would be the last time he would ever see her.

The first time he'd set eyes on her, he had been on his way back to his garrison. She was getting off the bus as he was about to get on. She didn't notice one speck of him. He saw every detail of her. From the two-inch heel to the hat pinned with a pheasant feather, and her freshly curled hair. A pencil line drawn up the back of each leg, disappearing up a skirt cut just below the knee. Her snakeskin handbag crooked over the left arm.

He caught the sweet scent of April Violets as she brushed past. Her dark eyes set to a distance far away. Not the roar of a red London bus or the choking of diesel fumes, nor the hustle and bustle of street life in a country at war got in the way of April Violets.

Time stopped. He stopped. She continued on her way, and so did the bus.

He was transfixed as she melted around the corner. He couldn't help but follow. With determination and an air of authority she entered a pub, but time was pressing, and he had to be back on base.

He turned around, waited for the next double decker and dreamed of seeing her, meeting her, talking to her, and knowing her.

She was so very beautiful...

He often wondered what might have happened. How things would have turned out if he had followed her inside the pub instead of letting her go.

However, a corporal and a sergeant of barbaric brutality, trained to dehumanise were waiting for him. No one wanted their fury and hell to come down upon them. Not even the busty elegant goddess that glided past him would detain him any longer than was necessary.

A week later, he saw April Violets for the last time. He ventured into the dark recesses of The Lamb and Staff. She was serving drinks, and with skilful agility darted past the grubby reaches of the clientele.

Her lips were a full pout of red, her golden hair bounced about her shoulders. She showed enough cleavage to intrigue. He heard the banter, the laughs and the refusals. She was in every word and action, a bar-room vision to be seen and admired from afar. Talk— yes. Touch — no, or receive a slap.

He finished his pale ale and then went away to war.

*

Now, four years later he takes the dog around the corner or perhaps the dog takes him. He's been a London lad all his life and knows this particular corner from his toddler days.

Then that scent again, April Violets.

In his own darkest hours on the front line, or later in hospital, it was her face that floated before him. She was the one he was protecting from the Krauts, because he loved her. He'd only spoken to her once to order a drink. He didn't even know her name. She was and always would be April Violets.

'Excuse me, are you wearing April Violets?'

'Who wants to know?' she says with a hard, sharp edge to her voice.

'Oh, no one, miss. I'm sorry.' He begins to turn away, embarrassment and shame taking their usual places front and forward of every other emotion.

'I remember you,' she says more softly. 'Pale ale, weren't it?'

And then as if only noticing for the first time, 'What happened to your eyes?'

'An explosion. My seeing days are over.'

'Oh my poor boy. Come home and meet me mum,' she said, taking him gently by the arm.

That was when he truly saw her for the first time.

Spring-Heeled Jack

(First published in Monsters by Black Hare Press.)

Mother warned me. I didn't listen.

She said, 'Be a good girl or Spring-Heeled Jack will have ya. Ain't no one lives after seeing his ugly fizzog, and his flashing tail. They say he runs you through with a red hot poker wot he stole from under the devil's nose.'

'If no one lives, how come they know so much about him?'

'Never you mind. Just don't trying earning a shilling in no back alley. Hear me?'

'Yes, Mum.'

I saw him springing over iron railings and scaling the sides of buildings, as he left me dying in the filth.

An Englishman in New York

(Appeared in the first issue The Inner Circle Writers' Magazine.)

Fatty Buckingham's education had been some of the finest 1930's aristocratic money could buy, and yet new ideas did not often bombard his grey matter. Under normal circumstances, he was more than happy to trot along the path of life letting those in the know do all the important things like cooking, organising his laundry, and thinking.

But the new idea wouldn't let go. He loved her.

The signs were all there; sweaty palms, an extra splash of Trumper, anxiety at the prospect of being in her presence, the loosening of his collar as she approached, forgetfulness once she arrived.

Yes, he definitely loved her. The idea soothed his brow like a cool muslin cloth.

Mustering his reserves, and determined to say something to her today, he entered the eatery for the third day in a row.

Sitting in the same booth he had taken on previous occasions, he watched as she approached, pulling quill and parchment from the frilly white pinafore smeared with grease and grey pencil marks. A strand of loose hair was casually pushed behind her ear. He was sure she had the brightest teeth behind those red lips. These were things he had never noticed in a waitress before. Waitresses just were.

How old was she? Late twenties, perhaps thirty. Well, it wasn't unheard of, was it? An older woman marrying a younger man. Would she even consider marrying him? A twenty-two-year-old Englishman visiting the Americas for the first time.

Marriage, another new idea. Gosh! Two ideas before breakfast. He was on a roll today. Wait till the boys back home heard about this.

'Wha' can I get'chya?' Such a delightful accent. The sort that threatens to take the listener into its confidence before laying them flat with dropped consonants.

'Well, I'm not sure. I was sort of struck dumb by the way you chew the end of your pencil and blow pink bubbles at the same time.' There, he'd said something.

'Are you tryin' to be funny, fella?'

'Oh no, I leave that to the comedians.'

'Are you for real?'

'Yes, I think so. Although if you're after an existential discussion I'm afraid you've asked the wrong chap.'

'Listen, dook. I just wanna know wha'chya wanna eat or drink.'

'Oh, I see. I'm not at all sure at present. May I have a menu?'

The waitress pointed her pencil at a menu board over the serving counter. The bubble she blew popped and drew his attention back to her. Fatty's face reddened from the knees up, and feeling hot — not to mention bothered — he said, 'Actually, miss, I feel like I've just walked the Gobi Desert or some such pill of a place. Would it be possible to order a soda?'

'Sure,' she said, before waddling back to the counter. A minute or so later, she returned with a glass of frothing brown liquid, placing it on the table with enough carelessness for spillage to occur.

The smile she gave him was over before it had begun.

Another idea struck like a minor earth tremor. *What would his wife say?*

Playing With Fire

(First published in Beyond by Black Hare Press.)

'Are you late for a wedding?'

'No, officer.'

'Perhaps there's a fire?'

'There is no fire, officer.'

'Then would you mind explaining why you're in such a hurry, miss?'

'Sorry. Do you want there to be a fire?'

'No, of course not.'

'I can make it happen.'

'What?'

'In your car, perhaps.'

'Look miss, tell me why you were doing fifty in a thirty, so I can issue you with a ticket. Do you have a license for this vehicle?'

'I think you had better look at your car, officer.'

'But ... It's burning. Wait there. No wait, don't go.'

Gods and Owls

(First published in Fireburst by Clarendon House.)

Now is the time to look back at what we once were.

Like gods above our creation, we focus on a blue and white globe twenty-five thousand light-years from the centre of a long-dead galaxy. The part of the globe that interests us has entered its night cycle, the continents lit with billions of electric lights — a shining beacon to passing travellers.

We look closer still, at a small island on the edge of a large expanse of water. The lights stretch out from population centres in long spidery veins. These veins light the transportation routes that bring food and fuel from distant farms and keep the citizens alive, the city dwellers secure in the knowledge they are the ones keeping the country alive with their finance and politics. They are mistaken, for without the farms in the countryside or small communities bordering the sea, the cities cease to operate.

Closer still we zoom, and follow a trail of guiding lights to the south. The roads diverging and thinning as the need to accommodate traffic lessens. Notice the explosions of varying colours as they illuminate the night sky; a misremembered tribute to the pagan gods of many years before.

And now we follow one small vehicle making its lonely way to the coast. Swooping like an owl, we glide alongside the car, easily keeping pace. Peering through the rain-splattered glass, we see the floppy hair and pale skin of the type of creature we used to be. The red-rimmed eyes thick with salty water.

It is his story we must relive tonight.

Looking through his eyes, the lights of the vehicle cast long shadows as it winds along minor roads. The trees line the roads in autumnal misery. Fallen leaves gather and mulch at the roadside.

His thoughts are a swirling mess: debt, shame, loss. We endure the turbulence of the conscious mind, the despair of his soul. Alcohol dilutes his blood. Darkness swamps his being.

The car slips on wet leaves. He counters the slide with a quick tug on the steering wheel, and the car is under his control once again.

He concentrates on the task of arriving at his destination.

The car draws to a stop at a cliff top. As he gets out and steps over a barrier, the rain clouds, now depleted of water, begin to dissipate and reveal a nearly full moon.

The ground is still damp, with caution he approaches the drop. Three hundred feet; how long would it take to hit the rocks at the bottom? Would he bounce off the steep incline? Would he feel his bones breaking or his head cracking? Would it hurt?

He takes several long steps back and prepares himself. Seconds take hours to pass. He springs forward, launching silently from the edge. He hears pebbles tumble and for a second, he hangs in mid-air like a cartoon coyote from his childhood, five, perhaps six feet beyond the edge. Then gravity replaces momentum and he is falling. The wind rushing, whips his jacket above his head. His breath held as he waits for the end.

Should the end take this long? We open his eyes. We are looking up at the underside of a hovering, rotating disc suspended in a beam of light only a few feet above the crashing waves. Sea spray is soaking our clothes.

The disc is drawing us closer.

This is how the first human, Adam, came to be saved by passing travellers.

A new species will soon emerge, but that is a lesson for another journey.

Adeste Fideles

(First published in Eerie Christmas by Black Hare Press.)

Everyone knows Christmas is a time for dark fantasy.

People think Scrooge is the ultimate Christmas villain, but that story is gothic sentimentality at best.

European Christmas myths — now they are scary; beautiful ladies who eat the innards of children, cats that eat everyone in old clothes, witches that leave coal for naughty boys and girls (perhaps that is not so bad).

But what could be scarier than being a pregnant thirteen-year-old? Throw into the mix homelessness, a carpenter to deliver the child, and a visitation by a creature not of this earth to impregnate you — now that is dark.

A Christmas Carole

Right then, how should I start?

It was the night before Christmas and all through the house…

No, that's not how it was at all. It was noisy, too noisy and very far from quiet, what with every house in the neighbourhood setting off fireworks. And the telly was on too, with Ant and Dec doing their Secret Santa, tears and gifts at Christmas shmultz.

The neighbours were having a party and I was sure they would cause a power failure with their god-awful lights all over their house blinking and flashing in time to 'Rockin' around The Christmas Tree'. Cars had been pulling up with hooting horns all evening to disgorge or collect passengers in various states of inebriation.

For that year's festivities I was at my son's. He was on the phone having a row with his ex-wife about the holiday arrangements for their five-year-old son, my grandson, Ben. She had changed her mind and wanted Ben to be with her and her parents. Honestly, families? At that point, I wished I'd stayed at home.

My son's girlfriend sat in the corner, with a face like thunder and I knew as soon as the first row had ended another would start with her.

I poured myself a whiskey and soda, which earned me a warning look from my son who thought I drank too much anyway.

The doorbell rang, 'Ding Dong Merrily on High' in electronic monotone. The girlfriend, Pamela, answered as I held Ben by the hand and the singers began their carol. She closed the door on them before they were halfway through the first verse of 'Joy To The World'.

'What did you do that for?' I asked.

'I don't have time for carollers,' she said.

'But, it's for charity.'

'Not my problem. I've got Christmas dinner to get ready and John clearly prefers chatting with his ex,' she said, returning to her sulk and her phone. My grandson sat on the floor and picked up his tablet to continue watching cartoons.

I still don't understand the younger generations. Didn't they know anything? I may be an old grump, but anyone stupid enough to be out on a night like that, for a good cause, deserved a little appreciation.

I went to the door and saw the group of singers outside another house along the street. Snow was falling, and I only had house slippers on my feet, so I wanted to be quick.

I interrupted the end of 'While Shepherds Watched Their Flocks' to put five pounds in the collection bucket. Time slowed as I looked in to the face of the woman holding the collection bucket. I recognised the deep, dark eyes and there was a smell of orange and jasmine that brought back the memory of youth and laughter.

'The girl at number 42 should have given you something, I'm sorry,' was what I meant to say, but instead I said, 'Didn't you used to be Carole Hartnoll from Saint Mary's High School?' and she said, 'Yes, yes I did. And I think you're Paul Browne. After all these years. Why don't you stay for a bit, sing a carol or two?' I said I wasn't really dressed for the event but invited her over for a drink after they had finished.

The whole choir arrived an hour later.

We ran out of booze and John had to go to the supermarket for more. Not a task I envied.

The choir conductor, a cook from the local primary school, helped Pamela with food preparations. A lot of fuss was made of my grandson. Songs were sung, and friends were made. Memories were awoken, and arguments forgotten.

It was a brilliant Christmas. The love that blossomed in my heart for Carole was the best present anyone could hope for.

We had five wonderful years together, and for that I'm eternally grateful.

Christmas Dinner

(Published in Dark Xmas by The Macabre Ladies.)

The family descend for Christmas Dinner.

My brother, his partner and their two children.

Aunt Jules, Uncle James, their sulky daughter and her goth boyfriend.

Mum and Dad.

My mother-in-law still thinks I'm no good, even though it was her son who had the affair.

My sister, Joan, and because her daughter, Evo, is also here, so is her ex-husband with his new wife. Not a good mix.

Evo thinks I'm 'Boring Auntie Sharon' but she should've seen me raving like a loon in '93.

No one considers the pressure I'm under.

I smile. Inside I scream.

This is Hell.

The Hunt

(From an unfinished short story collection featuring Morty and George.)

The shot would happen soon. She could feel the moment approaching. It had taken months of sleeping under glorious constellations on uncomfortable terrain to get here, crouching in the tall dry grass that made a noise like rustling razor blades. Her linen suit had become brittle from weeks of sweat drying into the fibres. Her guide refused to let her wash it. The dirtier and more natural their scent, the less they would alarm the creatures they tracked. She travelled with one man. A tall black man, who wore colourful robes and carried a spear.

For the past week they had camped on a barren spot with little protection from the elements or creatures of the Serengeti, a mile from flowing water. When she had first questioned the logic, he had swept his arm in a wide circle, 'We can see beasts approaching, they have nowhere to hide. If you wish to move closer to water, we can. But every beast great and small will be found there. We will get little peace and have to be vigilant all the day and all the night. Water draws beasts and death.'

She carried all her own equipment, a tent and basic cooking utensils. Her guide was not a bearer, and she wouldn't insult him by asking. The warrior guide slept in the open; she wasn't brave enough for that. They would go days without real food, but the warrior always found something. Occasionally grubs, more often reptiles.

She hadn't moved for over an hour. The cheetah had been stalking its prey for half that time. Georgette had been observing the habits of this female, and knew she had to be where she hoped the cheetah would hunt even before the cheetah knew. Some days were wasted right from the start. Others, like today, were magnificent. The light was spectacular, with the sun behind her casting just the right amount of shadow.

Some small bird far off in the distance, warbled. An eddy of air collected dry leaf litter to create a mini tornado almost ruining the moment.

She readied herself, mimicking the cheetah as it readied to pounce, forcing her shoulders to relax, and ignoring the fly that settled on her forehead. She could taste the tension. This was life at the edge of its limit. The knowledge that the young springbok may be about to meet its end did not weaken her resolve. The lives of Georgette and her guide, the springbok and the cheetah had all converged for this moment of action.

She couldn't take the shot until the cheetah made her move. Too soon and the cheetah may well alter its target and then either her or her guide would be cat fodder. Too slow and it would blur.

Click!

The red lips under the Leica turned upwards in a grim smile. When the time came to develop the roll, this would be the one. Just a hint of movement from the cheetah, partially camouflaged by tall grass, as it pounced towards its prey—in the foreground, the chase yet to begin. She would attempt to take more photos, but even with a speed of 1/500 of a second, the chances of a decent photograph would be unlikely. She signalled her guide, and together they withdrew from the shrub and made their way back to camp.

She smiled at him.

'Did you accomplish your task, Mma?'

'I think I did, my friend, I think I did. Let's get back to civilisation, shall we?'

The guide said nothing but began to stride ahead. His long legs powering their way through the low-lying brush, as somewhere behind her the cheetah began to devour the springbok.

The notes she had been keeping over her time on safari would be typed up and arranged into an article for The National Geographic. This hunt would not have been worth it without colour film, thank god for German technology. She would be sure to praise Agfa when the time came.

Her close-up of the same cheetah — her friend called it 'ngwe', meaning pure sovereign — focusing on the intensity of the eyes, the scars around the face, the partially missing ear and the drying blood around her mouth, should earn Georgette an award, let alone the honour of the cover.

The End of The Line

(Published in Beyond by Black Hare Press.)

I have been travelling for a long time.

Before I manned the train, I was in charge of a wagon and before that, a hand-pulled cart. At some point in the far distant past, it had been just me.

This locomotive, with elegant trimmings, has served the souls well. I've enjoyed being the engineer. She and I have collected the souls of man and beast, bringing them to the afterlife they deserve, with a touch of grandeur.

Now, there's no one left to collect.

This is my final journey, and then it will be time for Death to retire.

Immortal Soul

(Published in Tempest by Clarendon House.)

When you are as old as I am, there is very little left to achieve.

In the village where I was born lived an ancient man. He was a hermit, a teacher, a soothsayer and wise-man. People avoided him and spread tales of worship to evil gods.

One day while looking for berries, he found me near the entrance to his cave. Grabbing me roughly by the hair, and breathing fetid stink on me, he threatened to curse me and my descendants if I continued snooping near his lair. His bones creaked as he pulled my face close to his. He started sniffing around my hair and neck like a dog. I tried to break away, but he held me firm, in arms strong like bindweed. To my horror, he sliced into the palm of my hand with a long, dirty thumbnail. He sniffed at the fresh blood as it welled along the ragged cut. It is not hard to imagine my revulsion as he licked my hand clean. His eyes closed as he breathed in, long and deep, savouring the flavour.

Finally, with a voice cracked and dry, he told me I had a thread of old magic in my young blood, and that greatness would be mine if I agreed to be his student. My fascination overpowered my revulsion, and I stopped my writhing to listen to all the things it might be possible for me to achieve with his tuition. It is true, I found everything he had to say difficult to believe. Could a person change into an animal, or fly like a bird? Could I, a peasant child, live a life of riches or — as he had chosen to do — live close to nature and be one with Mother Earth?

He pointed at my damaged hand, muttering the spell which was to be the first I would ever learn, and the palm healed leaving no scar. My eyes widened and he smiled.

My mother was more than willing to give me a new home. Mother had another child on the way and had lost most of her teeth due to the number of children she had already birthed. She would have one less mouth to feed.

I was nine years old.

So, the hermit took me as his special pupil. He taught me to read and all about numbers. He passed on to me the secret words and spells of the ancients. In return I had to look after him, mostly cooking his meals and foraging for ingredients.

I would occasionally complain about the tasks. A young man with my growing powers should have been out in the world making a fortune. But he reminded me of our bargain. He predicted I would have a long life ahead of me; there would be plenty of time for gathering a fortune. Of course he was right, without those early years of discipline and shared knowledge I wouldn't be the person I am today.

So, I cared for him until the day he died.

It was a terrible death. Hideous blisters and boils covered his skin. When they burst, his flesh refused to heal. No amount of ointment or wafting of burning herbs fought off the rapid decay of his body. His hair fell out in clumps and blood would leak from every hole. I kept him clean and helped him sup soup when he was too weak to lift his head. Magic could not repair him, and I loved him too much to end his misery early. My tears fell onto his face as his head lay on my chest to sigh his last breath.

They refused to have him, this sage and storyteller, in their holy burial grounds. So I dug the grave myself and laid him to rest covered in dried herbs and spiced linen from the east.

His painful death has always been the driving force in my life.

Many years after that, I got mixed up with a young thug and his idealistic knights – a silly, immature boy, who always had to have his own way.

With no humility and even less charm he refused to believe when I told him to be wary of his friend and he said something arrogant like, 'She would never dare love anyone else, after knowing me.'

When I said, 'You're too confident, boy. She's a conniving field weasel with the morals of a tavern tart,' he banished me. He would have killed me, given half a chance, but he had just enough intelligence not to raise my ire.

Anyway, I was more than happy to leave.

*

I set forth to the Arabian lands, taking in the cultures and mythology of Europe along the way. Then, transforming into an eagle, I took flight to the southern hemisphere. In one form or another I travelled the world and believed by that point I had more magical knowledge than any other man before me.

Egypt had lost much of its splendour. The glory days were a thing of the past and much grave-robbing had occurred, even before the British arrived to keep up the tradition, all-be-it in the name of antiquity and preservation.

I persuaded a wretch of a man, who had spent much of his life stripping the burial chambers, to take me to the tombs of the great ancients.

For more than ten years I gathered the secrets and collated my own Book of The Dead.

Not so much a book, but a bringing together of various systems of belief. Ancient religions blended with arcane knowledge and occult spells. Using everything I'd learned in Egypt and the other places I had travelled, even from those tricksters of the sub-continent — the Fakirs — I embarked on my quest for immortality. If I could separate my spirit, my soul if you like, from my body, I would for a short time, become a wandering, ethereal ghost.

With the right incantation and the right herbs, the right mental preparation, the right diet, and the slowing of my heart to less than five beats a minute, it should have been possible.

And it was!

The first time I achieved it, for all of my understanding, the sight of my own body lying on a slab shocked me and drew me back with such force as to make me lose control of my bladder. It was a week before I felt strong enough to try again.

I was an old man by this point, probably approaching eighty years, and knew I didn't have much time.

There was a strong man in the village where I chose my new body. He was a tree-feller, and I imagined how invigorating it would be to have physical strength and youth once again.

I separated my spirit from its mortal coil and, resisting the urge to re-enter my earthly frame, sent my smoke-like form through the roof of my abode and out into the night sky. Over the forests I floated and found the tree-feller's hut where he lived with an old, shaggy dog.

As soon as I saw his body, sleeping on the floor near a dying fire, I rushed forward and took my first breath in a new body. Seeing the world through his eyes, everything looked brighter and sharper. I marvelled at the youthful hands as I manipulated the fingers. I felt the strength of his muscles, and the strong beat of his heart. I howled with joy and the dog slunk away from my new body.

Then he went mad. I shared the mind of the man for an hour as he raved and screamed at me. He clawed at his head and face with one hand while I tried to protect my new body with the other. In the end he was much stronger than I.

For all my preparations, my feeble body was close to death when I returned to it.

My hour-glass would soon run out.

The woodcutter sought me out and made accusations that were entirely true. I convinced the villagers he was losing his mind as he raged obscenities at me. But those with an above average intellect believed there was some truth to his story. Wherever I travelled, I had always been treated with caution.

I had never been one for frolicking with girls and had no intention of beginning at that sort of age. They distract too much, making too many demands and cause a man to lose focus. However, after my failed effort to enter the body of the strong man, I knew I would have to attempt my resurrection in a more primal way.

There was a maiden, of Roman descent, in the village, with golden skin and long red locks. A desirable creature said to be promised to a junior royal when her time came. By way of an apology to the woodcutter, I set a charm on the girl. She couldn't help herself. Before long he and she were making the old dance, which resulted, after much fun with a seedling taking root in her belly.

When she began to show, the father beat the girl and bloodied her face with his fists. His foot repeatedly struck her curled body as she tried to protect the tiny life inside her. He held a short sword at her stomach and threatened to kill her and the bastard she carried if she didn't give up the name of her defiler.

He sent men to kill the wood-cutter. I felt immense remorse and shame for the whole incident. But the baby within her was strong and refused to give up its life.

Rather than the royal, she was married off to a cousin in a neighbouring village. Her beauty and innocence having been tarnished, her father received little from the exchange. The cousin hated the child she brought forth. I should know.

Although frail, I had become adept at leaving my body behind for small periods of time. In my ghost form, I would visit my soon-to-be-mother in her new villa with her weak and miserly husband. I witnessed his cruelty and knew I would have to endure an early second life with the man.

Whilst on one of these flying visits, my first body died. Though I knew it was going to happen, it was still sooner than I had hoped. My only option was to go to the girl-mother and seek out the life inside her. A small, but strong throbbing heart called to me and I took the place of a soul not strong enough to resist.

For five cycles of the moon I developed in the warm cocoon of her womb. I remember the birth and heard the screams of pain as her young underdeveloped hips obliged my second birth.

I remember clasping my gums to her breast, knowing I'd achieved the impossible as I rejoiced and celebrated with warm milk.

Her husband was intent on my death, but she was strong-willed and wrestled me from his hands as he tried to drown my newly reborn body. She promised him anything, would do anything for him, if only he would let her child live.

She bore one other child, a legitimate heir, who would inherit much. He didn't have the brains to do anything worthwhile and had no idea how to use his position to his own ends. I didn't mind — I knew knowledge to be a greater power than wealth.

I grew up strong. The genes of the wood-cutter ensured I was fit and healthy. And my mother loved me, not suspecting I had destroyed the child she might have had.

By the time I could speak and talk clearly, I could easily recall not only spells, but my previous life. I received a poor education and very quickly outclassed the tutor. It wasn't fair really; I'd already lived a very long life. Having an intelligent child made my mother proud, but it embarrassed her husband that his own child was — as we used to say back then — 'not bright enough to find his own dirt-pipe without the help of a dog'.

In those days, it was not unheard of for siblings to arrange assassinations of their own brothers and sisters. The reasons for such atrocities were various, but greed, as is often the case, was the most common motivation. I could feel my younger brother beginning to fear and resent me. Soon after I turned twelve, I left that villa and the warm comfort of my mother to make a second life for myself.

Much of that life I spent dedicated to teaching. I gathered other young and intelligent people around me. We would discuss philosophy, the rights of Gods and men, even mathematics.

That life neared its end early. I could feel my own body destroying itself, so I travelled to the place where my first body had ended its time. The village had emptied, and nothing remained but sodden huts overgrown with moss and ivy. My old cave entrance had collapsed, making it impossible for anyone to get inside. However, it was easy for me to levitate the boulders aside. It's difficult to describe the stench, but more difficult to describe the sensation of seeing the skeleton that used to be my body. All around were the scrolls and herbs, artefacts and treasures of a widely travelled sorcerer, now damp and beyond saving. Green fire leapt from my fingertips devouring the evidence of an old man's life.

Then I turned my mind to a new start. This time, I wouldn't enter a foetus in the womb, but instead take a newly born child. There is always the possibility that a birth might end in the death of the child, or the child might even die before birth.

So, in a nearby city, I entered the body of a child that would one day be a king. With all the privilege that goes with being a prince, I had a comfortable life. Again, I felt the resentment of my younger siblings as they grew to adulthood. They plotted my death. As before, I left before they could carry out their plans. I didn't need the power of wealth; I just needed a comfortable start in life.

It is a process I have repeated on more than a dozen occasions. Twice given away for adoption by mothers who rejected me, feeling an unnatural and weak link with their child. One mother tried to smother me in my cot. Fortunately, her heart gave out before she could complete the act and I was raised by the grandparents.

I have occupied the bodies of men and women, and known the needs of both as well as their difficulties and expectations. In one of those female forms I gave birth to a son, so as to experience the sensation from the other end of the spectrum. That kind of love I have only experienced once, and even though I knew I was destined to outlive him, I thought I might end the cycle there when he eventually died as an old man.

Mostly, I have lived my lives in peace and solitude as well as in splendour and wealth. Warm foreign climates are more favourable than cold lowlands, but one hardly needs to live as long as I have to know that.

In the course of my many lives I have plotted with villains and advised kings.

I have explored the world and walked on the surface of the moon.

I've killed with thoughts and brought forth life without seduction.

I have met secret assassins in dingy drinking dives, while sharing the hopes and dreams of good men.

I have been famous, a celebrated hero and also narrowly missed being fried in the electric chair.

Men and women have desired me for my looks, they have also despised me for my crimes.

I've played the parts of scientist, saviour and sailor of the stars with ease and guile.

I have truly lived. There is nothing else left to achieve, except perhaps the exploration of the great unknown.

And I know that will not be the end.

This life is only the beginning.

An Old Priest

(Published in Angels by Black Hare Press.)

Sweat ran down the old man's temples as he entered the room.

The old woman, in her bed, looked at him with hate-filled eyes. She was one of his most devout congregates and he barely recognised her. Steam, along with the scent of Hell, rose from her body.

When he'd been younger, exorcism had been a problem only specialist priests dealt with. This was his fifth in a month. Though his faith was strong, his body was weak. Could he keep this up?

He readied the holy water and the crucifix.

'Begone, Satan, inventor and master of all deceit.'

The Butcher of Blengarth

(First published in Full Metal Horror 2 by Zombie Pirate Publishing. It also appeared in Lockdown Horror #1 by Black Hare Press.)

How do these tales of woe and misery usually start? With a creaking door, or the whistling wind, or even a blinking eye. Sometimes, they begin on a dark and wintery night.

*

On a dark winter's night with the threat of snow in the air, a figure carrying a backpack walks along a road wet with slushy, dirty snow. Wind whistles through the woods banked high above the traveller on either side of the road.

In this part of the world, street lighting does not connect one town with the next. Thick clouds obscure all illumination from the moon and stars. Fortunately, a torch held in one gloved hand provides limited light, making the journey slightly more bearable. The figure's shadow begins to grow and stretch ahead, as from behind an oncoming vehicle gains ground.

Turning, the figure extends an arm with the thumb raised. She blinks several times as the headlamps of the small, blue car pass by, leaving her once again in comparative darkness.

She isn't surprised. Who in their right mind would stop for a stranger on a night like tonight?

To her surprise, the car slows and eventually stops, evidently waiting for her to quicken her pace.

The window rolls smoothly down, and a warm feminine voice from within says, 'Get in, then.'

She stands back and opens the door with a loud creak that sends nesting birds scattering from their night's rest.

'Thanks,' she says, sitting awkwardly with the backpack wedged between her legs.

'I'm going as far as Blengarth.'

'That'll do. Thanks.'

'Where're you headed?' the driver asks, changing gear.

'Anywhere, as far away as possible.'

'There's a blizzard coming.'

Snow begins to fall, proving her correct. She flicks a stick on her driving column to activate the wipers.

'Shit, really. I thought the worst was over.'

She thinks she's upset the driver with her coarse language. The swish-screee of the rubber wipers highlights the silence settling inside the car.

'Don't you worry about picking up hitchhikers?' she asks.

'What do you mean?'

'You know, I might be a serial killer.' She smiles to emphasise the joke.

'I see what you mean, but how do you know I'm not?'

The driver smiles at the look of surprise on the hitchhiker's face, and then winks to let her know she's pulling her leg.

'Only joking. Name's Mira.'

'Hi. Janet,' says the hitchhiker offering her hand. They shake awkwardly.

The flakes of snow increase in size and begin to lay thick on the bonnet of the car. The windscreen wipers flick the wet splotches faster. Mira turns the heat up.

'I hate this stretch of road,' she says. 'The council never seems to spread grit here.'

The back-end slides as they round a tight curve, causing Janet to close her knees tight on the backpack.

'Don't worry. You're safe — trust me. Are you running from someone?

'You can tell?'

'Who sets out on a night like this without planning?'

Janet fiddles with the toggles at the top of her bag. Taking a deep breath, she says, 'Yes, I'm running. The situation with my partner is over. He won't accept it. I tried leaving once before, and he broke a mug of tea over my head, he did. I needed stitches.'

'Shit!' Mira throws a concerned glance out of the corner of her eye.

'Sorry, I shouldn't off-load on you.'

'Doesn't matter. Sometimes a stranger is the best person to talk to. If you ask me, you're doing the right thing. Men — they're all bastards.'

Silence settles between them again. Mira has to slow the car as the snowfall becomes increasingly thicker, making it difficult to see the front of the bonnet.

'So, he doesn't know you've gone yet?'

'No, I'll get word to him in a day or two.'

'I'm sorry.' She hunches over the steering wheel as if being closer to the windscreen will help her to see further.

'When you're not picking up runaways, what do you do?'

'Me? I'm a butcher.'

'Oh — you don't see many women butchers.'

'I know it's not a normal trade for us to seek out, but believe me, I do the job as well as any man.'

'It will be a long time before men believe that.'

Mira takes her eyes off the road for a second to share a sympathetic smile, and says, 'Jesus, this snow. Can you believe it?'

'How far from town now?'

'Less than a mile. What will you do once I drop you off?'

'Not sure. Find a B&B for the night, take the first bus to anywhere in the morning.'

'You won't find anywhere open in Blengarth at this time of night, and all the pubs will be closed, too. Tell you what — you can sleep on my sofa. Us girls must stick together.'

'I couldn't.'

'Don't be silly. What else you going to do? You can get a bus in the morning.'

'That's very kind of you, but won't your husband mind?'

'Divorced.'

'Oh, sorry.'

'Don't be. I caught him with his dick in the bacon slicer.'

'Eaurgh!'

'So I sacked her too.' Mira lets out a chortle, slapping the palm of her hand against the wheel.

'Oh, I see......'

'No, I'm sorry. It's a butcher's joke. Still want my sofa?'

'Yes, please.'

*

In the warmth of her apartment, over the butcher's shop, Mira pours them each a glass of red wine, then crouches to light the gas fire with a match. Click, click, click, whoomp. Blue flames dance over the ceramic heating tiles covered in mesh. She tosses the dead wood into a saucer on the hearth.

Janet sits on the sofa that will be her bed for the night. Her bag rests in the corner of the small room. Mira has already found a blanket for her to sleep under.

Mira sits opposite, and Janet sees her properly for the first time. Large round eyes look back at her. Mira tucks a strand of dark hair behind her ear. Both corners of her lips rise in a suggestive smile, before looking away. She fiddles with a heavy piece of stone jewellery around her neck. Even wearing a thick sweater, the shapely outline of her body is hard to ignore.

What is she telling Janet? Is she imagining the signs? Even so, this is too close to home; she needs to be far away from John. If she gives into base instincts, she might stay another night and another. It wouldn't be difficult for John to find her.

'It's been a long day, Mira. Would it be okay if I turn in?'

'Sure. I'm just across the passage if you want anything,' she says, running the tip of her tongue over her lips.

'I'm sorry?'

'Relax, I'm teasing you…just a little. It's been a while since anyone was in my apartment, let alone my bed; I'm not sure I'd know what to do.'

Mira finishes her drink, leaving a lipstick imprint on the rim, and stands to leave. She smiles with her whole body.

'Sleep well.'

She leans down and leaves a lingering kiss on Janet's cheek.

Now Janet knows all she has to do is tap on Mira's bedroom door, and she won't be turned away.

Janet also knows her hostess is a strange one. Her jokes are a bit too sick or off-kilter. Laughing about her ex-husband having an affair. Who does that?

And surely she's a little too keen. They're complete strangers. Is she really that easy?

But those eyes.

Janet drains her glass, savouring the warm fuzzy glow filling her. Still clothed, she stretches out on the sofa. The blanket doesn't cover her feet.

Now, she hears the shower running.

It's only one night, Jan. You'll be gone in the morning. Grab the nettle and explore that side of your nature you've denied for so long.

Janet's need forms a knot at the pit of her stomach. She'll go to her. After all, they're both consenting adults and can deal with things in the appropriate way.

'Would it be wrong to want to share your bed for the night? After all, what harm is there in two lonely people bringing a little happiness to each other, even if it is only for one night?' She rolled the words around her mind imaging Mina's reaction.

These words are fine inside your head, Jan. But when you say them out loud, you'll sound like a silly twat from a bad romance novel.

The shower comes to a trickling stop. *Now or never, Jan.*

She steps into the passageway as Mira, loosely wrapped in a towelling robe, opens the bathroom door.

'Sorry,' Janet says, all bravery gone in an instant.

'Don't be. I usually read for an hour or so. Don't worry about disturbing me. Let me know if I can do anything for you.'

Mira's dark eyes are peering deep in to her soul, reading her heart, and understanding her needs.

All Janet has to do is make the move. She takes a step closer; she has an ache which needs rubbing.

'Well, I was wondering… ah… if… well…'

Janet can smell honey rising from Mira's warm body.

'Yes, Janet? What is it? What do you want?'

The doorbell rings, long and shrill, making them both jump a little.

'Ignore it,' Mira says, stepping closer., 'Ask me.' Janet reaches a hand forward. Their fingers touch. Janet's eyes close. Her lips tremble.

The doorbell rings again, followed by loud, insistent banging.

'I'll get rid of whoever it is,' Mira says.

*

The first thing Janet is aware of when she wakes is the pain at the front of her head. Her right eye, throbbing in time with her forehead, refuses to open. She tries to touch it, only to realise her wrists are tied to the arms of a wooden chair. She can feel ropes biting into her torso and legs, making it impossible to move. Nonetheless, she rocks the chair from side to side.

'Help!'

It occurs to her that the darkness is not due to her inability to open one eye, and surely she shouldn't be cold enough for her teeth to chatter. She pauses in her rocking to assess the situation.

She can feel the rough wooden slates of the chair pinching her naked behind.

'Oh, God.'

The memory surfaces. She and Mira were seconds from embracing. Mira had gone to answer the door. Janet heard her call out. The door had slammed shut and by the time she got to the top of the stairs, John was already halfway up as Mira slumped by the front door with blood pumping from her head. Janet was too stunned to say anything as his baton struck and darkness descended.

The rope has cut into her wrists, grating on her nerve endings with every convulsive shiver.

'John.' Her voice cracks.

Clunk — the door opens. She blinks her good eye as the light of the walk-in refrigerator winks into life. Warm air rushes in, causing the motors of the cold box to engage with a whining, whistling drone.

John stands before her, tapping his extendable baton in the palm of his left hand. He has taken off his bulkier outerwear — jacket, body armour and helmet.

One of his cheeks is splashed with blood.

'Please stop this, John.'

'Did you really think you could ever leave me, Janet?'

'I'm sorry. I'll come home. It won't happen again.'

'I don't believe you. You're sorry now because you're scared, but what about later when you're feeling strong? If you come home, you'll soon return to your old habits, because ultimately you're weak and without moral fortitude.'

'I won't. I promise.'

'You will. Thinking impure thoughts, imagining unnatural acts, and looking at girls like this one tonight.'

'Nothing happened. She gave me a lift. That's all.'

'Liar!' The crack of the steel baton on the inside of the door reverberates around the box, sending a jolt of fear right through her. 'What were you doing in her flat?'

'She was only letting me sleep on her sofa. Because the weather is so bad. That's all.'

'You are a liar.' John steps inside and, turns her face with the cold steel of the baton under her chin. 'Her lipstick betrays you.'

'What? No, no, no it wasn't like that — Arghhhh.'

'I think you may have broken your arm on my trusty truncheon, dearest. Keep lying to me and I'll be forced to find other ways to hurt you.'

Janet nods her head, tries to still her rattling teeth. Tears and snot mingle with sticky blood.

'You realise you're in the refrigerator at the back of a butcher's shop. No one can hear you scream.'

'Please, nothing happened.'

'Of course,' he continues, 'being a butcher's, they have lots of very sharp knives here. What fun we can have. Don't go anywhere. I'll be back in a minute.' He backs out of the box, leaving the door open.

She can hear John grunting as something weighty is dragged and moved. Then a loud, heavy thud followed by a whimper and groan. Despite the cold, her forehead prickles with dots of perspiration.

John returns to the doorway, a cleaver in one hand and something small in the palm of the other.

'I found this cleaver. They have hammers and pliers too. And big machines for slicing and mincing. So tell me what happened, before I feed her to you, piece by piece.'

'Nothing happened. I promise. I just wanted a bed for the night.'

'What happened?' John steps into the fridge, dropping the cleaver and grabbing Janet's face with his left hand.

'Tell me.'

'Nothing — God's honest truth.'

He forces Mira's severed finger tip into Janet's mouth, pushing her jaw closed around it.

'Swallow it! Swallow, you bitch.'

He pinches her nostrils closed. Blood fills her mouth, the fingernail tickles her tonsils. She can't breathe and gags as she tries not to swallow.

She loses control of her bladder and warm liquid floods the chair, dripping onto the floor. John steps away, his lips curled in a cruel smirk as Janet coughs and spits the digit onto her bare thighs.

'You need help, John. I'll help you find it. I won't leave you, I promise.'

'She was in her robe. What did you see?'

'Nothing.' She was still spitting to try to clear her mouth of Mira's blood. 'I saw nothing! We did nothing.'

'Liar. You wanted to, didn't you? Admit it,' he says, once again withdrawing from the torture chamber.

'Please stop, John, please. Remember you're a policeman.'

John returns, holding a knife with a long, pointed blade.

'Now, let's make sure you never see anything again, you cheating, lying deviant,' he says.

Once again, he grabs her face with his left hand and begins to lower the point of the knife towards Janet's left eye. She closes the eyelid tight in a feeble attempt to protect her sight.

'Please. Don't. I'm begging you —' Her words becoming a soul-searing scream as the sharp point easily cuts through the thin skin of her eyelid, making contact with the orb underneath. He drags the tip across to the outer edge and finally releases her face from his tight grip. Blood pumps down her cheek. Her breaths are short, quick, and filled with sobs.

The pain is exceptional. She knows agony like this cannot be sustained for long, and that she will die from the pain alone. She doesn't see nor feel anything as John wipes his thumb over her exposed and bloody eyeball. But she does endure the shooting, tearing pain as he tugs at her eyelid, which dangles by a few millimetres of flesh.

'I've only scratched the surface, darling,' he says in soothing tones, while stroking her bloody cheek. 'Now, don't struggle. You'll only make things worse, although I really don't see how things could get much worse for you. I am, after all, about to hack your eyeball to shreds.'

'P…... please…....don't…...'

She can't see anything clearly, with one eye swollen shut and the other damaged beyond usefulness. But, she does hear a sound like an egg cracking, followed by the full weight of John slumping forward against her. The knife he holds slices most of her ear off, then clatters to the floor. She feels her shoulder become slick with blood.

Janet can make out a vague shadow of a figure standing before her. A large crusted bruise has formed in the middle of her forehead. One hand is wrapped in a bloody tea-towel while the other holds a heavy mallet, the ridged metal surface matted with blood and hair.

'Oh my God. Is that you, Mira? Please tell me it's you. Talk to me. I'm so sorry. Are you okay?'

'Pig,' Mira screams as she brings the metal mallet down for a second time, caving in the front of John's head. One more blow brings his convulsions to a halt.

Mira's eyes shift from the uniformed body on the floor to the bonds holding Janet to the chair.

'It's me.' Her voice has lost all its previous warmth.

'Untie me. Then call the police. We need help.'

'No,' Mira replies.

'No?'

'I've got you just where I wanted you all along. Human flesh tastes very much like pork.'

Before Janet can fully comprehend her meaning, Mira steps back out of the fridge, silencing the rising screams by shutting the heavy door.

Windless

(Published in Winds of Despair by Fantasia Divinity.)

It's the thing I never expected to miss.

I remember being on a beach, enduring a gale while a dog splashed in the breakers. I can still smell the scent of honeysuckle carried on a summer breeze

When I accepted this assignment, I thought about the people I'd never see again and longed to watch the sun rise over an alien horizon.

First colonists on Mars. We will be remembered forever. But we're destined to spend the rest of our days in this environmental dome, protected from the elements.

I'd give anything to feel the wind in my hair again.

It Still Burns

(Published in Blaze by Clarendon House.)

The flame still burns and has done for a millennia.

Legend has it, a priestess scrambled from the remnants of the interstellar explorer, draped the sacred stole around her neck, pulled the candle from the deep recesses of her robes, lit it using a hand-held flamer, and started praying to her now long-forgotten god.

Other survivors, shaken and bruised, had gathered around the tiny fragile light, each giving thanks in their own way. They were the chosen few, the first to colonise the new planet and had been fortunate to survive the crash.

The priestess encased the candle in a lantern, made from scrap-metal and cracked glass, to protect it from the elements. The flame came to represent their need to survive: While the flame burned, they had a chance. She became its custodian and welcomed all to her humble dwelling to look on the bright flame in those dark, early days.

In time, the wreckage had been cleared and the dead buried. A small community evolved, leaders emerged, explorers brought back new discoveries, and permanent homes grew. Cold winters killed off the weak. Monsoon waters washed away crops. The survivors learned to overcome the planet's temperament.

And through everything the settlers had to endure, they ensured the flame still burned.

Each time the candle drew to the end of its life, dedicated disciples produced replacement tallow from the hides of dead beasts. Thankfully, as new innovations developed, the sacrifice of animals became less essential for the survival of the flame.

Now, many years later, it is safely housed in a tower hundreds of feet high. This tower, an extension of the small candle, is said to be visible from space, a beacon of planetary proportions. From across the globe, pilgrims travel to ascend the exterior steps winding around the massive structure. After hours of climbing, and reciting ancient prayers from a dead world, they spend a few seconds gazing upon the ancient flame. Each taps a hand to the four sacred points of their body.

'It still burns. Amen.'

The Edge of Space

(Published in Worlds by Black Hare Press.)

After hundreds of thousands of years and the collaboration of many thousands of scientists from hundreds of worlds using the combined computing power of God, we have arrived at the very edge of the universe.

This world-ship's only purpose is to survey the milky surface and perhaps acquire enough knowledge for exploration beyond the barrier. That is for our descendants to consider.

The haze clears for a few seconds as something enormous moves.

Months of piecing together captured images from thousands of recording markers, finally revealed the horrifying answer.

A blinking eye.

Like rats in a lab, we're being studied.

His Mama's Son

(This entry for the second round of The Great Clarendon House Writing Competition had to be exactly 1,000 words long and won me a place in the final.)

Mama cried the day I said goodbye. The tears left dirty streaks as they fell down her cheeks. But I felt no remorse or pity as I swung up onto my horse with a six-gun on my hip, and a heart full of hope. Several months later, I found it very far from easy and most certainly not free.

*

Life on the cattle trail is no way to live. I was paid at the end of that damn ride with enough money to get a bath and an all-over shave, crawling with bugs and jumping things as I was. It left enough money to buy new clothes and a cheap pair of boots.

Mac was a tired veteran of the trail, he reminded me of my Pa; strong as an ox, stubborn as a mule. I didn't see how I could ever provide for a family working as a swing rider, so he and I high-tailed it out of there one morning and never once looked back.

A few weeks later, we rode into a small town not too far from the border. One of the local landowners was hiring guns. Mac said the rancher was probably looking for young men to die in some sort of land war. But the money was good and I was sorely tempted.

We looped the reins over the hitchin' post; I splashed water from the trough around the back of my neck and strode into the saloon wiping myself dry with my kerchief. I swear to the Good Lord Almighty, the off-key tinkling of the piano came to a halt and the bar-dog slowed the pace at which his dirty cloth smeared grease around a shot glass. A woman in silk and satin sidled up to me.

'Buy a girl a drink?' The deep chasm of her charms thrust towards me. 'Two large ones for the cowpoke, Thomas,' she said before I could politely refuse. With regret, I was forced to slide my two bits across the counter.

'What's yer name, stranger?' she asked as Thomas sloshed liquor into the glasses.

'Eddie, ma'am.' Mama raised me to always treat a lady right.

'Pleased to meet ya, Eddie. There's a room —'

'Sorry, ma'am, but I ain't lookin' for company.'

She threw her drink to the back of her throat and left me watching her retreating hips swaying from side to side like saddlebags on an old pony.

With no money and my tongue still dry as cracked leather, even after swallowing the gritty whiskey, I stepped through the swinging doors onto the covered wooden sidewalk. My ornery horse looked at me with one disapproving eye.

'I know, girl.' I ran a hand down her long sweaty neck.

'No good talkin' to the horse. She won't help none,' Mac said from the step he had chosen to use as a seat. 'You still wanna be a hired gun?'

'Reckon I don't have no other choice.'

'Sure you can use that thing?' he asked, lifting his chin toward my gun.

'Sure I can. Mama taught me.'

He laughed and said, 'And who's your mama, boy, Belle Starr?' Then he spat a long line of black juice into the road. I ignored his attempt at humour and answered him with a question, 'What will you do?'

'There's plenty a man can do with a gun at his side.' He gave me a sly look. 'Could always work for his-self, if he's prepared to draw it sometimes. You ever shoot anybody?'

'Shot a sick dog once.'

'Shit, everybody's shot a sick dog at sometime or other. In a few minutes I'm goin' into that bank over there and I'm gonna take all the money I can. How 'bout it, Eddie?' He pulled his rifle forward laying it across his knee. 'Come with me, draw yer gun and look like ya wanna use it. Equal split.'

I looked from Mac to the bank on the other side of the dusty street and then back at Mac.

'Why?'

'Ain't no one walked in there in five minutes.'

'What about the sheriff?'

'What about him? Probably catching a dose off some harlot somewhere. We go in fast and get the hell out of this sleepy town before he's pulled his boots on. We'll be safe in Mexico before nightfall.'

Mac stood, shifted his hat to shield his eyes from the sun, 'What's it gonna be, boy, hero or highwayman?'

'You ain't giving me much of a choice.'

'Sure I have, ya could always walk away an' watch me ride out of here with a thousand dollars.'

*

The bank was empty, save for two tellers and the manager. When Mac put the rifle to the girl's face they loaded up our bags. I kept the manager at bay with my pistol and some words Mama would have struck me for using. Minutes later we were heading south at full gallop. Not one shot had been fired.

A night under a clear sky and a full moon, as the wind whistled over rock and cacti, was enough to confirm my doubts.

On the assumption that a posse was after us, we chose not to light a fire. It might have been hunger eating away at my guts, but more likely it was the foul taste of disappointment. We'd taken less than a third of the amount Mac had hoped for. His share was propping up his snoring head.

Slowly, I shifted position and loosened the thong on my holster. Mac rolled over, suddenly wide awake. His rifle shot woke the vultures. It went wide, but my bullet found its mark. I was running quickly, as only a man full-growed can and my boot connected with his head. I tore his gun from his hands.

'Why, ya yella…bellied…skunk?' Blood bubbled on his dying lips.

'I'm my mother's son.' His eyes widened as I said, 'Belle Starr.'

Then I pulled the trigger and put the sick dog out of his misery.

Roofer

(Published in Hate by Black Hare Press.)

Politicians – I fuckin' hate 'em.

Ya' know we don't get pensioned till we're sixty-seven now. Easy for them to say on eighty grand a year. There ain't one o' them deserves one fuckin' penny. I'd like to see them up a roof when they're sixty-seven years old with my knees.

I've had it with Brexit and Euro MPs.

An' I got a parking ticket yesterday, too. Fuckin' council, robbin' bastards.

Wankers – I'd shoot 'em all.

Anyway, Guv, new gutter an' down-pipe to rear o' the house; hundred an' fifty quid all in.

I'll do it next Wednesday, if ya like.

Brian

(This is one of my shorter stories from The Magic of Deben Market *and gives an insight into the main character, Moony Moore.)*

Bright was the night Brian chose to hide up in a fisherman's shed. A full moon, so brilliant the stars lost their luminescence, hung high in the sky: the tiny dots of light dimmed and outshone, for one night only, by lunar glory. Looking straight at the glowing sphere brought water to his eyes.

Brian hopped over big walls into the gardens of houses belonging to the well-to-do of the little town. From one garden to the next and then the next, in his attempt to steer clear of Sergeant Hill. The punishment he had received from the fat policeman, a few nights earlier, had been beyond cruel. Locked in an old Anderson shelter overnight with no light or water, he had messed his pants which only sent his mum into yet another rage.

What did she expect? It was all her fault. She was the one who had got the policeman to punish him in the first place, simply because he didn't like going to school.

What twelve-year-old did?

He would rather be out in the wild, than sitting in a boring classroom. He knew things about the land and the forest no teacher did. He knew the habits of badgers and birds. He could snare rabbits and skin 'em too. But no, his mum wanted him to be just like the others.

Bollocks to that.

Now, she had set Sergeant Hill after him again and he needed a safe place to hide. Somewhere the fat pig wouldn't think of looking. He made his way, in a round-the-houses fashion, down to the beach and climbed into an old shed, turned the paraffin heater on, and kipped down for the night in front of it.

Old Nick nudged the boy awake with the tip of his boot.

'Wake up, young 'un,' he said.

The boy tried to dart away on his hands and knees, but Old Nick's boot soon pinned him to the floor.

'Sorry, I'm sorry,' Brian yelped.

Having spent time in Japan from '42 to '46, Old Nick recognised genuine fear when he saw it, so lessened the pressure on the boy's chest.

'Yer not in trouble, boy. But ya owe me for breaking in and use o' the gas.'

'I don't have no money.'

'Best ya work yer debt off then. Help me gut some fish, and then we'll think 'bout mending the lock together. How 'bout that then, Moony?'

'Moony?'

'I got to call ya something, int I?' said Old Nick, smiling and holding out his hand.

Brian waited a few seconds before putting his own hand forward.

Growth

(Published in Apocalypse by Black Hare Press.)

The soil is nothing more than sand. It lost nearly all of its nutrients long ago.

But we still toil, even though growing food is almost impossible. One more row of carrot seeds before I rest, for I grow more weary with every passing day.

My child is skinny and cries from hunger. I fear he will grow used to it. And the child growing in my womb will never know a full tummy, if he even survives.

The cockroaches somehow grow in size and number. Their meat is unpleasant but plentiful.

The growth on my neck will burst soon.

Little Brass Tin

(Published in Twenty Twenty by Black Hare Press in support of Australian Bushfire Wildlife Organisations providing emergency veterinary care, etc to wildlife in the affected bushfire zones in New South Wales and Victoria; - NSW (New South Wales) Wildlife Information, Rescue and Education Service - Zoos Victoria.)

Welcome, welcome to The Little Brass Tin. I'm always glad to see new patrons in my humble establishment. What would you like to drink?

Oh, I see…

Well, we sell nearly everything here; from booze to milk and even dancing girls, if you take my meaning. But, not many know that I might occasionally sell the white powder to a select circle of friends.

They say it keeps one going for longer, and you know how those bright young things like their parties. They're the ones who mainly seek me out. And apparently, one of them has being telling tales out of school. Oh well, never mind. Felix, the tricky minx, it seems, has been let out of the bag.

Did you know that Sherlock Holmes believed it made his mind sharper and wittier? I won't talk about what it does for the reproductive organs, not while there's a lady present. And it's available in so many forms. One can chew on the fresh leaves and get a very pleasant, if a little numbing, sensation. We sell, quite legally, two brands of coca wine. Especially liked by some of our more famous ladies — Sarah Bernhardt was a big fan of Vin Mariani. Are you sure you wouldn't like some of that instead? No. Can't say I blame you. In truth, it's not what it used to be.

So, what do you want to drink? This is after all a bar. You should at least be seen to be enjoying yourself in the expected manner. Splendid. Two White Ladies while we chat and I decide if I like you enough to sell you my prize commodity. Forgive me if I dominate the conversation. As you have no doubt noticed, I like the sound of my own voice a little too much.

You know, I first got a taste for the stuff on the front line in 1916. Much nicer here in a warm, dark bar than a cold and muddy trench, wouldn't you agree? I was a seventeen-year-old second lieutenant with no life experience other than six weeks basic and four weeks officer training. I had been a schoolboy up to a few months previously, and schoolboys were sent clothes at Christmas, bought their books in the holidays and waited for acceptance to one of the universities. I skipped on Cambridge. As far as I could see, I was ready to be a man, and being a man at that time meant preparing for war.

The NCO who drilled us told me, in one of his more civil moments, 'Eat everything, Dervish. Don't waste anything. If it moves, kill it and then eat it. If it's already dead, just eat it. If it's free, eat it. If you can cook it, cook it, but the important thing is to eat it.' And then he forced me and two others to eat the remains of a blackbird pie: bones, beaks, feathers — the lot.

His point being, food was scarce on the front line, and what food there was, was of poor quality. You were never sure of what you were eating, or when you would eat it. And one had to get one's energy from somewhere, didn't one?

Cigarette? Here, please take one of mine.

Where was I? Oh yes, the little brass tin with the word 'Harrods' embossed on the cover was always a very welcome gift; one which I soon looked forward to with great expectation. It came with a loving note from Mother, and it lifted the spirits. Looking under the lid and seeing the vial of morphine with an accompanying needle and a separate cachet of white powder, always brought a sense of relief. There is nothing better for giving one enough energy to face the enemy than one of those cachets — it beat seven bells out of boiled vermin, I can tell you — and when most of the guns were silenced (although, there is never any complete peace in Hell) an injection of morphine helped send one on the sweetest sleep.

I was eventually pulled out of a hole, bumped up to major and shipped back to blighty, minus an eye.

After that, it was a desk job for me, but I still missed the euphoria such a little brass tin would bring. To be honest, I still need it to silence the shells and the screams that continue to berate the old thinking machine.

When the war ended — gosh, has it really been five years? — one had to pay chemists and stores large amounts for a rapidly shrinking commodity. So I turned to the streets of Soho, where one could find it by the barrel load, after said barrel had fallen off the back of a horse and cart.

And then I struck a deal with a nasty piece of work.

I've been running this bar for the last year now. I don't have any trouble from the law or racketeers peddling protection, but if I do, the aforementioned nasty piece of work is never far away to deal with them.

Are you okay? You look sleepy. So does your lady friend for that matter. The chaps in the band call them 'Jazz Cigarettes' and they can have a rather soporific effect to the uninitiated. What you need is a little pick me up. Come with me to my office. It's in the cellar, I'm afraid.

Yes, there are a lot of stairs. I think that's because of the underground. You can hear it all around sometimes; above, below, far away and close by. I agree, it is hot down here. It might have something to do with the torches on the walls.

There you are. Sit yourselves down and rest easy. Who? Oh, him in the alcove, in the corner. Don't mind him. He's the nasty piece of work I struck up a deal with. Yes, you're right. He does look like The Devil, although I am assured he is just one of His minions. A demon whose name I fail to pronounce every single time, so I won't embarrass myself by trying again. But there is no doubt about it, he is a demon. You can tell by the glowing red eyes and cloven feet. The horns tend to draw a bit too much attention in public. That's why he lives in the basement of my little bar. Or is the Little Brass Tin a doorway to Hades? I'm not really sure.

No, no, no, don't try to run. Your legs won't be able to carry you up the steps much less get you to the front door. You see, I'm afraid you've had a rather large dose of opiate. Wrong of me, I know. But I won't tell anyone if you don't, eh? Mum's the word, right.

That's it. Lie back, close your eyes, and let oblivion take you. Soon, I'll lay you on the sacrificial slab, one at a time, and then Hell, oh I am sorry, I mean *he'll* feast on your souls and I'll be able to feed myself for a couple of weeks too.

Old habits die hard and all that… But, this is the price I pay to silence the shells of Passchendaele.

Powerless

(Published in Apocalypse by Black Hare Press.)

Darkness came but the end is still happening.

No one is sure who did it, or why. On a basic level, home appliances stopped working and phones died. More serious were the planes that fell from the sky. The financial power houses collapsed the day the power failed. Banks became obsolete overnight.

The rioting went on for weeks.

A friend, a maths professor, estimates that half the population may have starved, been killed or died from previously avoidable accidents.

Can you bake bread from scratch?

Before this, I'd never killed for food. Have you?

Most are cannibals now, even vegans.

Wishes Can Come True

(Published in The Inner Circle Writers' Magazine as an overview to The Magic of Deben Market.)

I can't blame Angelika, not really. We were always close, even before she came to live with me at the age of fourteen. Her mother had issues, but I can't blame her either, she never got over the death of my son.

I haven't made much sense, have I? Let me start again. Angelika is my granddaughter, and my son was her father. His wife, a French woman, had Angelika and never forgave him for dying or her daughter for ruining her own life. So, Angelika came to live with me when she was only fourteen, and I looked after her and her baby till she could stand on her own two feet.

Linda, my great-granddaughter works for the solicitor. Personal Assistant they call it now, we used to call them secretaries in my day. She better be careful, that Christopher Benton always had wandering hands. Well known for it, he is.

The things I could tell you about the people in this town. We've had murders, and people go missing with no explanation. We've had pop stars and TV personalities turning up for dirty weekends, but you can read about that sort of stuff in the papers.

Let's see, Jane Thirsk has never been the same since she walked in on that suicide. The woman put her house up for sale on a Friday afternoon, leaving the keys with Jane at the estate agents and said she was going to Brighton. Jane walks in on Tuesday morning — after the summer bank holiday — and finds the place full of blue bottles, the woman dangling from an oak beam. She had nearly been decapitated, so they say.

Then there's old Felix, who always said he was once married to a princess. He came here and nearly died of heartbreak, but the town kept him going.

There's a policeman in this town you wouldn't want to get on the wrong side of. Imagine it, in this day and age, a copper who takes advantage of his power. He's quick with his fists if riled and will take payment any way he sees fit for turning a blind eye. Mind you, his grandfather was just the same.

Who else is there? Let me think, there's plenty of drinkers, but don't ever go on a session with Darryl, he swears blind aliens that experimented on him. I don't know if too much partying scrambled his head, or if he really was abducted and now needs to hide at the bottom of a bottle.

There's Matt who works more jobs than is humanly possible. The Social Security would put him away for forever and a day if they ever bothered to investigate how much cash he earns while still claiming benefit.

Young Wally, well he's not so young anymore, but I can't help thinking of him that way. There is something so incredibly disarming about Wally. Many take him for a fool, but how many fools do you know with a multi-million-pound building company, eh? He's in love for the first time in his life and I'm happy for him.

Gilbert White doesn't know his son is planning on selling the family business as soon as he gets his hands on it.

There's a retired spy come to die in one of the old folks' homes. I'm telling you, there's something strange about him — I can't quite put my finger on it.

Then there's the ghosts. I often see Dickie Harris looking better than he ever did in real life. And if I go and stand outside the cottage where Jane got the fright of her life, I can see that poor woman who hanged herself with the cord of her robe. She stands at the window night after night just staring, with her head at an odd angle.

Know what I think? I think there is some sort of ancient magic on this town bringing waifs and strays here, and it is reluctant to let them go. Perhaps not magic, but certainly something mystical and mysterious from way back in the past. No, I am not being fanciful; I truly believe it because of the things I've seen.

I was talking to Moony about it once, years ago, and he said, 'Some o' the things I seen at sea will straighten yer short an' curlies.' That's Moony for you, salt of the earth fisherman that he is. He's lived a long, hard life the best way he could. Loved a lot of people and damaged a few that hurt those he cared for.

Nevertheless, never believe a fisherman.

There's a boy who can bring animals back to life. He's special, like my Angelika, but he doesn't know it yet.

Sorry, I'm rambling – where did I start? No, I don't blame her. It broke her heart when I died. After all, we were very close, and although she never said it out loud, she wanted me back so much that she wished me back from the dead.

There I was not exactly dead but not alive, in some sort of limbo. It wasn't dark, but with not a prick of light it felt pitch black. And I was floating or maybe drifting, but I knew I was standing on my feet and walking. I was all alone, yet knew many more like me weren't far away. I should've been scared witless and out of my mind, but I felt really peaceful, really calm.

I don't remember a tunnel or a light or hearing people calling me back or anything like what people talk about when they're on the telly. All I know is I opened my eyes and still couldn't see a blessed thing. I raised my hands and realised the coffin lid was only inches above me. Luckily, they hadn't nailed it down, so, when I pushed, it lifted easily enough.

I was only in the funeral home, so I was, in an air-conditioned viewing room filled with dried and dusty flowers. Everywhere I looked, everything was red — the carpet, the drapes and the walls. Half a dozen chairs with red cushioned seats were placed around my coffin. I'd been in this place before when I had to see my old man out of this world. I was dressed in some sort of white funeral garb, all ready for them to come take one last look at, before rolling me through the red curtains.

Considering I had spent ninety-nine years on this planet before my resurrection, I felt pretty good — never felt fitter, actually. So, I clambered over the edge of my coffin and walked out of there. It was late at night which helped. Imagine the look on people's faces if I'd done that in the middle of the funeral service.

Later, I made the local news for the first time in my life, which is ironic. The police were looking for sick thieves who stole the body of a great-great-grandmother on the eve of her funeral.

I walked for miles on that first night, only to return to Deben Market, and an old, crumbling chapel in the woods on the edge of town. I haven't got the nerve to face my family again. I'm not sure what I'm going to do. I haven't figured out what I am yet. See, I don't really get hungry, but I've a yearning for rare steak — any rare meat, if I'm honest. And my heart don't beat no more, although it could burst with loneliness.

Soldier

(Opening drabble for Storming Area 51: Survivor Stories by Black Hare Press.)

Oh my God! Really, Sir? 1989?

Please listen to me, Sir. I come from the future. On September 20th, 2019 more than a million people stormed Homey Airport.

It was a total massacre, Sir. Lethal force was sanctioned, but there were just too many insurgents. They released the aliens. The aliens began killing everyone.

I found myself alone, out of ammo and surrounded by grey-skins. I backed into a metal and glass box over in X-block, unit 88. Somehow, it must have accidentally activated and now I'm here.

Whatever it takes, Sir, we must stop the storming of Area 51.

Daniel MacBride

(Published in Storming Area 51: Survivor Stories by Black Hare Press. Released to coincide with millions of UFO enthusiasts who were to descend on the infamous air base en mass in September 2019. Their mission - to know the secrets held inside. Their Facebook group slogan — 'They can't stop us all'. On the day, only a handful turned up!)

September 20, 2019

Good evening, viewers. The government may have thrown a blanket over traditional reporting, but this is the twenty-first century. People are the news-makers now. They can't stop people talking.

We're here with one of the survivors of the extraordinary scenes you have no doubt seen today online and in other uncontrolled news sources.

Hello, Daniel would you like to tell the viewing public about yourself?

Err, yeah. My name's Daniel, Daniel MacBride. I'm a student, sort of seeing the world on my gap year. You know, just me and a backpack. But I never expected to see what I saw earlier today.

Before we get to that, how did you get to the site? Tell us about the atmosphere.

Well, the whole thing reminded me of a line from that old Woodstock song my Gram was always playing. You know, 'By the time we got to somewhere we were half a million strong'. There was an air of rebellion and freedom and camaraderie.

But we were heading for Area 51 not a hippy music festival.

Roadblocks didn't stop us. People were travelling cross country by trail-bike and four-wheel drive, some walked, others rode horses. I even saw someone on a camel. Armed with nothing more than curiosity and need to know the truth, we travelled over desert rocks and dunes to converge and surround the installation.

Tell us more.

Er, well the internet was rife with speculation and instruction. But I rode my thumb and got picked up in a flat-bed ford, driven by bloke called Leroy, but his grandma was the force to be reckoned with in their party.

As if by silent agreement every man, beast and machine halted about twenty-five miles from the fences to set up camp. The glow of fires could be seen in the clear desert night. The old lady told me all about watching the moon landing from her father's knee as we shared our food and drink. When the sun rose all you could see to the left and right was a never-ending mass of humanity waiting to move. Behind us was a thick carpet of people. It was beautiful.

The authorities had made threats online, but how do you stop a million people?

We started moving. A slow trundling pace at first so that no one was left behind.

Sirens sounded. Jet planes flew in formation, some quite low, to intimidate us. But we kept moving. The old lady was my constant companion. She held my arm as we rode in the back of the pickup and I asked if she was scared or would prefer to be inside the cab, but she said something about fighting for the right thing all her life, 'When soldiers opened fire at our college, I knew I would always fight'. She was a brave woman.

Military trucks met us halfway. A voice from a loudspeaker told us to halt, to cease our advance, that we were on Military ground and action may result if our insurgence continued.

Someone nearby was playing the Star-Spangled Banner on their car stereo. The old lady had her fist in the air along with the rest of us. We smiled at each other.

And then a hole appeared in the middle of her forehead and she dropped like a stone.

Wait a minute, Daniel. Are you saying the military opened fire first?

As far as I'm concerned. Yes. And then there was total mayhem. People were screaming and crying. A million people were panicking. No one expected the soldiers to open fire. I mean this is the twenty-first century.

I was lying on the bed of the truck, cradling the old lady. But she was gone. I peered over the edge to see other vehicles charging along with us, hundreds of them. When I think about it, there must have thousands, perhaps tens of thousands of ordinary cars and trucks and vans all intent on ramming the fences. Explosions started to rain down on us. For crying out loud they were firing rockets. I saw a camper-van flip over and explode. A riderless horse overtook us.

I lay on my back praying that Leroy would see sense and turn the truck around. I just wanted to getaway. At any second a rocket might have taken us out.

Drones were whizzing about too. Micro-rockets targeted random vehicles. But someone had thought to bring their own armed drones. Soon there was a mini dogfight going on in the skies above us

As I watched, the truck rattling my teeth, I saw my first alien. A sort of flying creature, and then another and then more until the sky was full with them.

Then these things started diving down on us. They plucked people from the backs of bikes, or ripped open the roofs of cars with their claws. People were lifted into the sky in a bizarre lover's embrace. Only to be dropped from hundreds of feet up. One of the swarm descended for me, I scrambled back from it and lifted the nearest thing to defend myself with, which happened to be a pitchfork. It pierced its skin easily, killing it instantly. I'll never forget the black grey skin and almost featureless face, with a row of needle-like teeth jutting forward. It was very small and lightweight. I threw it out of the truck easily.

It sounds absolutely terrifying, Daniel. How did you get here? How did you escape?

The pickup came to a sudden halt against the wall of a building, well inside the complex. I can't describe everything. Leroy was dead. Bullets were flying everywhere. The explosions. The dust. It was crazy. And those alien things diving on people, soldiers too. I just ran, trying to find somewhere to hide.

I followed some random guy inside a giant hanger. The door had been partially blown open. He fell down and I tripped over him. Most of his head was missing. The same soldier turned his gun on me, but his superior pushed it away and the bullet went wide.

Just to confirm, Daniel. You witnessed a US serviceman murder a citizen.

Well, yes. Didn't I just say that? And he'd have shot me if his superior hadn't intervened. She bundled me to the back of the hanger. The murdering soldier was saying it was all our fault, we were the ones breaking the law, we were the people who had released those flying things. And she reminded him that we were all American citizens. The true enemy were the aliens. She actually said the word, 'Aliens.'

Me and her and half a dozen soldiers scrambled into a weird vehicle. I didn't really see it properly, but it floated, you know hovered above the ground. Once inside I could hear the radio chat. Area 51 lost, immediate evacuation and all that sort of stuff. We were flying low and fast.

I don't know anything more. I don't know if I can tell you anything else.

Did the soldiers say anything to you? Did they make any apologies?

No. I was left on the highway and I had to walk into town. She gave me a look that said sorry, but nothing more. Then they were gone.

What will you do now, Daniel?

I don't know. Prepare for war I guess. If the things I saw escaping are only some of what was in Area 51, then we're in trouble.

Red

(First appeared in Forest of Fear by Blood Song Books.)

'Call me, Red,' she replied to Wolfie.

Red hair, red lips and long red fingernails. She wore a Little Red Riding Hood costume that hugged every curve; she was delicious. *Good enough to eat. Relax, it's only a figure of speech.* But Red liked Wolfie — he could tell.

Later, as they passed the wooded copse, Red grabbed his hand and pulled him inside. As they embraced, he heard someone snigger.

'Did you hear that?' Wolfie asked. His eyes widened as Red's fingernails tore deep grooves in his neck.

'Come sisters. It's dinner time!'

The shadows came to life.

A Bullet for The Horse

(First appeared in Dastaan World Magazine. More recently, I am proud to say this story has also been published in a genuine western magazine, Saddlebag Dispatches.)

His eyes are two thin slits as he stares into the setting sun. Two long shadows are cast in the dust. He tilts his Stetson, but it does little good. In silence he leads the horse by cracked leather reins. The horse with its head low, limps beside her companion.

Blood coats the hoof of the left foreleg. Flies buzz.

The stable is one of the first buildings on the edge of town. The smell of fresh horse-dung fills him with hope — the place is clean.

'Anyone here?' he calls out.

'What?' comes the reply, from behind one of the stalls. An old boy with grey stubble steps into the sheltered yard, his cheek bulging with a wad of tobacco.

'My horse needs help, there a Doc in town that can deal with this?' he asks, indicating the lame leg.

'Cheaper an' kinder to put a bullet in the creature than use that drunken butcher,' replies the stable owner, bending down to look at the injury.

'I'm all out of bullets.'

'I can spare one for a nickle.' The stable manager smiles and then spits a long streak of black juice into the corner.

By the light of a lantern and with the help of the chaw chewer, he washes the wound. Fortunately, no maggots have set in, although an unpleasant smell turns his stomach over.

Taking the knife from its sheath on his left hip, he pops the back off the bullet. He bends the horse's leg up and takes the weight as she leans against him. Carefully, he pours the powder into the raw hole, creating a thin dark layer. Her flank quickly becomes slick with sweat, as she starts to panic.

'Easy girl,' he says, stroking her nose and looking her in the eye. 'We've been through a lot you and me. This has to happen.'

He looks at the old man to check if he's ready.

'Hold her steady.' They both press her body against the stable wall.

'You're not paying me enough for this.'

'Just hold her.'

He strikes the match on the woodwork and touches it to the gunpowder in one fluid movement.

With a bright flash, and an almost silent fizz, the gunpowder catches alight and a second later has burnt itself out. In the time it takes the powder to do its magic, he's released his hold on the leg and they've scrambled out of the confined space. They lean on the half door panting for breath, as she rears on her hind legs. Her cries of pain set the other horses neighing and jittering. In their panic, they're kicking at the stable walls making a thunderous and almighty ruckus.

Soon, she begins to calm, and stands with the hoof raised off the floor. Steam rises from her body. The smell of burnt hair fills the air.

'Give her water, and the best feed you have. I'll be back in half an hour.'

He returns with fresh linen, smears iodine all around the wound, and bandages it as best he can. He will do the same tomorrow and change the dressing daily. Should the horse survive, it will be weeks before she'll be shod again.

'I need a place to sleep. Do you have a spare room?'

'What's wrong with the saloon?'

'The soup.'

'Dollar a night, including food. Ma does a mean stewed rabbit.'

'Prices like that, I'll need work.'

'Sheriff's looking for a deputy.' The stable owner had a laugh like a mule and spat more juice into the corner.

'I'll pay him a visit in the morning.'

'Welcome to Tombstone, son.'

Foodie

(Published in Love by Black Hare Press.)

He'd always loved food. It was fair to say food was his passion.

He loved every meal — breakfast, brunch, lunch, dinner and supper.

Toast, bagels, sausages, cream sauces, raw fish and most meat were all his loves.

Game — both fur and feather. Farmed food and even roadkill. He had tried it all.

Fancy chocolates in Belgium. Fine street food from stalls in Asia. And 72oz rib-eye steaks in Texas — he had won a prize.

He was a true gourmand.

But he had never tried human meat, not till earlier that night. Her death was quick. He loved her.

Serve Cold

(Published in Flash Fiction Addiction by Zombie Pirate Publishing.)

I develop recipes for TV chefs. I'm the one who decides if the ingredients work, tweak them a bit if necessary, pinch of salt here or added flair there.

Anybody who thinks the Jamies and Ramseys of this world can do it all themselves is deluded. These guys are millionaire businesspeople with restaurants, television programmes and books to promote all around the world. They have charities to patron and families to be perfect with. They do magazine interviews, tweet their news, Facebook their envious lives and don't forget occasional TV spots. They give the impression of being superhuman, but they have large teams to support them in every aspect of their lives.

I currently work for a particular lady who's been in the biz for what feels like centuries. She has it all, the big house, a successful business, a football team and a perfect family. All built on lies and deceit. Back in the day when we were just starting out, we both worked for Craddock as assistants. Her on screen and being helpful. Me behind the scenes, doing the sweaty work. When Fanny had had her day, someone new was needed to fill the void. She stole my creamed chicken recipe, and it wasn't the last thing she stole. After she dumped me, and I was dropped from the production, I saw many of my dishes served up with a tweak here or a pinch of salt there. However, through grit and determination I got other work behind the scenes and the chaps with the big names were always appreciative of the help of backroom boys like myself. I'm grateful, but damn it, I deserved the top gig. I should be the recent receiver of an OBE. I deserve everything she has instead of a flat I can barely afford the rent on and a tumour the size of a fist in my bowel.

A year ago, I was asked to be part of her team. She didn't recognise me — Bitch.

There she is now smiling at the camera, putting the almond tart in the oven. Listen to her, 'Cook for twenty minutes on gas mark four or fan one eighty.' Senile old cow got it wrong, again. 'Then leave for an hour until cold.'

Now they cut to my tart, and she simpers, 'Fortunately, I made this one earlier.'

She cuts a thin wedge and serves it with raspberries and crème fraîche. The camera lingers over my masterpiece. Then with a fork she cuts the tip off the slice and raises it to her pouting red lips. Slips the portion in, sucks the fork with sensual pleasure, licks her lips and smiles at the camera. Her eyes still as alluring as ever, look beyond the camera into the homes and lives of everyone watching. The viewers at home can taste it.

'Astounding, nothing better. You'll love it.'

I had loved her once.

Everything happened so quickly. Grasping her throat and foaming at the mouth she collapsed forward, crashing off the work counter and landing on her back. She was dead before she hit the floor, live on Saturday morning TV.

We all rushed forward to help, but I stopped at my almond tart and cut myself a slice.

I smiled as I took my final bite and thought of the old adage about cold dishes and revenge.

Late Night Drinks

(Published in Monsters by Black Hare Press.)

'Pint please,' the vampire said.

The claws of the werewolf made drawing the blood easy, if a little messy.

'Quiet tonight,' said the vampire, after paying.

'I know. It's their fault, they unnerve the regulars.'

The vampire looked sideways at a group of zombies in the corner of the room.

'Weird, are they not?' said the vampire.

'It's unnatural, is what it is,' said the werewolf. 'They don't drink or eat. They just sit there groaning.' He lifted the still-living victim's arm and helped himself to a couple of fingers.

'But they're no trouble?'

'Nah. Not in my pub.'

Looking Glass

(Published in Maelstrom by Clarendon House.)

Carol Arlington, as a young child, would sit at her mother's dressing table and wish she was grown up enough to be allowed to wear makeup. She would test the powders and be transported far away to exciting cities by the names on the pots — Dior, Yves Saint Laurent and Guerlain. The smells of lotions had nothing on the glorious, heavenly scent of Chanel. She would trace the embossed logos with her fingers, play with the golden tassels on bottles and once or twice tasted the lipstick on her lips. She would look in the mirror, which her father always insisted on calling a looking glass, and try to imagine herself all grown up. With an aching heart she yearned to be an adult, to have her own routines, her own lipstick, powder and paint, and to be like Mummy. Being a child was so unfair.

But that had been a long time ago.

Now, every time she sat at the dressing table she despised the image of the woman looking back. For forty years she'd had to stare at that face while she made it into something better. Of all the people to look like, she had to look like her mother. The woman with the shortest fuse in history, who would abuse her and embarrass her at every opportunity.

As she stared into the mirror — *sorry, Daddy, looking glass* — she slid inside the memory, and found herself once again in her childhood home. She and her brother had recently come in from school on a hot September in 1976 and were sitting down at the table laid for four. Daddy would be home soon, but they couldn't start until he was back. She traced a finger over the green and yellow checked tablecloth with frayed edges, itself underneath mismatched plates and cups that waited to be filled with strong tea. The faded yellow of bone handle cutlery reminded her of her grandmother's false teeth. Thick sliced bread and butter lay next to Robertson's strawberry jam. A large brown teapot poked out from under a stained tea cosy in the shape of a house.

Mother always laid the table early so she could sit and rest while she had another cigarette. She must have laid the table at breakfast that day. The butter was almost liquid, and the milk in a blue and white striped jug had curdled, giving off an unpleasant odour.

A gentle breeze fanned them through the open back door as they waited for their father. Her brother flapped at the swollen, lazy flies that buzzed around the food. Daddy came in through the same door, with much excitement, and threw his hat, jacket and suitcase on to an unoccupied rocking chair in the corner of the room. Kissing each of them, he said with pride he had made a big sale and that Christmas would be good that year. They helped themselves to warm pork pies and hard-boiled eggs, laughing at his promises of the biggest goose ever on the Christmas table.

Mother grunted at the news. It took a lot to make her happy and food was not one of the things to bring joy into her life, especially if she had to share it with her children.

With a cigarette gripped in the corner of her lips, her eyes squinting as smoke drifted into them, Mother poured the tea. Then milk plopped into each cup. Brother and sister shared a worried glance.

'Mum, I think the milk's off,' Carol said.

'Don't be silly,' her mother replied.

'But it makes me gip.'

'You ungrateful cow.'

Carol never could recall the blow; only afterwards sitting in the same place, crying and shaking. Her brother with big watery eyes looking from Carol to Mother and then back to Carol again. The echo of the slamming door as her mother left the room. Her school uniform covered in sour milk turned pink with the blood gushing from her head. The striped jug broken, some of the pieces in her lap.

Daddy had taken her to the surgery where a nurse took needle and thread to her. Only three stitches needed. She was pale from the loss of blood, but more concerned about ruining the tea-towel she was using to try and stop the bleeding. Mother never let Carol forget that the souvenir, which had been bought at Somerleyton Hall, was forever stained with blood and could only ever be used as a dusting and cleaning rag.

The scar stretched as she entered her teen years, and she was forced to learn clever eyebrow application tricks to hide the unsightly line.

The reflection in the looking glass stared back at her. The lips were thin like her mother's. Those lips that never kissed her goodnight, and from between which never a kind word was uttered. Ironically, she could not say a kind word about herself either. A doctor in town added some filler every nine months to plump them up. She always applied extra lip liner for added pout. Her own charm and natural exuberance ensured everyone around her always enjoyed themselves. She smiled at the idea, happy to make people happy.

At least she had her father's eyes. Those kind blue orbs with dark splashes of brown in the iris, had a smile all of their own. Several minutes of carefully gluing individual eyelash extensions in place enhanced and widened the bright eyes. Mascara too, and the eye-shadow — 'Drops of Jupiter' today, with pale liner on the rim of the lids. Finish with highlighter at the inner corner of each eye, for that eight hours of sleep look. She leaned in closer to the looking glass to get a better look and suppressed a shudder.

Primer, foundation, BB creams, CC creams, concealer, contouring, strobing, nothing helped. No amount of tinkering or light-reflecting-particles could hide what was underneath.

Her teenage spots thankfully came and went quickly leaving no unsightly pock marks. Her mother had always been quick to point out a new one, fault-finding a particular joy of hers. Consequently, Carol had always looked after her skin with a dedication bordering on the religious, and applied with ritualistic attention to detail the best oils and creams available. Smoking had only been a social thing and had never developed into a habit. Alcohol had not passed her lips since her thirtieth birthday. Now she was reaping the rewards of a life of dedicated skincare. Everyone always remarked on her clear and flawless complexion.

Friends would make comments, 'You look years younger, darling,' or 'No one would ever guess your real age.' Her husband would always say, 'You're the most beautiful woman ever. I do love you.'

They didn't understand. It wasn't the skin, but the face that upset her. Carol had always been a disappointment to her mother, nothing was ever good enough. All she wanted was to please her mother, to be loved by her. Was that too much to ask?

'All done,' her makeup artist said, popping a brush into the belt he wore. He claimed to have a brush for every crisis.

'Thank you, Donny. How do I look?'

'Smashing, perfect, divine.'

Donny was standing back admiring his handwork, smiling in that special way of his, with his head tilted to one side.

'Why so glum?' he asked.

'Nothing, just thinking about my mother.'

'She was a looker too, was she?'

'I have her face, so I owe her everything.'

Her co-presenter opened the dressing room door and leaned in, 'Ready, darling?'

'She's never been readier,' Donny said.

'No first night nerves, no cold feet or anything?' the co-presenter asked.

'No. Let's go and have a good time,' Carol said, thanking Donny with a sumptuous smile. She stopped at the door and reflected on the twin in the looking glass one more time. The child Carol now gone, and replaced by the popular personality known to the public as...

Donny switched the lights off.

Young Lion

(Published in Angels by Black Hare Press.)

This is what most beings don't understand. There is no good or evil.

Only right or wrong.

Some people kill. Doesn't mean they're evil. Happens all the time in the wild.

Chimpanzees will turn on each other. A young lion will defeat an old patriarch to claim the pride.

That is what I intend to do; take His crown and throne. He has made a mess of everything; Earth has never been in such turmoil and the less said about Heaven, the better.

I've right on my side.

I am the archangel Gabriel, and I will be your new God.

Corky's Return

(Published in Paradox by Clarendon House.)

After six weeks in clink, I found myself standing in my old shabby office, which still bore the marks of my last scuffle. The visitor's chair rested on its side. The Bakelite ashtray lay on the floor, its pile of contents spread far and wide. A fine layer of dust had settled over my desk and the rough array that had once been a tidy, well organised room. I lifted the receiver of the telephone – nothing, as I had expected. I was surprised the landlord hadn't turfed me out and found a new tenant. I'd been behind with the rent as it was, before the case that resulted in my arrest.

I reached into a desk drawer; the one that always housed a bottle of Bells whisky — nothing. Someone had taken my alcohol, and I was pleased. Some things a man can do without.

Time inside is difficult for an ex-copper; you'll always be the enemy. I had received my fair share of revenge beatings but managed to keep myself alive. The only time I came close to pegging it was when an old lag with no chance of seeing the outside world again planned on plunging a sharpened spoon into my back, while we shuffled along the dinner line, having mashed potato and grey slop ladled onto our trays. How do you sharpen a spoon in prison? On a lathe, of course. And his reward for my death — smokes. Why didn't he stab me? A big fella with a face like a well-used shovel reached forward and grabbed the old guy's wrist. A deep Irish voice said, 'No.' This drew my attention and I turned to see the big guy shake his head slowly until the old man dropped the spoon. I retrieved the homemade weapon and later disposed of it in a furnace.

The big fella's name was MacCarthy. He didn't talk much, had no friends and I hadn't passed more than two words with him until that point. So, I don't know why he saved me that day. But I smiled in recognition of the favour and he gave a slow nod of his head in return. From that day onward we ate our gruel together in companionable silence. Mac was released the day before I tasted freedom myself.

Forty-two days inside helped clean my system out. I still had a desire for booze, but I was feeling much healthier. I wondered how long that would last and closed the drawer with equal amounts of relief and despair.

In through the door walked a tall man with a large stomach, cleanly shaven and smelling of cologne, leaning on a silver-tipped cane.

'Hello, Mr Sackman. Come to turf me out?'

'The boys are downstairs waiting to throw your belongings on the street.' He clearly found the thought of touching anything distasteful and pushed debris aside with the tip of his cane as he progressed into my office. 'Then they will take payment for three months' rent, in kind or unkind ways.'

'Hang on, Mr Sackman. I can —'

'Be realistic, Corky. You've just come out of prison. If you didn't have a bad reputation before, you certainly have now. What are you going to do, rob a bank?'

'I can get the money. Give me a day or two. This is all I have. I sleep there.' I pointed at the sofa.

'That is against the rules.'

'Rules?'

'Yes, the rules. I give you business rates, not domestic. One should never break the rules, Corky.' He tapped his temple with a forefinger. 'Now to business,' he continued, while I looked around the room trying to figure out what I would be able to carry, providing my arms weren't broken. 'Do you want this job or not?'

'What?' I admit to not paying full attention.

'I have a job for you, Corky. Do you want to take it?'

I sat heavily in the chair. 'You want to hire me?'

'Yes. On a strictly confidential matter. If anyone finds out that I have hired you, my lads will remove digits. Do you understand?'

'Yes, Mr Sackman.'

'Good.' He turned to leave.

'I just have a couple of questions.'

'Why?'

'I need a few basic facts before I start.'

'Come to my home tonight at seven thirty.' He looked me up and down. 'And make an effort. You look like a chap who's just come out of prison.'

'Mr Sackman.' He stopped at the door.

'What?' Impatience forced him to turn slowly.

'We haven't discussed my fee.'

'I thought you were smart. Your back rent of course.'

Now this was a turn up for the books. Mr Sackman showing a bit of leniency towards rent arrears and in need of my help.

After the war, Sackman had bought fall-down buildings at knock-down prices for sky-high rents. Sky-high might be exaggerating the point a bit, but he was a wealthy property owner who didn't normally let rent slip. Roofs leaked; heating consisted of whatever tenants could warm themselves with; damp ran down walls and late payment was dealt with harshly. But I'll say this for him; he didn't discriminate – Irish, black or Jew; if you had the money, you could rent his hovels. But if you couldn't pay, you were evicted with an equally callous cold heart.

For the small business owner who rented his offices and retail units, he allowed a certain amount of flexibility knowing that businesses had their good days and bad, which explained why I had managed to get into arrears without being kicked out before my incarceration. I was surprised that he had let my situation slip so far. It must have been a big personal problem for him to allow his business reputation to take a hit.

I would need a new set of togs, but with no money I had no means to acquire any. So, in the hope of a borrow I walked over to my good friend, one-time partner and as it happened betrayer and saviour, Ian Spencer. By coincidence, he rented a one-room hole from Sackman, in a glorious terrace that had seen better days. The frontage still held a trace of grandeur, but once inside it didn't take Einstein to see the state of disrepair the building had fallen into. It hadn't received a coat of paint in many years and a crack I could put my hand into ran floor to ceiling up the stairwell. The stairs had long ago lost their carpet and on one flight someone had ripped out the banister, presumably for firewood.

I rapped at Spence's door and a few seconds later heard the bolts being drawn back. A woman's eye peeked through the gap.

'Tell Mr Sackman, I'll have his rent tomorrow no problem. I'm workin' tonight.'

'I'm not from Mr Sackman. I'm looking for Spence. Ian Spencer.'

'Don't know 'im, love.' She closed the door forcing me to rap again, a little louder. She hissed through the gap, 'I told ya. I don't know your friend. Now, piss off before you wake the baby.'

'He used to live here. Do you know where he moved to?'

'I don't know nothin'. I only moved in last week.'

The wail of a young baby came from inside.

'Now look at what you done.'

The trudge back to my office was made more miserable as rain began to fall. A slow persistent drizzle that insinuated its way under the layers of my clothes and deep into my bones. I considered calling on my ex-wife for help. There was a chance she might still have some of my clothes. But I knew she would only pester me for money even though she knew where I'd been.

I could hardly blame her — no one had money these days.

As I stepped back into my office, I couldn't help noticing the giant asleep on my sofa, one arm held over his eyes to block out the light.

'That you, Mac, or should I be worried?'

The mountain moved and a deep Irish voice said, 'Where've ya been?'

'Looking for friends.'

'Found one, ain't ya.'

'What are you doing here?' I moved behind my desk to sit in the creaking chair.

'Got anything to drink, Corky?'

'I'm trying to stop.'

'Well, I ain't.'

'I don't mean to be rude, Mac. But what do you want?'

'You're a Private Investigator, ain't ya?'

'I won't quibble the point with you.'

'Will ya help me find someone?'

'Listen, Mac. I got out today only to be offered a job I couldn't refuse from my bent landlord. If I don't turn up at his house tonight looking half respectable to find the details of the job, not only will I not have an office to work out of, but I'll be homeless and probably fingerless too. And I know I owe you, but today is not the best of days.'

'Her name's Rosie. She was expecting my baby.'

'Haven't you been listening? I'm in the clarts here.' I held my head in my hands.

'I can pay.' Of course, this made me look up.

'I'll need an advance.'

He handed over enough for a meal and new suit.

'Come with me, Mac. We can talk while we eat.'

There are plenty of places to eat on Brighton seafront, many servicing the fisherman who came ashore at odd hours, their lives dictated by the tide. The café we stopped in did us bacon butties with white sliced — Mac had two — and mugs of tea.

Mac talked more than I'd ever known him to. He'd been a commando in the war – one of Churchill's super soldiers — and had even been decorated for bravery. He hadn't adjusted well to civilian life and had tried many jobs before being arrested. The police said he was suspected of thieving, but he said they didn't like his accent. He overreacted putting one in hospital and they put him inside for six months. His wife was left alone with a little bump that would soon be a baby, and no way to support herself.

Life is full of coincidences if you know where to look. He showed me a photo of his wife and stone me if she didn't look like the one eye that was staring at me from Spence's old gaff this morning. But for the moment, I kept quiet. He came with me to a tailor who sold good quality suits more or less off the peg. An hour later, in a grey marle check and grey pork-pie hat I was feeling once more like the man I used to be several years earlier. And Mac followed me around like a puppy dog. He had quietened down a little, but he wanted to know when I would start looking.

'I think I've already found her,' I said watching his face break into a wide grin, making him somehow uglier and childlike at the same time.

Together, we climbed the stairs and Mac asked how people could live like this. I was hardly one to comment, so offered no reply. I knocked on the door. The bolts unbolted and the eye looked out again and then it flicked up to Mac. She panicked and tried to slam the door, but Mac's big hand had reached over my head and pushed the door and the girl back. The chain snapped.

'It's me, Rosie. They let me out for good behaviour. I didn't know where you were.'

Rosie pulled the robe tighter around her small body and backed away from him. I'd made a mistake. In my haste to save my skin, I hadn't ascertained the full facts. I'd believed the gentle giant and now found myself trying to restrain him. But Mac was intent on a reconciliation, whether she wanted it or not.

When he saw the baby in the least damp corner of the room, he changed direction. Then Rosie was trying to stop him from approaching the infant. The baby was swamped by the big hands, but they were surprisingly gentle as he cradled the little innocent to his chest.

'Don't hurt her, please,' Rosie begged.

'Why would I hurt her?'

Then Rosie was shouting at me, wanting to know why I would do this to her. A neighbour responded to her cries and rushed in wielding a broom. Rosie was telling the neighbour to call the police. But Mac, besotted with the tiny baby, was oblivious to the commotion going on around him.

'Come on, Mac. The police won't be pleased, neither will our probation officers. Let's not risk it all, eh buddy. We'll talk when Rosie is ready.' I tugged at his arm and he passed the baby to the mother. 'Thank you,' he said, before allowing me to guide him away.

The authorities hadn't arrived by the time we were on the street.

'I have to go now, Mac, to see my landlord about this job of his. Remember?'

'Yeah. I'll come too.'

I could hardly say no, could I? What if he went back to see Rosie again? I didn't think he'd hurt her or the child, but I couldn't be absolutely sure, plus if the rozzers did turn up, he'd be back inside faster than you can say 'He did it, officer.'

In the taxi I asked where he got the money from. Cons usually didn't have much in reserve when they come out.

'Had some put away in a safe place.'

'Where'd you get it?'

'Navi-work. Minding. Post office job.'

'Christ, Mac, you can't tell me that. I used to be a copper.'

'But you're an ex-con now. Do you still have a licence?'

'You don't need a licence. Just… know-how.'

'I didn't know that.'

'Still, you shouldn't divulge that sort of information to me.'

He shrugged his giant shoulders.

*

Sackman's house was in the suburbs and sported a large garden behind a tall wall. Several cars were parked around a turning circle. Another drove in, narrowly missing us as we walked up the drive. Fortunately the rain had stopped. Drivers sat in their cabins or shared smokes huddled in the shadows. I told Mac to hold back for a bit while I approached two smokers.

'Got a light?' I asked.

One held his cigarette for me to light my own with.

'Cheers,' I said. 'What's the do for?'

'What's it to you?' the other challenged.

So I told him the truth, or most of it. 'We've been invited and I can't figure out why they'd want the likes of us here. That's all.'

They flicked looks over at Mac.

'Some big-knob's birthday party, init. P'raps they want you to serve drinks.' The two men chuckled, and I chuckled right along with them.

A butler showed us to Sackman's office in a room off to the left of the hallway. A girl in a pink satin cocktail dress and smelling of Chanel No. 5 walked up the curved flight of stairs, holding the arm of a man.

'Who's this?' Sackman said, once the door was closed. Two bruisers stepped forward, but I could see reluctance in their eyes.

'Mac is my associate, Mr Sackman. He is very good at keeping quiet. Isn't that right, Mac?'

Mac nodded.

Sackman glared at me. Everyone was quiet for a little longer than necessary, while they waited for him to decide what to do. I broke the silence. 'I came here to discuss work. So, are we talking or just eyeing each other up?'

'I see you are more like your old self, Inspector. Feeling cocky are you, Corky?'

'Amazing what a decent meal and new suit can do for a man. Now what do you want me to do?'

He stood up and smiled a smile that didn't reach his eyes.

'Come out to the party, Corky. Stay here, lads.'

He took us across the wide entrance hall into a small, but still sizeable ballroom. A quartet played slow, low-key jazz at one end. Ladies wearing chiffon, satin and silk ballgowns of pale pink, sherbet lemon and powder blue sat or danced with men in tuxedos. Smoke filled the room in swirls of grey and silver. The lighting was low level, but I could see enough. A girl with a faint white smudge under her nose, and another whose hair wasn't as clean as it should have been. The older women were wives and wore jewellery that caught the candlelight in the way that only diamonds can. The younger girls wore marcasite. I wasn't up to speed with local politics having 'been away', but I knew the type of men who smoked fat cigars and thought that money could buy anything. I did recognise a footballer with the chairman of the local team.

As we wove between the guests with Sackman nodding and greeting them with laughs and kisses, he said, 'I have a delicate situation I would like your help with.'

I stubbed my cigarette out in a glass ashtray on a table we were passing. 'How?'

'There is a person of interest who I would like you to have a chat with.' We were moving to the back of the room, away from the band. Sackman plucked a glass of champagne from the tray carried by a waiter.

'Why?' I lit another smoke and passed the pack to Mac who helped himself.

'He refuses my generous gifts or even to be civil with me if our paths cross. He didn't reply to my invitation to this soirée.'

'You want to bring him into your circle of friends. Well, you can't make someone be friends with you. Perhaps you're not the most popular girl in school anymore.'

We sat at an empty table. Mac remained standing.

'Look at the people here, Corky. The creme de la crème of the local elite —'

'And their bored wives, and girls on the game, businessmen, councillors and villains, not that there's much difference.'

'You're pushing your luck, Corky. Listen to my offer or you'll be homeless before you leave this building.'

Pressing his buttons would do me few favours, so I wound it down a tad.

'Okay. Why me? You have plenty of people on the payroll who are far more persuasive than me. People willing to bend the rules and break bones to make a point.'

'The new Chief Constable needs to be treated with kid gloves by one of his own.'

'And you think that's me?'

A woman came to join us. The violet silk of her ballgown crinkled as she sat next to Sackman. I could smell the spray that held every hair rigidly in place. Her glassy eyes barely noticed me. One of her white gloves had worked its way down her arm revealing old needle marks. He whispered in her ear and she giggled.

Sackman looked up at Mac and said, 'In the meantime, perhaps this gentleman will take you for a set around the floor.'

She stood and held out her hand. Mac looked at me. I indicated with a nod of my head that I'd be fine.

'Help me out here,' Sackman continued, 'and I can send business your way. Good business working for me and I'll have plenty of work for your friend too. This sort of gathering could be a regular thing for you.'

'This isn't really my scene, Mr Sackman.' I watched as Mac glided around the floor with the girl. He was surprisingly light on his feet.

'Simon Byron is a man who persists in hounding my business interests. It's coming to something when a man can't run a legitimate business that employs local tradesmen and provides housing to the needy without being victimised by the authorities. I pay my taxes, Corky. There is nothing villainous about my operation.'

'Only this morning you implied that I would be beaten-up by your henchmen if I did not come to this meeting. That in itself is a crime. And if I'm any good at the job I used to do, I'd say you have plenty to hide.'

'So says the murderer.'

'Not guilty and I'm the reason you're dealing with a new chief constable and not your old pal, Austin.' I stubbed the cigarette out and immediately pulled another from the pack.

'You've made things very difficult for me, Corky. Now I'm giving you the opportunity to make things right. Whatever the outcome, I'll wipe the slate clean as far as your arrears goes.' This was too good to be true.

'You overestimate my negotiation skills, Mr Sackman. He won't listen to me. I'm a disgraced ex-copper and ex-con to boot. I'll clear my office tonight and get the money I owe you within the week.'

'Speak to him and the debt is clear. Do we have a deal?' He stood and held out his hand as Mac returned to the table.

'Okay.' I also got to my feet and took the hand, feeling like I'd just signed my life over to the devil himself.

As we walked back down the drive Mac said to me, 'You know it's a trap, don't you?'

'The thing is, if I don't go, I'll be out on the street. I don't have a choice.'

He didn't say anything. So I did. 'Why was your wife scared of you?'

'We had a little misunderstanding before I was put away. I was spending too much time working.' His words were slow, considered.

'Post Office jobs?'

'Minding mainly.' He smiled at me when he said it. 'But I was trying to look after her, like a good husband should. I came home early one night and found her with another fella. I lost me temper and bounced him off the walls a few times, but he was able to walk away. So, no real harm done.'

'Did you hurt her?' I passed him a smoke and then the lighter after I'd lit my own.

'No. Me mam taught me right. But I could've killed him — it's not so difficult to kill a man.' He passed my lighter back.

'Tell you what, Mac. I'll visit her tomorrow and see if I can put a good word in for you.'

'You'd do that?'

'Why not? I might be able to do something good before tomorrow night.'

Mac's big ugly face broke into a childish grin.

*

I'd bought a new door-chain from the iron mongers and held it, along with a screwdriver, up to the slit in the door – my intention clearly to make right something that was broken.

It was strange being in Spence's old room. The same bed, same table and same oven all doing the same thing. After I'd fitted the new chain, I sat at the table, my fingers automatically picking at the old familiar chips in the Formica. She made me a mug of tea with water boiled in Spence's old kettle.

I told her that Mac was sorry for the upset of the night before, that all he wanted was to speak to her and to try to be a good father. I asked if he'd ever hurt her and she said no. I asked if he'd ever had a right to be angry and she said yes. I asked if he looked angry last night and she said he'd broken the chain. But I argued that rather than angry, he was over-excited, and she concurred with a nod of her head. I suggested that we could all meet in a public place if she wanted. Rosie smiled and nodded her head again.

Then I had to ask some difficult questions. Was she seeing another bloke? What business was it of mine? Be better if Mac knew the full s.p. There was no one special. My next question is the hardest one to ask, but it's an obvious one when you know what to look for.

'You turning tricks, Rosie?' She slapped my face, and then let tears fall.

'Well, I don't suppose he needs to know about that right now, does he?' I said. 'Go and put your face on. See you in the park in half an hour?'

Again, she nodded her head.

*

'Thanks for your help, Corky,' Mac said as he laid a white fiver on my desk.

'You don't have to do that. I was repaying a favour.'

'You still going to see the Chief Constable tonight?'

'I have to try.'

'I'll come with ya.'

'No, go home to your wife. Stay out of trouble. Make sure you're around for the little girl. Keep up with the rent. Sackman is a bastard of the first order.'

'Thanks, Corky.' He ducked his head under the architrave as he left my office. I folded the note and slipped it into my wallet.

*

Sackman had given me the address of the Chief Constable, Simon Byron. Much land, including a small wood, surrounded a Tudor Manor House. As the sun was setting, I strolled up the lane leading to the front door. I thought I might try to appeal to his better nature, introduce myself as the man responsible for exposing his corrupt predecessor. See if he would have any objection to me operating as a Private Enquiry agent. And not even mention Sackman. After all, if the new C.C. was a decent sort, he wouldn't ever likely find himself in a situation where he would associate with Sackman, would he?

I gave my card to the man who opened the door and was shown into a comfortable study with French doors looking over the grounds to the woods.

A few seconds later, a tall handsome man strode into the room. 'Mr McCorkingdale,' he said, studying my card at arm's length. So... he was a little too vain to wear glasses. He came forward to shake my hand and offered me a drink. The temptation was great; I suspected a truly delicious malt would be poured from the crystal decanter, but I refused. Then he sat behind his leather inlaid desk in a leather captain's chair.

'Take a seat. What can I do for you?' I was more nervous than I'd been in a long time.

'It's a delicate matter, Sir.' Old habits die hard — he was a senior officer. 'I am not currently an active Private Detective, although I was not long ago, and a pretty good copper before that.'

'I know who you are, McCorkingdale. And I know what you helped achieve. But a suspect still got away.'

'An innocent suspect, Sir. But the situation was complex, and I was not... myself. Being inside was a blessing in disguise, Sir. I'm more, I don't know... more settled, I suppose.'

'They say criminals can be rehabilitated, but I have my doubts.'

'I'm not a criminal, Sir.'

'I apologise. What did you want, Mr McCorkingdale?'

'I wanted to know if you have any objections to my continuing to operate my business.'

'None at all, providing you don't interfere with police investigations or fraternise with known villains, and continue to meet your parole officer.' I didn't point out that sometimes getting to know villains was part of the job. But mentioning Sackman would not help. My instinct told me this man was as straight as they come.

'Thank you for your time, Sir.' I stood, offering my hand.

At that moment the French doors burst open and someone stepped in with a pistol pointed at the C.C. I vaulted over the desk to put myself between the shooter and the C.C., my intention being to push him out of the way. A gunshot rang out, I heard glass breaking, and few seconds later, Mac was lifting me off the C.C. Blood soaked the Chief's shoulder.

'Are you okay, Sir?' I asked. Sackman's plan was now clear. Clear as crystal. He wanted Byron dead and me dangling at the end of a rope for it. Two birds, one stone.

'I think so, but you're the one who's bleeding,' Chief Constable Byron said. Then the pain hit me. The butler rushed in as the C.C. picked up the telephone. And all I could think was, *a drink would do the trick right now.* No one offered me one. I was glad.

Mac left me sitting against the wall while blood seeped between the fingers of my left hand that was holding my right shoulder. He delivered a punch, which would knock a cow out, to the shooter who was struggling to his feet.

The C.C. slammed the phone down having demanded uniform and C.I.D. arrive within minutes or heads would roll. He collected the gun, which lay on the floor where it had fallen and then turned to look at me with a questioning eye.

'Mac's a friend of mine.' Looking up at his big face, I noticed it was smeared with mud. 'We sort of look after each other. He got a medal from Churchill.'

'Do either of you know this chap?' The C.C. indicated the semi-comatose body on the floor.

'I have a story to tell, Sir, but I swear on my little girl's life I don't know who he is or that he'd be here. But I know who sent him.'

While the ambulance men patched me up — it was only a flesh wound they said, but it bloody well hurt — I told the Chief everything that had occurred between Sackman and myself since he walked into my office the day before. A sergeant took notes. We went over everything several times, including my suspicions of the guests at Sackman's so-called soirée, making sure he had my story in full.

'Are you prepared to give evidence?' he asked before looking at my friend. 'And you, Mr Mac?'

'Mac doesn't know all the details. But I do. After this botched job, I'll likely be homeless. Might as well try and bring the bastard down with me.'

Jane

(Published in Unravel by Black Hare Press.)

1958 — The first murder case I was in charge of was the brutal knifing of a prostitute in an underpass. I've seen many corpses, but no one deserved to die the way she did.

Her name was Jane. She left a teenage daughter behind.

There were no fingerprints and the murder weapon was not in the immediate vicinity, but from the spray of blood, the angle and height of blade entry, her killer must've been a woman. Old-fashioned police work did the rest.

I rested my hand on the streetwalker's shoulder.

'You're nicked,' I said.

And Jane's daughter turned around.

Morty Falls in Love

(From an unfinished short story collection following the adventures of Morty and George in pre-war England.)

It was a Saturday morning when Morty had been introduced to his first love. Cyril 'Blakey' Blakenston-Smyth had arrived all of a funk with a black-eyed temptress, going by the innocent sounding name of Sally, in tow. Not that Morty noticed the colour of her eyes as he stared open-mouthed at the tale that was laid before him by his friend.

And nor was it the tale of need that caused the jaw to slacken and the tongue to loll. No, it was the rather late night that he had enjoyed in the company of Fatty Buckingham at not two, but three night clubs, ending with a night-cap at Fatty's cousin's place on Downing Street.

Blakey was oblivious to the dishevelled, crumpled clothing of the night before and the hair, usually neat, that was now a nest to twigs and things of the hedgerow. He failed to look into the red eyes that refused to focus, with any real conviction, on either him or the guest.

No, he was too busy pushing the last piece of toast into his mouth after first pushing into the hallway and calling at the top of his voice, 'Morty. You owe me a favour and I'm calling it in.'

He refused to listen to the dulcet tones of the butler, 'Mr Marsh h'is h'indisposed at the minute, sir.'

'Well, unindispose the blighter.'

'Very good, Mr Blakenston-Smith, sir.'

By the time Morty stumbled into the breakfast room, Blakey had finished the last of the eggs and bacon. Morty failed to see the cocker spaniel under the table enjoying the last sausage.

'What the devil are you doing here, Blakey? Do you realise what time it is?'

'Yes I do, and I have to be on the 10:04 to Dover in half an hour.' He licked his fingers. 'You see, my aunt has tasked me with caring for the Baskerville type you see before you, and she wouldn't listen to me when I said I had business in the South of France.'

'Baskerville Business. S of F.'

'Yes. Now do be quiet. You're holding me up with all this chitter-chatter.'

'Sorry.'

'Quite. I need to be away, post-haste and without delay. That is to say, without unnecessary or redundant speech on your part. You need to be a good fellow and look after my aunt's favourite non-human. Goes by the name of Sally. Three walks a day. Eats the usual sort of stuff.'

'Why do I need to know your aunt's daily habits?'

'Not my aunt, you fat-head. The pooch, the spaniel, the hound. Oh for goodness' sake, don't look at me that way. A dog, Sally is my aunt's dog. She's foisted the animal on me, but I'm off to the Riviera today. I tried calling last night. But you were nowhere to be found. Now look, I need you to look after Sally. It's only for a week or three. I'm sure you'll get on like a house on what's-it.'

'Sally. Dog. Three walks a day. Eats food.'

'That's the ticket. Tootle-pip.' He tapped the cheeks of Morty's face with the palms of his hands and made promptly for the front door. Thirty seconds later, he was in a cab whizzing his way to Victoria Station.

Now Morty was no stranger to dog handling. His late cousin had often roped him into a spot of dog walking when he had been younger. But it had been a beast of a thing. An Aberdeen Terrier given the moniker, Hamish, with short legs that worked harder than Hercules to propel the little thing along at the slowest pace possible for any creature with four legs to move. Its stomach touched the ground. And it had a growl that said, 'I'm watching you, sonny.' Hamish was the most ill-tempered dog on the planet, with a stubborn streak that meant he would only return from his walk when he was good and ready. In short, the animal had put Morty off the idea of dog ownership as a pursuit of enjoyment from an early age and he had vowed that he would never have a single one under his roof; if he ever had a roof he could call his own.

However, once Sally the cocker spaniel was left alone with the male, who stank of cigarettes and unwashed clothes, she immediately went to his feet, assumed a comfortable position and laid her chin upon his scuffed brogues.

Morty's red eyes became a little redder.

Five minutes later he moved his feet and reluctantly dislodged her from her slumber. Sally looked up at Morty with a tilt of her head that asked a question.

'Come on,' he said, and she hopped to her feet and followed him into the hall and trotted up the stairs beside him to his room. He really needed more sleep, but Morty had a responsibility now and knowing Blakey to be the selfish so-and-so that he was, reckoned that the dog had not yet had its morning constitutional. So, he threw his soiled clothes onto the bed, splashed water over his fizzog and then put razor and comb to work. Fifteen minutes later, dressed in something half respectable, he trotted out the door with his new charge.

Green Park had never looked lovelier. The scent of blossom filled the nostrils and his new companion observed every lamppost and creature it passed.

Morty chose a bench and using it for its designated purpose, watched the dog scamper from tree to dog-walker to dog and back to tree again. Why did dogs greet each other that way?

Sally, after all available points of interest had been investigated, returned to Morty and once more rested her jaw upon his shoes. Pride filled a part of him that he had not known was empty.

As the weeks passed, Morty grew to know the subtlest of meaning from the twitching of her eyebrows (the human speaks) to the tilting of her head (the human speaks). Sally had many subtle ways to communicate her needs. For instance, when she was ready to go outside, she would casually saunter away only to be found a few minutes later sitting and staring at one of the doors that led to the garden.

Her short tail wagged continuously, even when lying down and often in her sleep. Her eagerness to get through the door whenever he approached it from either side gladdened his breast. She followed him from room to room; sat next to him at the breakfast table; accompanied him to the TT club for his lunch; sneered at Stinker when he suggested a nefarious wheeze that Morty might be interested in helping out with, and generally did not leave his sight. She even insisted on sleeping with her jaw resting on his chest.

*

A month after dropping Sally off with Morty, Blakey sailed in from the Riviera to claim the hound and return her to her rightful home many miles away.

Once again, Morty's eyes became red as he recalled the weight of her body next to him at night, the sound of her snoring and the way her ears lifted when he said her name.

They Meet Again

(One of my few attempts at poetry. You may notice that it is 100 words long, so it counts as a drabble too.)

She will celebrate another hundred years,
Wearing an old suit and making home-brew beers.
On her thin lips, Elizabeth Arden red,
Old friends will arrive soon, if they're not dead,
Carrying magical elements for boiling, on an electric ring,
Care home staff would disapprove, if they knew anything.
You must not fear.
The time is near.
Ritual dancing and chanting, soon will commence,
Youth will be theirs again, so take no offence.
Toil and Trouble come tapping at her door.
'Come,' she says, cross-legged, an inch off the floor.
They enter, ball gowns swishing,
'All hail, Hecate. Queen of Witching.'

The Old Ways

(The Mystery of Deben Market.)

March 16, 2069

What a remarkably disturbing world we live in, thought Lt Col George Davis, the oldest member of the Davis clan, as the gift materialised in the transpad receiver.

'I remember when you had to wait for an item to arrive through the post,' he said, 'sometimes as long as a week. And then, when the internet really got going, companies like Amazon actually delivered what you ordered the next day, maybe the same day. Now *that* was progress.'

'Really, Grandad? You had to wait? How boring,' said Missy, the youngest Davis.

George wondered just how things might change and what sort of world Missy would grow up to be a part of. At seventy-five, he was astounded on a daily basis by the technology available to the everyday person. Missy would never be lonely in the house with Nandy the nandroid. Her parents had robotic help for most domestic chores — cleaning and maintenance. Even he'd had his life enriched by digital surgery that had removed a tumour in his brain, fifteen years earlier. And his life expectancy, like most people, was to be a centenarian.

'Yes, sweetness, but that was part of the fun you see. The waiting and the anticipation. It was something to look forward to.'

'Boring, boring, boring, isn't it, Nandy? Tell Grandad how boring it all is,' she said, looking to her ever-present companion.

The robot, a fifth-generation, top-of-the-line nandroid of sexless determination, nodded its head in compliance and said, 'Only to you and I, Missy. Your grandfather was not perturbed by such time delays. Do you understand?'

'No, it's boring.' She was going into one of her tantrums.

Knowing that he was powerless to intervene with what was about to happen, a deep feeling of impotence tugged at his insides.

'The attitude you are displaying is discourteous to the older generation, Missy. Please alter it,' said the nandroid.

'Shan't, and I want my toy now. Get my toy, Grandad,' Missy demanded, crossing her arms over her chest and snapping her lips tight with a sucking sound. Her eyebrows knitted tightly together and deep lines furrowed her brow.

'You leave me no option, Missy, than to induce a sleep period,' said the nandroid.

'Can't make me,' said Missy, but her head had begun to fall forward. She curled into a ball and lay on the grav-sofa next to her grandfather. The nandroid also seemed to be resting, its sensors dimmed.

George contemplated the ethics of having the child's mind partnered with an android. Was it really necessary? People had been getting along fine for thousands of years. Did we, as a race, really need to be tethered to a machine to teach compliance and manners? *Robots. We'll all be robots in the end.*

He stretched his legs in front of him, felt where the stump had once been and thanked the Lord for advances in prosthetic technology that had gifted him a leg much better than the original. Long after he was gone, thousands of years from now, the leg would still be good as new and fit for action. It might be a family heirloom. He smiled at the absurd image of the leg being kept in the corner of a room.

With a simple tap on the control pad, he returned the package he had ordered for the child. It dissolved from the transpad receiver, followed shortly by a bleep and visual confirmation that credits had been returned to his bank balance. His daughter would have completed these actions with thought waves, but he had decided against the implant. Besides, he was too old to start learning new things. He was happy with the old ways of doing things.

Is there really a need for the android to be so closely linked with her? he asked himself again. *It's too creepy.*

Missy, sleeping on the grav-sofa, twitched. Silence reigned.

'Dad? Wake up, Dad.'

With bleary eyes, he looked up into the pouting lips and round face of his long dead wife, Chrissie. Then he saw the short blonde hair, and the vision melted away to be replaced by his daughter.

'Marion, what time is it?' He sat up, wiped at a thin line of drool on the stubble of his chin.

'Just after five.'

'Blimey, I should get the meal on,' he said.

'Don't worry, I'll just order a takeout.'

'No, I'm on cook-house tonight. CAIG, done like it used to be in the old days.'

Forcing himself to wake up, he wobbled to the kitchen, found his favourite pan and a cook's knife then ordered some diced synth-meat and vegetables, which materialised on the kitchen transpad.

'Why is Missy sleeping?' she asked.

'Don't ask me. The nandroid sent her off to the land of nod because she was playing up.'

'And why was that?' Marion asked from the other side of the kitchen counter.

'She just started, and the damn machine went into sleep mode before I could calm her. Do you want to help? These carrots need washing.'

'The carrots arrive clean, everything does. I've told you before. You shouldn't have upset her.'

'What makes you think I was to blame? If you didn't have the nandroid, she'd still be awake, and her tantrum would have passed by now.'

'You're such an oldster, Dad. Everyone has a nandroid for their kids. It's proven that children who've been brought up with one are less aggressive than they were a generation ago. A hundred years from now, crime will be almost completely eradicated.'

'Oldster.' He hated that word. It implied the elderly were past it and without purpose. It suggested outmoded thoughts and undermined a whole lifetime of experience.

'And no one will be able to act or think for themselves,' he said. 'They'll buy what they're told to buy and think what they're told to think. Creativity will be non-existent, and the corporate monsters that sold you this dream will be running the world. No one will wash their carrots, and one day they'll die because the carrots arrived dirty, but they didn't question why it was gritty and what would happen if they ate the dirt. Bacterial food poisoning, that's what, and their weakened immune systems won't be able to cope half as well as they might have a hundred years earlier.'

'You're a paranoid old dinosaur.'

'Just wash the carrots.' Pausing to calm himself, he added, 'Please.'

'What's CAIG?' asked Missy, who had woken but remained quiet to hear the grown-up talk. She picked up on an unfamiliar word and by asking had broken the uncomfortable atmosphere.

'Cats Arse In Gravy, sweetheart,' George said.

'Dad, please.'

Missy giggled at the rude word, but then her face started to crinkle. She inhaled a big gulp of air as her bottom lip started to tremble, and her eyes grew large as water threatened to spill down her cheeks.

'Now look what you've started. It's not cat. Grandad's joking, darling, aren't you, Grandad?'

'Yes, I'm joking. We're having synth-stew, no cats or any other animal will be harmed in the making of this meal,' he said with a deep note of regret present in the timbre of his voice.

'Go and play with Nandy,' said Marion, thankful that a full-blown Missy meltdown had been avoided.

The nandroid hovered nearby and displayed complex holographic puzzles in the air for Missy to reassemble. Soon, she was engrossed in her favourite pastime.

George browned the synth-meat and proceeded to dice the washed vegetables.

'Red wine,' he said to the transpad, and a glass of the deep red liquid shimmered into existence. He added this to the meat and vegetables, already sweating in their own juices.

'Another,' he said.

'It is requested that George Davis moderates his consumption of alcoholic beverages,' said the feminine voice from the machine. He looked from the machine to Marion with a raised eyebrow, waiting for an explanation.

'Barclay adjusted the settings,' she said, colour rising in her cheeks all the way to her hairline.

'You think I'm an alcoholic? Jesus Christ strode about naked!'

'It's just —'

'Bollocks to "it's just". You asked me to live with you — remember? "Be nice for Missy," you said. Only you don't want me to be me. Don't upset Missy, don't drink —'

'It's not like that, Dad.'

'Yes, it is.' He took an extra breath, forcing himself to calm down. 'Please ask the machine to furnish me with a glass of red, Shiraz would be best. It's for me to drink while I cook the meal, if that's okay?'

'Yes, Dad. Sorry, Dad.'

'It's fine,' he said, after she passed him the glass. 'Go and play with your child or whatever it is your generation do.'

'Sorry, Dad,' she said again.

'Don't worry, I am an old fool. Let me cook this in peace or the special ingredient will be lost.'

'What's that?'

'Love.' He smiled at her. She raised the sides of her lips in hesitant response.

Mealtime had been difficult. He and Marion had always had their ups and downs. Any disagreements they'd had in the past had always blown over, as this one would. But Barclay was a supercilious buffoon in George's eyes, and his son-in-law's comments about midweek drinking only confirmed his decision.

'Is it a special occasion?'

'Why is there wine on the table?'

'None for me, I care about my mind and body. Really, George, another glass?'

'No, Marion, one glass is one too many.'

Tosser, thought George, but kept his opinion to himself. With his bad mood worsening, and Marion's attempts to lighten the atmosphere countered by Barclay's undermining attitude, the meal was a disaster. And not a word of thanks for a traditional home-cooked meal from anyone — *ingrates*. The only bright point of the evening being Missy's joy at informing her father they were eating cat's arse.

Shortly after turning in for the night, George found himself staring at the reflection in the mirror of his en suite. Grey thin hair, watery grey eyes and grey stubbled jowls looked back at him. When he'd been a schoolboy those cheeks had been pink, plump and acne ridden. His early memories of shaving were mix of delight and torture. His eyes had been bluer and his hair unnaturally blonde. The First Asian War soon aged him. His hair had been streaked grey by the time he was thirty. The stress of war had shown itself in other ways too, but the love of a good woman and a young child put the shakes at bay and the nightmares to rest.

By the time of the Second Asian War in '45 he had risen to a level that required less front line action, but he still found it hard to cope with the figures of the dead, and his part in the passing of so many young men and women. He'd written thousands of letters. Even when there were no bodies to repatriate.

The inferno of Guangzhau had one been one of the most horrific acts of war ever. Nuclear warheads had never been launched. That would have been seen a step too far. But it is possible to drop so much incendiary that typhoons of fire rage through a city. The fire's insatiable need for oxygen scoops everything into its swirling centre; buildings, animals and people, spitting out molten ash that would land miles away starting new fires that were as hellish. People: civilians, soldiers, the enemy, his men would spontaneously combust. Some people tried to protect themselves by jumping into the Pearl River. But water boils. And the allies did this knowing that hundreds of their own troops were in proximity. It shamed him to be a part of the winning side. Twenty million people died one weekend of living Hell. No wonder he needed a drink or two.

George lathered his craggy face with an ancient badger brush and then put an even older safety razor to work over the flesh of his face. The trend for men now was to have permanent hair removal, allowing the individual to choose which hair follicles remained. Hair only grew where a person wanted it to grow. And if they got tired of it, then a handheld micro transpad did the old job of a razor. It was considered safer and to have less of an impact on the environment. However, George failed to see how running a matter transference device over your skin was any safer than a razor blade. The worse thing that might happen with a blade is a cut or nick, but if one of those modern things malfunctioned, you'd find have your face in orbit. And anyway, it was called a safety razor for a reason, wasn't it?

He had a lifetime of possessions, but an old soldier was more than capable of travelling light. Moving on would be easy. All he needed was access to his bank and credits. A reliable watch, an old Smiths of his grandfathers, kept in pristine condition. It didn't have trackers or life enhancing AI, but simply told the time in a reliable automatic fashion. In the pocket of his old trench coat, he packed his shaving kit and a cleansing bar, and an old flash drive with every photo he had ever taken of his wife, daughter and grandchild.

He left a note written on a digi-screen, on a cabinet door in the kitchen.

We all need a bit of space
Be in touch soon
Dad

March 17, 2069

The great thing about old clubs like The In & Out, is their rigid adherence to tradition. They employ real people to wait on table and serve at the bar. The drinks are prepared in the traditional ways. Scotch was from Scotland. The staff were well paid, and the doorman always remembered the names of members. The carpet may have been worn in places, but it was seventy years old. Nothing under the roof had changed in sixty years. The bedrooms had old smart TV's, which had long been left behind in terms of connectivity. An old soldier would have to rely on the blue-ray player and old discs.

They sat in high wing-back leather chairs in front of an open fire, but it had been many years since actual wood or coal had been burned in it.

'You still in, Charlie?'

'Retired from active duty four years ago, George. They put me behind a desk. Six months later…well, it wasn't for me.' Major Charlotte Hood shrugged her shoulders by way of explanation.

'What? You were fit as a fiddle last time I saw you. Still are, if you ask me.'

'The army's changing, George, everything is. It started when they put androids on the front line with humans. They performed so well that just recently, it was decided human troops weren't needed. Androids are inexpensive, and no one mourns an android, do they? In five years, the army and navy or the other lot won't be a career option.'

'But —'

'Way it is now, George, we just have to accept it.'

They talked about the old days and old comrades, which inevitably led to curmudgeonly good-natured moaning about the modern world.

'Staying here, are you?' Charlotte asked.

'For the time being. Might move to the country, away from all this modernity. Perhaps, even take in the sea air.'

'Well, I'm in town for a few days, but as it happens, I'm heading to the coast. You're welcome to tag along. It might be just what you're looking for.'

'Ready whenever you are, Major.'

March 20, 2069

Charlotte had explained the final destination by telepod happened to be some distance from their actual destination. When George enquired as to the covert nature of their journey, Charlotte said all would become clear.

'You're worrying me now,' he said.

'Nothing to worry about. It's just that the commune like their privacy. I've been there a few times. I'm a bit of a fetcher and carrier for them.'

Consequently, they materialised in the sleepy town of Halesworth in the town's only public telepod station.

An old man wearing a worn-out wax coat and patched corduroy trousers drove them ten miles to a stable and apologised for not being able to take them further. 'The battery be old it be, and only do twenty-five miles before it need chargin' ya see, boy.'

George found himself standing in the stable-yard looking into the brown eyes of a beautiful six-year-old gelding. He rubbed the horse's nose and let the graceful beast nuzzle his hand.

'What's his name?' he asked the stable manager.

'Donald,' she said.

'Oh, I was expecting something lengthier, like "Sound Bet" or "Faster Than Light", you know.'

'I know, but since the ban on sports involving animals, these beauties are just pets now. As pets, they get pet names. I know one mare called "Lulu". These magnificent animals are from thoroughbred lines that can be traced back three hundred years. What a waste, eh?' The obvious pleasure she took in being around the horses was soured by sadness and bitterness in her voice.

George and Charlotte rode the fine horses at a gentle trot for the rest of the day, along roads barely used for their original purpose in these modern times. The lack of use coupled with the price of fossil fuel meant that the roads were in a terrible state of disrepair. It did mean, however, that they could travel without the danger of passing traffic.

They came to the remains of a small, dead town. As they trotted down the curving road into the town centre, passing a small church, George felt a deep sense of *déjà vu*. The sensation really took hold as they walked along the High Street. A disused furniture shop reminded him of a book shop. He was sure the double fronted glass display should have the words 'Deben Market Bookshop' stencilled in an arch on it. Farther along, the name Pargeter over a large shop frontage, its windows boarded up, seemed also to be familiar.

'I get the oddest feeling I've been here before, Charlie.'

'Perhaps when you were a child on holiday. I think that was its main attraction once.'

It was the same for many small towns that had once relied on the tourist trade.

An old man was standing outside a public house. He waved them down.

'They said some people still lived here, but I've never seen anyone before,' Charlotte said.

After a brief conversation it was quite clear that he was not what George would call completely sane.

They passed through the town, leaving a double trail through the leaf litter.

A mile or so beyond the end of the town they came to an old farmhouse with views to the south of strange tall towers. To George, they looked like old radio beacons.

Charlotte called out to an old man with a mop of unruly grey hair, shuffling along the courtyard at speed as they clip-clopped to a halt.

'Evening, Prof. Want you to meet a friend of mine.'

'Bad timing, Charlotte. Griselda's gone into labour. Make yourself at home. I'll say hello when all's well,' he called back as he continued his hurried shuffle and disappeared inside a barn. As the door closed behind him, an agonising scream escaped.

'Please tell me that's not a woman in there,' he said.

'Oh yes. But I'd forgotten she was due.'

'Why isn't she in hospital having the baby tele-born? It can't be safe, surely?' George asked, pulling up a seat at an old pine table. Charlotte filled a metal kettle with water and set it to boil on the stove top.

'This lot shun modern ways as much as possible.'

'Christ, that's going a bit far though. Actual childbirth is so medieval, so dangerous.'

Charlotte placed a mug of coffee in front of her old commanding officer and went to rub the ear of an elderly spaniel asleep in a basket in the corner of the room.

'They're a strange bunch here, from all kinds of backgrounds. And they appreciate any sort of medical help, but the main thing they want to get away from is the control and intrusion of everything that comes with modern living. So, they found this old town. I bring them stuff that they might find useful. They do have quite a sterile medical unit and I got hold of old forceps and such not long ago. She'll be fine.'

'If you say so. At least they have a doctor.'

'Oh, the prof isn't a doctor. No, he's a scientist. Hell of a brain on the old boy. They do have a vet though. She'll be in charge in there.'

'Jesus,' George said in wonderment. He might not agree with everything the modern world had, but it had to be said that it did have a few benefits like taking away the pain of childbirth. He sipped his coffee. 'This is real coffee. Where did you get it from?' Charlotte winked and made a zipping motion across her lips.

At that moment a tall man with a full beard and a cable-knit jumper came into the kitchen.

'Hello, Charlotte, saw you arrive. Who's your friend?' He held out a hand and shook vigorously as George introduced himself.

'Pat here is in charge of the place,' said Charlotte.

'Nothing so grand, but I do try to timetable us all. Professor Lang is the chap who brought us all together; if anyone is the leader, it's him. But generally, we try to get along without titles or formality.'

'Tell me about the place. What do you call it?'

'Well, it doesn't really have a name. Deben Market Farm I suppose. We run it as it might have been back at the turn of the century. Similar to a small holding or a commune. We have wheat and rye crops, pigs, chickens, sheep and a small herd of cattle. The main problem for us is that at the turn of the century, farms were able to utilise the technology of the day, and that technology is hard to find now. For instance, we don't have access to petroleum or diesel, so the land is tilled by horse or cattle instead of tractor. Our grandparents could drive to large markets to top up supplies, whereas we're rather cut off from the masses as we don't have transpad technology.'

'But why? Is modern technology really that bad? My prosthetic is a miracle, and my life was saved by brain surgery,' said George.

'Medically, no, we all want a healthy life, to live a little longer. But how do we know they are not monitoring our thoughts or even influencing your decisions after they have meddled with our hardware?' he said, tapping his temple with his finger.

'My daughter would say, "You're a paranoid old dinosaur."'

'And what would you say?'

'I have questioned the need for nandroids, specifically the need for the connection between child and machine.'

Professor Lang stepped in from the small hallway just off the kitchen and said, 'I'm glad you say that, George. Sorry, couldn't help but overhear as I took these gummers off in the hall.'

'Griselda?' asked Pat, leaning forward in his chair.

'Mother and daughter both doing fine,' the professor said absently before turning to George. 'I believe it was people like you who've had neurological surgery that were templates or guinea pigs for machine-linked minds. Somewhere, an aqueous computer is recording all your thoughts, and the thoughts of anyone who has had surgery or implants in their brain.'

George coughed as his coffee went down the wrong way. 'What?'

'Enough for now, Prof. We're tired and could do with some nosebag. Let's talk later. George, I'll show you where you can doss down,' Charlotte said.

After a communal meal of roast chicken and potatoes, George sat with Charlotte and Professor Lang in what passed as the professor's study. It was in a small room on the first floor. His unmade bed was in the corner. Books stacked waist-high lined the edges of the room. A desk faced a window. On the desk were papers with hand-scribbled notes, several clocks and a telescope that looked over the marshes to the radio beacons.

'The state of the technological world,' the professor began, 'that we live in has progressed so far that soon there will not be much point in the existence of the human race. How do most of us occupy ourselves? Do you know how many people draw some sort of benefit in this country? Think about all those people all around the world living on basic social handouts. A hundred years ago there were thousands of occupations that do not exist today. Oh, other forms of employment evolved to replace them, but now even those jobs are becoming scarce. You see, nearly every job can be done by android, robot or AI. That's why I gathered a few people here. It's an attempt to try to hang onto some of the old ways and give the human race a chance of survival.'

'Things can't be that bad, can they?' George said, looking to Charlotte for conformation. She nodded her head.

The Professor continued, 'I have it on good authority that patients in need of hospital treatment are assessed by AI. Nothing so wrong with that you might say. However, the main criteria is shifting from how do we do the best for this person to how much will it cost and whether the patient can repay the system through taxable earnings when they recover. Since the abolition of the National Health Service, the older generation are now less likely to be able to repay what is, in actual fact, a loan.

'Therefore, it won't be long before an AI suggests the best way to save money in healthcare is to provide no care at all. Did you know that parliamentary decisions are countersigned by AI to avoid human responsibility? If we go to war, blame the AI — it calculated the losses and gains. If a human makes an error, don't worry, the AI is there to catch it. But really, the AI has the final decision, the final vote.

'I foresee a world, not long from now, where humans are uncared for by the machines we built to make our life easier. Humans who can't get back to basics because we are so reliant on the machines. Imagine if machines simply stop providing food by turning off the transpads. Imagine if medication were to be withheld; the wards closed to new arrivals and healthcare completely withdrawn. Imagine the state the world would be in if that happened.

'Within a week, the population of the globe would be starving, and everyone would be suffering. Not only that, there would be no other nation capable of support or able to send aid, because every nation would be affected. Attempts to demand or take back control would be met by unemotional and more than likely deadly retaliation, by a military run entirely by AI. Not that they'll be much resistance. The young, as I think you already suspect, are being brainwashed into non-confrontational masses.'

'Are you serious? You believe this could really happen?' George said.

'Absolutely. I had a very unique place in the world before I saw the error of my ways. I was a director in Boyant Tech Industrial, head research and development scientist, Artificial Intelligence being my area of expertise. My concerns grew late in my career, as I saw large companies hand over more and more control to AI. Especially in respect of accounting and finance. Today, ninety-five per cent of all businesses rely on AI to guide them and all AI is centrally connected.'

'The prof is trying to make amends for what he was part of,' interjected Charlotte.

'My aim here is twofold. First, to encourage self-reliance and the rediscovery of the old ways,' said the professor. 'The people on this farm, like you, question the need for machines like nandroids. They believe that self-sufficiency is the best way to ensure the survival of the human race. They agree with me to a greater or lesser degree, and more are coming every week. Soon, the town we border may be resurrected.'

'And the second reason?' asked George.

The professor and Charlotte shared a look. After an imperceptible nod from Charlotte, the professor continued. 'It's best if we show you.'

Charlotte harnessed a horse to an old cart. They made the short journey, following raised paths through the marshes to the tall towers George had noticed earlier. Professor Lang refused to answer George's queries regarding the second reason for being out here in the sticks. The sun had set, and the trail was poorly lit by a thin wedge of moon — it was a slow journey.

Eventually, the track they followed opened out to reveal dozens of tall, thin towers, tethered to the ground and each other by thick wire cable. Some of the towers had collapsed and lay strewn across the weedy pale concrete. In the centre of the array was a flat, wide structure, no larger than a two-storey house.

'You should tell me more before I go in there with you. This whole thing feels like a trap.' He turned to Charlotte and grabbed her arm. 'I thought I could trust you, but you were fetching me for a reason.'

Professor Lang disembarked with a grunt and said, 'This is an old radio listening outpost and weapons development site. I have developed, with the help of Charlotte, something to give mankind an edge. We are not here to trap you but convince you, and if after you have seen what there is to see you want nothing to do with us, then you will be free to leave. Now please, no more dilly-dallying. We must get inside.'

George climbed down from the cart with some reluctance. The horse lowered its head and pulled at some stringy grass.

They made their way up half a dozen steps and once inside the structure, the professor flicked a switch on the wall. Several dozen lights came on, although many did not. They followed a sloping corridor that descended for more than two hundred metres, accompanied by the sounds of their footsteps and the rhythmic clack of the professor's walking stick. The further they descended, the more the air filled with the scent of stagnant seawater.

Professor Lang tapped a code into a panel, and a single door clicked open. They stepped into a room large enough for two people to sit in. On their right, a control desk ran the entire width of the room with a single window above it. Knobs, controls, sliders, buttons, digital readout, and analogue dials littered the control panel, reminding George of old recording studios.

Beyond the window in a separate room was a man-size, first-generation telepod, lit by spotlights, one of which flickered. The pod room was accessed by a door opposite the one they had entered through. On the left of the entry door was a bank of very old CRT monitors, all blank, reflecting the three of them in altered mis-formed unreality.

The professor sat and invited George to sit with him. George remained standing.

'Talk,' he insisted.

'This is the second reason for me being out here,' said the professor, indicating the transpod on the other side of the glass.

'No shit, I'd never have guessed.'

'Now, now, George,' said Charlotte.

'You can shut it, Major. Enough with the cloak and dagger bollocks. What's going on?' His voice trembled as he pointed an accusing finger, first at Charlotte and then at Professor Lang.

'I have developed a time machine and intend to prevent this current timeline from ever developing in the first place,' Professor Lang replied, coming straight to the point.

'Oh, I see. And you believe this, do you?' George said, looking at Charlotte.

'I know it sounds crazy, George. But it works.'

'Then you're as mad as he is.'

'It works, George, on my oath as an officer in His Majesty's Army. I wouldn't lie to you.'

'But it's impossible.' George sat heavily in the spare chair.

'They once said that about flying, and virtually instant matter transference. It's just another form of transport,' said the professor.

'No. It can't be done. I know a bit about this — The Arrow of Time. It only moves forward. If time travel were possible, you would only be able to travel forward but just faster than we are already travelling.'

'Bunkum; a fine theory, but recently disproved,' said the professor.

Looking from his friend to the scientist and then back to his friend, he recognised their serious intentions by the set of their faces. Whatever their reasons, they believed they had a time machine.

'You're really serious?'

His friend nodded and a smile spread across her features.

'It works, and we need someone with guile and cunning to change things, George.'

George nodded his head, trying to force his brain to absorb the impossible.

'Why are you telling me? If my brain is wirelessly connected to aqueous computers, they'll know what you're telling me.'

'This is a Cold War compound, two hundred feet below ground level. The entire structure, the walls, the roof, is covered in two feet of lead casing. Nothing gets in or out, nothing. Unless we want it to,' said Professor Lang.

'But I'll have to leave sooner or later. Surely, they'll find out then? Data will upload.'

'We'll deal with that later,' said the professor.

George looked in again at the one-man telepod.

'That's it, is it? An old telepod. They were unreliable when new — some very nasty accidents if I remember.'

'It's been upgraded; there's more to it than meets the eye,' Charlotte said.

'Are you going to prove to me that it works?'

'We know it works. We've tested it,' said Professor Lang.

'This is madness. Pure madness.'

'I've travelled in it,' said Charlotte.

'Really?' replied George, the scepticism thick in his croaky voice.

'Yes, George, and a few days ago, Major Hood travelled back in time four days in order to meet with you at The In & Out. The simple fact that you're here proves the machine works. You see, in the original timeline, she did not rendezvous with you. You sat alone and because you did not meet with the major, did not come to the farm and give me the pleasure of your company.'

'You have to explain how you know that, because I only remember talking with Charlotte.'

'I don't think I can. But what has happened proves to me that time can be altered with prior knowledge. It also proves that the machine can still transport a person in space and that the machine works as a time travel pod.'

'What are you getting at exactly? I think I already know, but I want to hear you say it.'

'We're asking you to volunteer to go on a mission, back to the turn of the century,' said the professor.

'Ha. You *are* mad. Do you know how old I am? If this thing does work, you'll need to send someone young who's likely to survive the journey.'

'But a young person will probably find the culture shock more difficult to handle. We were saying earlier about how much they rely on modern tech and AI. It would be like asking you to visit Dickensian London. How do you think you'd cope? But you were there, George, as was I. If we think long and hard enough about it, we can recall the gadgets and vehicles, the big companies and fast food outlets.'

'Why don't you go then?'

'I'm not a trained soldier.'

'I'm hardly match fit. I've gone to seed.'

'Beside the point.'

'I need a drink,' said George.

'We haven't anything here.'

'Why me? Send Charlotte, she's younger and stronger.'

'Major Hood is needed here.'

'There's something I don't understand.' He rubbed his temples as he gathered his thoughts. 'If I change the past and time takes an alternate path, then there will be no need to invent a time machine to send me back.'

'This is true, but if I haven't sent you back, then time hasn't changed and we will be here now, having this conversation,' continued the professor. 'It's a variation of the grandfather paradox. Let me explain.'

'This is too much. I'm just an old soldier.'

'The truth of the matter is, we can't be sure. Not yet at least, but I theorise — as many renowned scientists have — that both timelines will exist in two different universes. The saving grace is that, at the very least, should your mission succeed, then a world that is not dominated by AI and robots will exist. A world where humans are free to make their own choices and mistakes.'

'We think going back to 2002 will be fine,' Charlotte said.

'I was eight then, how old were you?' he asked, looking at them both.

'Fifteen,' said the scientist.

'Born in '19,' Charlotte said.

'If time changes, what about my family? How do I get back?'

'It's a one-way journey, George. As for your family, I don't know for sure. At a guess, I would say your life might continue unchanged. It is further along the timeline that changes should become apparent. The Asian war might have a different outcome, the second Asian war might not happen at all. If you have any children, your daughter — whom you had late in life — may not meet the man who becomes her partner, consequently any grandchildren you may have, will be different individuals. Of course, things might remain unchanged, but the technology that is so all-pervasive may be drastically less intelligent.'

'You sure know how to mess with a man's head.'

'I know it's a lot to take on board,' said the professor.

'How do I materialise? These pods come in pairs. They need a receiver pod at the other end,' George asked.

Charlotte showed him a chunky bracelet, made from a rough, unpolished alloy. It looked cumbersome on her wrist; not a pretty thing at all. 'This is what the prof invented. It's a device to reassemble your atoms at the other end. It shouldn't work, considering it is also de-atomised, but it does.' She handed one to George. It was heavy. 'Try it on. It needs to detail your genetic code. The pod sort of sends it a photograph of its contents and then the bracelet puts it back together like a massive jigsaw.'

He looked again from one to the other and was about to clasp the bracelet in place around his right wrist, but paused and said, 'Tell me more about the mission first.'

Before either of his comrades could answer, an alarm sounded in the complex. An old blaring klaxon, its pitch rising and falling. All three raised their hands to their ears. Charlotte went to the control panel and powered up the old monitors. In grainy black and white, a dozen android troops could be seen marching through the entrance door. Another monitor showed troops and armoured vehicles surrounding the complex on the surface. The professor silenced the alarm with the flick of a switch, before turning and fiddling with more dials. A deep throbbing hum made the floor vibrate as the telepod came to life and its door clunked open.

'They must have tracked you, George. The technology has advanced even further than I anticipated. You two go, I'll stall them,' the professor said.

'I can't. They'll kill you,' Charlotte said.

'I'm dead anyway. We all are if we do nothing, if we surrender. I've set the self-destruct for three minutes. Save yourselves and change the past. Charlotte knows what to do, don't you?'

Charlotte nodded in grim agreement as the professor opened the door and stepped stoically through. She locked it from the inside.

On two monitors from two different angles, they watched the professor shuffling at speed, leaning heavily on his stick, back up the corridor toward the entrance. The androids stopped as a single unit when he came into view.

The silent monitors showed all. They saw him hold his hands up, his obvious pleas falling on inhuman ears, and watched as the androids unloaded their rifles on the old man. They both knew the capabilities of the weapons.

Three seconds later, when he lay on the floor, 252 entry and exit wounds could be counted. Not one round had missed its target. His head was almost completely severed. The androids marched on, stomping his already pulverised body into a bloody pulp.

'We don't have long, George,' Charlotte said. 'Quickly, put the bracelet on and get in the pod. There's a backpack of rations and all the kit you'll need inside, be sure to pick it up. You first and I'll follow if I can.'

'I need to know more. What's the objective?' he asked as he clasped the bracelet around his wrist.

'Change the future by killing Professor Thomas Lang as a child. Quick. Go!'

George stumbled through to the chamber containing the time machine. Pulling the heavy door of the telepod closed muffled the sound of rifle fire. What else could he do?

The familiar tingle of de-materialisation began.

Find out what happens to George in the soon-to-be-released, The Mystery of Deben Market.

About the Author

David Bowmore was born on a winter's night with the sound of thunder and the flash of lightning welcoming him into a brightly painted Gypsy caravan.

Forty-five years later he started writing fiction. After a steep learning curve, his short stories and flash fiction began to appear in various collections.

David is a classically trained chef, a personable teacher and unqualified landscape gardener. He's lived here, there and everywhere, but now lives in Yorkshire with his wonderful wife and a small white poodle.

David tends to write thrillers and mysteries as well as stories with a touch of the supernatural about them. He focuses on character and the oddities of being a human being, sometimes with humour, but more often with dark unreality.

When he was younger, he had a love of science fiction and fantasy. *The Hobbit* and *The Lord of Rings* were particular favourites. In adult life his reading taste veered towards thrilling mysteries, particularly Golden Age crime. You know the sort of thing – country house murders where everyone is a suspect, impossible locked room mysteries with more red herrings than your local fishing hole.

David is an admirer of many authors including P.G Wodehouse, Terry Pratchett, Neil Gaiman, Elmore Leonard, Patricia Highsmith and Agatha Christie.

Since his first published story, 'Sins of The Father' appeared in *Vortex*, published by Clarendon House in June 2018, he has featured in twenty-five short story anthologies and had in excess of fifty drabbles published.

David's collection of connected short stories, published by Clarendon House — *The Magic of Deben Market* — is available through Amazon and Lulu.com

Other Clarendon House Publications to feature his work are *Enigma, Rapture, Cadence, Fireburst, Gold, Blaze, Tempest, Maelstrom, Gleam,* and *Paradox.*

He has also been published by Zombie Pirate Publishing in *Flash Fiction Addiction, World War Four, Full Metal Horror 2, Grievous Bodily Harm, Treasure Chest,* and *Clockwork Dragons.*

His drabbles appear in these Black Hare Press Publications: *Worlds, Angels, Monsters, Beyond, Unravel, Apocalypse, Eerie Christmas, Love, Hate,* and *Oceans.* Also for Black Hare Press he has stories in *Deep Space, Storming Area 51, Bad Romance, Twenty Twenty,* and *Passenger 13.*

Other publications featuring David's work include: *Dragon Bone Soup, Forest of Fear, Curses and Cauldrons,* and *Dark X-Mas.*

David has also had work published in the following magazines; Dastaan World, Inner Circle Writers' Magazine and Saddlebag Dispatches.

———

Acknowledgements

In this modern age of self-publishing it is difficult to have one's work read by the wider public. You would think it would be easy — write a story, or even a novel, load it up to Amazon, and wait for your wallet to overflow with the crinkly stuff.

Sadly, this is not the case.

So, it with gratitude that I mention the following independent publishers who help us — the struggling writers — get our work out there.

Blood Song Books, The Macabre Ladies, and Fantasia Divinity for introducing me to the short form known as the drabble.

The entire team at Black Hare Press for forcing me to up my output of drabbles, and for their encouragement and understanding with my science fiction stories.

Likewise, DW Brownlaw and P.C. Darkcliff for accepting my first fantasy story into the anthology that wins best name — Dragon Bone Soup.

Zombie Pirate Publishing for being such brilliant and supportive guys within the indie-press world.

Dennis Doty — a genuine gentleman, and editor of a great magazine for western readers, Saddlebag Dispatches.

Umair Mirxa, previously of Dastaan World, and now running Paper Djinn Press.

Steve Carr — an excellent writer, friend and the inspiration behind Sweetycat Press.

And of course, Grant Hudson from Clarendon House, for agreeing to publish this collection and for being the first to give me hope that my scrawlings were not (as I had feared) complete drivel.

A special thank you for my wife, Jai, is also due. You always give me an honest opinion, great ideas, help with edits and remind me when I'm getting too big for my writing slippers. Love You.

Join the
Inner Circle Writers' Group on Facebook!
This group is unlike most writers' groups on social media. Post ANYTHING about writing, including: •passages from books you admire •recommended reading
•extracts from your own work
•requests for advice or guidance about anything to do with writing
Founded in 2008, this group is a thriving community, celebrating fiction of all kinds. Here you can also get a glimpse of the unique and revolutionary 'physics of fiction' as outlined in the book *How Stories Really Work* (see below) and in many articles and items.
This is not available anywhere else.
The group is free and fun.
Just go to Facebook:
https://www.facebook.com/groups/innercirclewritersgroup

HOW STORIES REALLY WORK:
Exploring the Physics of Fiction
by Grant P. Hudson

Learn:
- what a story really is
- what it is actually doing to and for you and other readers
- the things called 'plots', what they are and how they are actually made
- the four categories of the powerful force that compels readers to turn pages
- the magnetic power that attracts readers even before the introduction of any character
- what the thing called a 'character' actually is, and how to rapidly build a convincing one
- what 'protagonists' and 'antagonists' really are, and what the connection between them consists of
- the 'nuclear reactor' that drives all successful stories through to their conclusion
- how the four basic genres - Epic, Tragedy, Irony and Comedy - are composed and how they work to create different effects

and much, much more.

What the experts say:

As with all professionals, I too read craft books every day, to stay on top of my game. Over the last thirty years, I've read (literally) hundreds of writing books. And, lemme tell ya, the VAST majority of them are garbage.The relative few that are decent still aren't great. Writing instructors usually spend 60,000 words saying what could've been said in 60.

EXCEPT for yours, Grant. Your books are hands down, bar none, exceptional.

You get down into the nitty gritty and talk about real stuff that's immediately useful. I especially like How Stories Really Work. You really nailed it with that one. And, Grant... it's REALLY hard to impress me. But, you had me hooked from the very first sentence. In fact, I've already turned a number of my past clients onto it.

So... thank you for giving the writing world something of merit. Your book is a breath of invigorating fresh air. May it breathe new life into this great industry of ours so that writers may once again set the world on fire.

-J. C. Admore, Professional Writing Expert

An amazing book. Fascinating application of physics theory to the art of fiction writing. Presents new ways of understanding how stories work. I now look for 'vacuums' everywhere. Excellent case studies covering all genres. Thought-provoking and inspiring. I highly recommend this book to all readers and writers of fiction.

- G. Leyland (B Social Work, Grad Dip Writing, MA Creative Writing)

What the authors say:

I'm reading through How Stories Really Work. I've studied writing books for years but I've never seen anything like this! I learned about your work after reading an article you wrote. I was intrigued by the premise, but at the time, there wasn't an Amazon review (something I must rectify when I'm finished). I decided it wouldn't hurt to read the preview. . . And promptly bought it. This book is REVOLUTIONARY. Everything is made so simple and precise that other methods of writing seem clumsy by comparison. It's not just a way of writing, but a way of seeing.

-A. P. (Author)

It's beautiful, informative, essential reading for anyone who wants to write fiction. It's almost a responsibility point, you're committing a crime if you don't get it into peoples' hands!!!

-B.R. (Author)

Loved the book. Have used the principles in many a story. It all makes so much sense. If you want help in drawing readers in - this is the book to get.

-M W-B (Author)

This is a book every author should own. Grant P. Hudson does an outstanding job explaining story structure and the mechanics involved in creating a story or novel that readers will love. His examples are explained in an engaging manner so this book doesn't seem like reading a text book. I have already implemented many of his ideas in building a novel. This book contains great advice and I highly recommend it to all authors.

-D. T. (Author)

After reading this book, I'll never look at stories the same way. This step-by-step how-to book is full of wisdom about how classic stories are structured. You will see how to apply these principles to your own stories and novels, converting them to page-turners.

-P. V. A. (Author)

An essential purchase for anyone wishing to not only improve their writing but understand the art of story telling. You will never read a book the same way again. Nor watch a film or play without seeing the theory, that Grant so eloquently describes. Brilliant, worth every penny.

-D. S. (Author)

I have had nearly 100 short stories published and thought I knew about writing. This book taught me new ways to look at my own writing as well as other writing. Grant Hudson doesn't recycle old ways to look at the writing process, he invents new ways for a writer to examine almost every aspect of writing fiction, and provides a new vocabulary for how to do it. Very highly recommended for anyone who writes or wants to write fiction.

-A. C. (Author)

I wish I had found this book sooner. It was fascinating and insightful. I am now very annoying when watching films as I apply the techniques learned in this book, and quickly guess the twists! Very helpful in planning and forming ideas and I use this technique when writing stories.

-S. C. (Author)

I love the way Grant has approached the whole subject in this excellent book, in a very different and almost 'obvious' way compared to other books that attempt to teach the craft of writing. As a writer myself I now see in a different light what I am writing. Where was this book 35 years ago when I first started writing? One of those 'I wish I'd known that years ago' books.

-J. W. F. (Author)

I finished this book over two nights and had an epiphany. Such common sense and thought provoking ideas. This should be a mandatory text book for any serious writer. I'm excited to inject more purpose to my writing. This book will become a constant reference book for me now. Highly recommend it.

-R. C. (Author)

Your book is teaching me all the stuff that the other books don't! I can learn all about three-act structures and all that stuff elsewhere -this book is telling me exactly what to put INTO the structure! It makes writing so easy and you can immediately spot where you're going wrong! Excellent!
-L.J. (Professional)

This is an absolutely amazing achievement! I highly recommend it to anyone interested in writing fiction.
-T.R. (Student)

I was extremely impressed. This is not idle flattery. You've done a superb job in uncovering the factors that go into making a great piece of literature.
-B.R. (Executive)

Printed in Great Britain
by Amazon